In a Pale Blue Light

In a Pale Blue Light

a novel

Lily Poritz Miller

Sumach Press
Toronto

In a Pale Blue Light
by Lily Poritz Miller

First published in 2009 by
Sumach Press, an imprint of Canadian Scholars' Press Inc.
180 Bloor Street West, Suite 801
Toronto, Ontario M5S 2V6

www.sumachpress.com

Canadian Scholars' Press Inc. gratefully acknowledges financial support for our
publishing activities from the Ontario Arts Council, the Canada Council for the Arts,
the Government of Canada through the Book Publishing Industry Development
Program (BPIDP), and the Government of Ontario through the Ontario Book
Publishing Tax Credit Program.

Library and Archives Canada Cataloguing in Publication

Miller, Lily Poritz
        In a pale blue light : a novel / by Lily Poritz Miller.

ISBN 978-1-894549-83-7

        I. Title.

PS8576.I54I53 2009   C813'.54   C2009-904502-8

Cover design: Liz Martin
Interior design and composition: Em Dash Design

09 10 11 12 13   5 4 3 2 1

Printed and bound in Canada by Marquis Book Printing Inc.

To my parents

Sarah Shapiro
and Joseph Poritz

All the world is a narrow bridge…
and the main thing is not to be afraid.
RABBI NACHMAN OF BRESLOV (1772–1810)

· *preface* ·

This story has been fermenting in my mind for many years. I first began writing it in the winter of 1971 when I was living in Montreal. I had left New York where I worked as an editor and thought I would take a respite and devote myself to writing. But a meeting with Jack McClelland took me to Toronto the following spring, where I embarked on an eighteen-year endeavour as senior editor at McClelland and Stewart, editing the books of many major writers.

The intervening years served my story well, and when I took up the manuscript again I found it was still alive in me. Many things had changed and new discoveries had been made. In 1992 I began travelling to Eastern Europe, seeking out the ancestral *shtetlach* of my parents, and I developed a strong emotional bond with their homeland. Though my parents were no longer alive, I now knew so much about their early years in Lithuania and subsequent journey to South Africa. As a child growing up in South Africa, I had little awareness of the impact of the Holocaust on their lives and the loss of their beloved families whom they had left behind when they immigrated to South Africa in late 1929.

With a deeper understanding of my parents and the world they encountered when they arrived in the new land, I continued my own journey of retracing my years of growing up in South Africa in the late 1930s through the outbreak of World War II. It was an era when the Jewish immigrants from Eastern Europe were rebuilding their lives in the new land, and a time when the black and coloured people did not resist their fate.

Though my story is drawn from memory, it is a work of fiction and I have allowed my imagination to transcend reality.

Lily Poritz Miller

· one ·

It had rained all night, softly, silently, and now in the early morning the hibiscus and primroses that laced the trellis on the side of the house were quivering. Dew like teardrops shimmered on the honey-suckles and red and yellow roses, and the lone bird of paradise stood proud and silent.

The couple from next door were passing the house, their little boy wedged between them, but on this day they walked on the other side of the cobblestone street. Signing in the language of the deaf, their hands moved forbiddingly towards the big white house, but no sound escaped from their lips. The boy ignored their warnings and stepped into the street towards the gate beside the red stone steps, but his mother snatched him back.

They reached the corner, turned to cast furtive glances at the house that stood shuttered on the dead-end street, then vanished down the hill.

The sun burst out, luminous in the sky, and a breeze swept down from Table Mountain. A group of children rushed forward, two boys and a girl, their skin golden from the Cape Town sun, their eyes stealthily set on the gate.

"*Ouma* says not to go there today," the girl cautioned her brother.

"Me want to play wid Sayer!"

"No says *Ouma!*"

"Did he get dead — Sayer's daddy?"

"Shoo!" warned the girl.

At that moment the shuttered door of the house opened and the three children fled.

Libka peered out into the day's light, squinting as though it stabbed her eyes. Small for her age, but solemn beyond her twelve years, she stepped onto the cement stoep in bare feet. After a few moments she sat down on the top step, nestling her back into the stone wall. Here she sat as though in a trance. The spell might have lasted were it not for the appearance of a troupe of children. The sister with the two brothers had returned, but now they were accompanied by a menagerie of children from the surrounding streets. They hovered around the gate, the smaller children climbing onto the railing to get a peek. A flaxen-haired boy rattled the gate and it sprang open with a clash, bringing Libka to her feet.

"We come to play wid Sayer," the boy announced, standing before the open gate.

"Not today," warned Libka.

"You say dat yesterday," shouted another boy, coming to the foreground.

"Go away!" Libka shouted. *"Voetsek!"*

"Then he can't climb Tante Sannie's pawpaw tree no more."

The boy blew spit bubbles, and the smaller children joined in, slime slipping down their chins, bravely swinging on the gate. This had been a house where the gate was open, where shutters welcomed the sunlight. The neighbourhood children had always played freely among the flowers and toys, plucking fruit from the trees.

A small boy ran out of the house. His golden curls fell about his face and shoulders and his cheeks were polished from sleep. Seeing the children in their brightly coloured clothes, joyously swinging on the gate, his eyes grew large and he ran towards them.

"No, Shneyer!" Libka's dark eyes held him back.

Shneyer looked down at the children. "Lemme go play ..."

Now Libka stepped forward and flung her arms out, sending the children scattering into the street; but in moments a group returned, planting their feet inside the gate, chanting:

> Sayer can't play! Sayer can't play!
> Not today! Not today!
> His daddy is dead dead dead!
> So Sayer must stay in bed bed bed!

The refrain caught on. "Dead dead dead. Bed bed bed," the children called, running through the street, the little ones screaming the loudest.

"Voetsek!" Libka shouted, bounding down the steps. "Scram!"

She watched until the last of them disappeared around the corner before she slammed the gate and raced back up the stairs. Taking her brother Shneyer by the hand, she gently pushed him inside. "Go play in your room."

Turning to close the shuttered door from the stoep, she paused by an inner door and, with a quick look over her shoulder, tiptoed into the front bedroom. Though her father now lay in the Pinelands Jewish Cemetery, she could still smell the mustiness of death. As she lingered in the dim room she heard a cackling sound and Dina crawled in, wearing only a bib. Libka lifted the infant onto her hip and hurried back onto the stoep, drawing the shutters closed once more.

Down below, at the foot of the gleaming red stone steps, Maputo had appeared, burnishing the brass plaque on the gate.

The large man looked up at Libka, his smile radiating love. "My little missus feels gloomy."

"Soon the people will start coming again," Libka said nervously as she descended the wide steps, Dina clinging to her.

"They come to honour your father," Maputo said gently. "Have Elsie dress up your little sister."

Libka carried Dina along the path past the rosebushes and multicoloured flowers and turned into the lane that separated her house from the towering dwelling of the neighbours. At the end of the lane near the courtyard she saw Elsie throwing mealies to the rabbits in the hok.

"Look at you!" the coloured woman scolded her. "Not even shoes on your muddy feet and soon the guests will arrive." She threw a last handful of mealies to the rabbits. "Here, let me tend the baby and you go make yourself proper."

When Libka pulled a face, Elsie shot her a reprimanding look. "Now don't cause no more problems, Miss Libka. Your mother is counting on good behaviour."

"If my father died, is this a reason to celebrate?"

"Enough, now. You know it is the Jewish tradition to receive those who come to pay their respects for the dead."

Elsie scooped the baby out of Libka's arms and patted her naked behind.

"I wish I could just disappear," mumbled Libka.

"Hush!" Elsie opened the wooden gate to the courtyard and scuttled away with the baby.

Libka meandered back to the front of the house and sat down on a step, watching Maputo rub the plaque to a glow, humming a mournful tune as he stroked the inscription "The Haven."

"I'm tired of smiling at all those people who keep coming every day."

"I mourn with you, Miss Libka, but we must remember that the good master has gone to the great heavens."

"I wish I could believe that, but when I go into that eerie room ..."

"You must look upwards, my young missus. Mysteries dwell in the sky that we mortals cannot behold."

Libka stroked his arm and turned to enter the house. People would soon be arriving and she still wasn't ready. She went into her room and was tugging a comb through her tangled hair when the first knock on the door echoed in the entryway.

———•———

Into the house moved a constant stream of people. They chatted beside the white pillars on the stoep, but as they entered the passageway, their tongues froze. The house was dim and solemn on this bright summer day in December and, according to tradition, the mirrors were turned to the wall.

On a low stool in the sitting room, a black lace shawl draped around her shoulders, sat Sara Hoffman, the widow. Dina crawled before her, wet diapers sagging below her belly. Positioned at the entrance to the sitting room to greet the visitors were Libka and her elder brother Beryl, with Golda hovering behind, smiling shyly. And in the dining room Shneyer peeped from behind the sideboard where Libka's swimming trophies and blue ribbons were displayed alongside Beryl's accolades for rugby and cricket. The sliding doors between the dining and sitting rooms had been opened for the occasion, and people were flowing through the area in a hum of Yiddish and broken English, smiling with large gold-capped teeth.

"You're too young to lose your father," Mrs. Reznik whispered to Libka. "Watch over your mother. She's all you poor things have left in the world."

"You'll have to grow up fast," Mrs. Rashkowitz cautioned. "After all, the oldest daughter."

The red-nosed Batya Boyarsky sniffed into a lace handkerchief as she addressed Mrs. Rashkowitz. "Such a tragedy! Five small children left without a father. At least Yosef lived to see the Bar Mitzvah of his oldest son. Beryl is a nice boy. But *ver vais* what Hitler did to the rest of the family, to all our people."

All week Libka had heard these gloomy words and now she felt she had to free herself. She eased her way through the crowd. People were picking from a table spread with *shmaltz* herring, hard-boiled eggs, *challah* and potato *knishes*. Others elbowed each other to get to the side table where cheese blintzes, *taiglach* and apple strudel were displayed. Wherever Libka turned, she caught snippets of conversation.

"I wouldn't move too close to that Motel Shmerl," Mrs. Goldstein whispered to Mrs. Davinsky as the two women glanced at a ruddy-faced man with a gleam in his eye. "Chana Gitel swears that at the Bar Mitzvah of her son, he gave her behind a *knip*."

"And I understand his Masha had all her teeth pulled," Mrs. Davinsky replied, "but it didn't stop the babies from coming. Nine they have already."

"I hardly recognized her when I saw her at Velvel's unveiling. Not a tooth in her mouth. How does she eat?"

"You think Motel Shmerl can afford to install her with gold teeth? The way he's struggling with his variety shop in Wynberg! And I hear he cheats customers. He must have been kicked out of the railroad in Durban, so he came back to Cape Town. Goes from one thing to another and can't make a living."

At the other end of the room Libka spotted the glamorous Miss Ingrid. She remembered how the Swedish lady had sat at her father's bedside during the last weeks of his life. Libka had known her since she was little. It was Miss Ingrid who had first taught her English from the fairy tales she read when they lived in the rooms above her father's workshop.

Next to Miss Ingrid stood Mr. Oberg, the tall Scandinavian man whom her father had known when they were students in Leningrad. Mr. Oberg had always looked like a rugby star, but now he seemed old and bent.

As Libka tried to navigate through the crowd, she was greeted by her father's accountant, Mr. Adelson, who stood solemnly beside his wife, Hinda. When she saw the sadness in his eyes, she lost her reserve and had to bite her lip to keep from crying.

A distinguished-looking man in a dark double-breasted suit with silver specks in his black hair entered the sitting room and shook hands warmly with Beryl.

This did not escape Mrs. Stein, who elbowed Mrs. Donsky beside her. "See that," she whispered, "Abraham Garfinkel, the shoe manufacturer from Camps Bay."

"What a tragedy," Mrs. Donsky whispered. "He's not the same since Hena's death."

"You don't ever see him at functions. Only once I saw him in *shul* at Rosh Hashanah."

"And a match is out of the question," said Mrs. Donsky. "I understand he won't hear of it."

Of all her parents' friends, Libka liked Mr. Garfinkel best. She remembered how he and her father would play chess far into the night, and the summer the families had spent together at the seashore in Muizenberg. Despite her shyness, she was moving to greet him when she felt a tug from behind.

"I've been looking for you," Mrs. Peker said accusingly. The stout woman with a mop of bleached-blond hair pulled Libka aside and dragged her into a bedroom, shutting the door.

"Let's see your dress. I don't think it fits right." She twirled Libka around, scrutinizing the black cotton dress, which had the mourning tear at the collar, just like the other members of the family.

"It's snug on top," Mrs. Peker said. "You're starting to develop." She tugged at the bodice.

"I have to wear this dress this week while my mother is sitting *shivah*."

"Well, it doesn't look good." Mrs. Peker's teeth were smeared red from the rich foods. "You wear a bra?"

Libka shook her head, and the woman fingered her midriff. "I think it's time. My Sally was already wearing a bra before she was thirteen. How old are you, anyway?"

"Twelve."

"You still go to Hebrew school at the Sea Point *shul?*"

Libka nodded, wriggling to escape the pinching fingers, but Mrs. Peker did not release her.

"Listen here, now that your daddy's dead, you children should keep an eye on your mother. When I was your age in Lithuania, I was already feeding six younger mouths." She wagged a finger. "And don't allow your mother in the kitchen. It's not suitable for a white lady in South Africa."

"She likes to cook for us," said Libka.

"How can the *shvartze* servants respect a white woman who meddles in the kitchen?"

Libka edged towards the door.

"An exception once in a while," Mrs. Peker continued, blocking her path. "Like my cheese blintzes. Did you taste? They're going like hot cakes. The *shvartze* have no *seichel* for such things."

Libka rolled her eyes. Mrs. Peker spoke about the blacks like someone who had lived in South Africa forever, but the Peker family had arrived in Cape Town on the same vessel as Libka's parents. They had set out from Lithuania fifteen years ago, in December 1929. Four of the daughters had been born in the old country, and a son and daughter followed in the new land. Mishka Peker, a timid man who struggled with the English language, delivered milk on a bicycle in the wee hours of the morning.

Finally Libka freed herself from Mrs. Peker's grasp and ran into the garden. There under the primrose trellis she found her sister Golda with Anya Steinberg, a girl with green eyes and black hair bouncing at her waist.

"Get into the house!" Libka fumed at Golda. "It's your turn to entertain."

"Don't look at me like that," her sister pleaded.

"I've had enough. The stupidity! Parties for the dead."

Anya straightened to her full height of four foot eleven and stood before Libka, her hands on her hips. "So what are you going to do about it?"

"All these people do is stuff their mouths and gossip," Libka said. "Is this called respect? They don't care that my father died."

"Mommy's only observing our Jewish traditions," said Golda.

"It's easy for you to talk. Who has all the responsibility while you just act so innocent?" Libka shoved her sister against the hedge. "Get inside and talk to Mrs. Peker."

Anya burst into laughter. "You're jealous because everybody prefers your sister."

"We don't like you corrupting her," said Libka. "How about associating with people your own age?"

"Like you? No, thank you."

"You know my mother's against you."

"We'll see about that." Anya turned away and grabbed onto the trellis. She dangled among the primroses, her sleek black hair swinging back and forth.

"Watch out!" Libka warned. "My father built that trellis."

"Please, Anya," begged Golda, "don't break it."

But Anya only swung more defiantly.

"Now I know who you take after," said Libka.

Anya jumped to the ground. "Who?"

"It's too bad about your father. No wonder all your brothers and sisters ran away. And don't think we'll let my sister sleep over your house anymore ... to protect you."

"Little mouse," sneered Anya. "You're jealous because everybody hates you and you have no friends."

· *two* ·

The daily visitors slowed to a trickle and Libka had to face going back to school. She strolled from her house in Green Point to the tram stop ten minutes away. The area held a mixture of inhabitants. At the crest of the cobblestone street stood Libka's house. From there she went down the wide avenue, where the Dutch colonial houses were a powdery white with the occasional splash of colour from flowerpots in front. Though it was not a Boer district like the Newlands where she had lived before, several Boer families lived here, the children flaxen-haired and blue eyed. Libka would hear them talking in Afrikaans, which she now understood as it was compulsory to learn this language at school. A number of English families also occupied the area, their simple homes kept prim. Then a bleak street of shanties veered down towards Main Street. Here children played in the lanes between the shacks. There were no shutters over the soiled windows and sometimes a torn curtain would part to reveal a yellow-skinned face.

"Don't loiter along York Road," Beryl always warned Libka, "and avoid those coloureds. They're worse than the blacks and half the time those scoundrels are drugged on the dagga they smoke."

"Just mind your own business," she would retort.

On Main Street stood a tavern with a sign "No Dogs No Jews." Along the way was the Malay store, which carried fruit, vegetables, sweets and toys; the dispensary, which emitted the smell of antiseptic; and the house of "the crazy lady." The imposing white structure was set far back from the traffic, encircled by high stone walls and meticulously trimmed hedges. Libka would peek through the openings in the gate to see if the strange lady was coming. The woman had a large, square frame, her grey hair shaved like a man, and she was always loaded down with shopping bags. She would come bouncing along the promenade towards the gate, her chirpy monologue interspersed with laughter. If she spotted Libka, she'd signal to her, but Libka would skip away.

Sometimes Libka would see the woman moving among the shanties on the street of coloureds. The children would run to her when they saw her coming. She would stop at each hovel and lift goods from her bag.

Today there was no sign of the crazy lady. Libka waited for the tram, and when it stopped, she climbed up the steps. The European section in front was almost empty because many of the white people travelled in big cars; but the rear was crowded with coloureds, blacks and a few Malays. Some women were standing with heavy sacks and babies tied to them, but they dared not take a seat in the white section. Libka felt ashamed when she sat down.

When the tram pulled up in front of Promenade High School in Sea Point, Libka rose to get off. The school stood on a hill midway between the mountain and the sea, a grey stone structure encased by walls eight feet tall with towering trees further obscuring the view. A breeze raced down from Table Mountain, and sometimes at high tide the students could hear the rumbling of the waves.

Just as she hopped off the bus, a chauffeured white limousine pulled up and Ruth Freedman jumped out with her sister Myra. Ruth was a classmate of Libka's but she swept by her, followed by her sister.

Libka flushed at the insult. Though she might have expected some sympathy so soon after her father's death, she wasn't really surprised. They had treated her this way ever since the day Ruth's chauffeur had driven Libka home after school. As the polished limousine cruised along the street populated by the Cape coloureds, Ruth had looked fearfully out of the tinted windows.

"You live in a coloured district?" she asked, aghast.

"No, my house is further away."

Even when the limousine pulled up before Libka's stately house, Ruth did not relent.

"Where do you swim? It's so far to the Sea Point Pavilion."

"I prefer Three Anchor Bay, anyway," Libka answered. "It's less crowded."

"And smelly! Ooh!" She pinched her nose. "The water's dirty there."

That was the last time Libka was allowed to have lunch with Ruth and Myra. Once the word got around to the other Sea Pointers whose mansions faced the ocean, they turned their backs on her. She was no longer welcome on the hill where the girls sat cross-legged on the grass as they removed brimming sandwiches from ornamental boxes. Libka's lunch consisted of mashed banana on *challah* or simply bread and butter. If her mother was in a good mood, she would sprinkle on a little sugar or chocolate flakes. When a classmate caught Libka licking the flakes off her bread, it became a source of amusement for the girls. "What is your wish for luncheon today, my young missus?" they recited to each other as they circled around in the playground. "Do you favour a mealie-meal sandwich or a dab of chocolate flakes?" The girls laughed hysterically, collapsing onto the grass and clutching their stomachs.

And now, on the first day back since her father's death, things were no different. Libka forced herself through the motions of going to class, enduring the hours until she could return home.

But things weren't much better there. It seemed to Libka that since the death of her father the house was in perpetual darkness. Sunlight no longer penetrated, the shutters were often drawn and a musty odour permeated the rooms.

"Mama!" she would call as she neared the kitchen, but she did not expect an answer. She would call her mother only to alert her, hoping to eradicate the gloom of Sara's haunting wail. At any hour her song of sorrow would drench the house and echo, even in the black of night. Who was it that started this? Had Maputo caught her lonely chant, or had she taken it from him? Yet Libka knew that the chants were oceans apart. Maputo's song was one of joy, of hope, of eternity. Maputo could laugh up at the sun when he sang; he could feast upon the heavens, for he saw his master as clearly in death as he had in life. But Sara's wail was of sorrow and doom.

Libka reached breaking point when she came home from school one day and found Sara crouched on a stool, Dina crawling in a sodden diaper.

"I'm sick of this!" She flung the satchel from her back. "Get off that stool and start acting normal."

Libka's anger frightened Dina, who began to wail.

"Look what you're doing to the baby, to everyone. I'm leaving. I'm quitting school and leaving."

Sara's red-rimmed eyes looked up, pleading. *"Sha!"*

"There's no light in this house," Libka fumed. "No sun. Can't you even open a shutter?"

Libka ran to the window and unfastened the latches, flinging the shutters free. The thud of the wood against the concrete unnerved the infant, and her wail rose to a scream.

Libka fled to the room she entered each afternoon, the room of her father. His scent still lingered, a fusion of rumpled sheets and eau de cologne. "Daddy," she whispered, and opened the bottom drawer of the dresser where, amid his undergarments, lay the silver box of old European coins, medals and mementos, his eyeglasses and gold fob pocket watch. She peered through the small round lenses with the wire clasps and put the watch to her ear to hear it ticking.

She was startled by the creaking door, then spotted a pair of eyes staring out of the closet.

"Shneyer!" She threw the glasses and timepiece back in the box and closed the drawer, flustered at this intrusion into her private moment. "What are you doing here?"

Her brother shrugged and withdrew into the closet.

"Come out of there!"

She took his hand and pulled him out. "Is that where you hide when Mama can't find you?"

His cheeks had lost their glow and his golden curls were matted.

"What do you do in there?" Softening, she took his face in her hands.

His large blue eyes gazed solemnly up at her.

"You don't even play with your friends anymore. I saw Kevin outside. He said, 'Shneyer doesn't come out to play.' Don't you like him anymore?"

"Why his daddy and mommy talk with their hands?"

"Because they can't talk like us. They're deaf."

"But they not dead?"

"No."

Shneyer stepped back towards the closet.

"What means dead?"

"Come," Libka said, "I'll take you to the Malay shop for some sweets."

"But what it means?"

"Gone away." She bit her lip. "It means gone away for a long time."

"Daddy is dead?"

"Yes. Now will you come out of there?"

Libka led her brother back into the kitchen.

"Guess where I found Shneyer?"

"Aw, Shneyerel," Sara said, rising from the stool. "Where you been, *mein kind*? I was looking for you all over. Lunch you didn't even had and it is already almost suppertime."

"Where do you think he was?" Libka asked. "With you behaving like this, wouldn't anybody hide in a closet?"

"In a closet?"

"In Daddy's closet."

"I was only playing hide-and-seek from the boogeyman," said Shneyer.

"What boogeyman?" Sara pleaded.

"The boogeyman that hits you with a stick and locks you up."

"What is he saying?" Sara eyed Libka. "There is no boogeyman," she told Shneyer. "You imagine, my child."

"Will he come in this house and hit us? Like he did to David Copperfield?"

"Aw, aw," Sara exclaimed in relief. "Golda's book you are thinking of, the one she read to you, yes? That's only a storybook. No boogeyman will come to us. Don't be frightened."

"He can climb through the roof."

"No, *mein kind*." Sara drew Shneyer into her arms. "I think you are hungry and sleepy. Come, I will wash you up and make something nice. Maybe fish and chips and chocolate pudding for dessert?"

As Sara led Shneyer to the bathroom, Dina crawling after them, Libka eyed her mother's old black garment. "Put on something decent," she called after her. "No wonder Shneyer has nightmares."

· three ·

The first person she saw when coming home from school was always Maputo. "Maputo, my friend!" Libka would call as she reached the gate.

His smile lit up his face.

"Ah, my young missus."

Today she lingered at the gate, admiring the way the red stone steps reflected the sunlight. The garden was in full bloom. Red, yellow and ivory roses nestled together, their petals soft and velvety. The buttercups fluttered in the warm breeze and a ladybird took her seat on a dahlia. Along the brick panelling on the edge of the flowerbeds grew a myriad of tiny flowers, their colours forming an embroidered fringe. The bird of paradise stood apart, guard of its empire. Chameleons slithered along in disguise on the freshly pruned hedge; and the gardener was slumped under the vines near the rabbit hok, spitting pawpaw seeds against the wire fence.

Libka watched as Maputo breathed in the sweet juiciness of the garden and glowed with pride at his polished steps. Then he stooped once more to add a final stroke. His torn woven shirt, worn by the master in better days, was soaked from the heat of the sun, and his skin was beaded with sweat.

Now his eyes fixed on his most prized target, and he lovingly extracted the brilliance of the brass plaque set on the gate.

Libka sat down on a step. She wore the navy blue tunic with the white calico blouse, and the blue-and-gold tie. The school badge was sewn on the breast pocket of her blazer. Her feet were encased in brown oxfords and her shoulders hurled back by the satchel laden with books.

Libka despised the severity of the uniform and submitted only to a degree. Her hair, which was required to be braided, hung loosely around her face. She had once been severely reprimanded for this, and her knuckles were chopped with a metal-edged ruler. But now that she was in high school, the punishment was the cold eyes of the headmistress.

"Take your hair out of your eyes," her mother would plead. "How can you even see?"

Libka had tried knotting her hair in back. One day she went to school that way, but when she returned home she ripped off the ribbon. Now as she sat before Maputo her hair flowed freely down her back.

"How did it go in the school today?" Maputo wanted to know.

"I wrote a poem on my way home. It's in my head."

"Maputo!" came the shrill call from the lane leading to the rabbit hok as the coloured woman appeared, the baby in her arms. "Don't come tell me you're not yet finished with them steps!"

"Elsie, it will be finished. If not by three o'clock, it shall be done by the hour of four."

Maputo bent to his work and took up his chant:

> My *baas*, he left the earth,
> Only yesterday he was here ...

"I ask you to stop this hawkin' of yours," Elsie shouted, waving a rag at Maputo. "My head's splitting from listenin' to you. And the baby's not stopped crying. It's all on account of you casting them evil spell."

Maputo flashed a grin at Libka.

"I cast no spell, Elsie. It's not yet ninety days our good master's soul has left us, and me remembers him more on this day than when the *baas* was among the living."

The woman grimaced, shaking the rag so the dirt sputtered into Maputo's face. "Oh rot! Get movin'. The yard needs cleaning and this is *not* my territory."

"You got a sharp tongue, Elsie, but I see something else in them eyes of yours. You're grievin', Elsie, you're grieving for our master."

"I's doin' nothing of the sort. I got enough troubles for m'self, and don't you make me start up again, Maputo, or so help me I'll have you out!"

Elsie scurried up the steps with the baby and for an instant Maputo looked up into the sun, then he resumed his work.

As he polished the plaque, he chanted a hymn. Libka leaned back and watched as he lifted his glowing face to the sky and sounded the refrain.

> My *baas*, he left the earth,
> In the great heavens he now dwells.
> May the good Lord, may He,
> Look upon my *baas*
> As Maputo had looked upon him.
>
> My *baas*, he left the earth,
> Only yesterday he was here.
> And the veld, it stretches out,
> And my *baas* is no more here.
>
> I will weep for him,
> As I weep for my flesh and blood.
> May the good Lord, may He,
> Look upon my *baas*
> As Maputo had looked upon him.

Though his song held mystery and he tried to console Libka, she would always remember his agonizing cry the night she tapped on the door of his little room in the courtyard and whispered "My daddy is dead."

Today Libka's mood was especially dreary. It had been inspection day at school and the teacher had criticized her dirty nails and untidy hair. During lunch break she had hidden behind the caretaker's shed to avoid being caught alone while the other girls formed a circle on the grass, laughing and chattering as they ate their lunch.

As she sat near Maputo, she kicked off her heavy oxfords. "If only I could make myself disappear like the chameleons."

Maputo looked up at Libka, sweat glistening on his face.

"My little missus don't look too cheerful today."

"Why should I be cheerful? I hate school. At morning assembly they keep reading out the names of the boys killed in action."

"It is a sad time."

"It seems like everybody is dying in this war."

"We must trust in the Lord, Miss Libka. Peace will come again."

The gate rocked as Beryl bounced forward in his school uniform. Maputo moved aside to allow him through. "Good afternoon, young master."

Beryl nodded curtly and took the steps two at a time, then eyed Libka scornfully. "Don't block the entrance. And how about putting on your shoes?"

"How about keeping off Maputo's clean steps with your dirty shoes?"

Beryl hovered over her threateningly, then rushed into the house.

"The young *baas* speaks the truth. It is not fitting for you to sit here conversing with me."

"I don't care what's fitting. I'd rather talk to you than to him. Why do we have these stupid rules? Everything is all wrong in this country. I hate it."

"Is that a proper thing to say, Miss Libka?"

"You should hate it even more, Maputo."

The black man's face turned grave. "For me to be in this household with the good master's family is a gift from the Lord. Before you were born, Miss Libka, the *baas* took me into his home and provided for me."

"I miss my father."

"But you must remember that the Lord has taken him into the heavens and is watching over us all."

As he hummed, Libka thought how lucky they were to have Maputo in their lives. But her thoughts were cut off by Mrs. Peker's voice wafting out from the front room.

"Sara, what you got servants for? You're not in Lithuania no more."

"Rivka, in Lithuania I didn't do much housework," came Sara's reply.

This was a gentle hint to her *landsleit*, who had worked as a maid in Sara's family inn. But Mrs. Peker did not catch on. "Don't you want your children to fit into this society?"

Libka rolled her eyes. Mrs. Peker was always interfering in their lives. And since her father died, she had become almost a daily fixture in their house.

Though Mrs. Peker could not afford a home in Sea Point, she took steps to overcome this. The European names of her children had been changed: Bashka became Betty, Chana was Annie, Hena was Helen, and Sheina was Sally. The last two, who were born in South Africa, were suitably named from the beginning: Naomi and Sheldon.

As soon as the daughters reached puberty, they were groomed for their future. Ships were entering the Cape Town harbour with sailors from America, and the dressmakers would be outfitting the girls according to styles in American film star magazines. Mrs. Peker encouraged her daughters to go down to the docks to meet the sailors. "It's important for girls to socialize and mingle. You never know. In the house you won't meet any prospects," she'd say. "And now with the war it will only get harder. The white boys are dying out like flies. I don't know why they don't send the *shvartze* to war. Of what use are they! The way the war is going, there'll be ten girls to every white boy."

Mrs. Peker's pride and joy was her daughter Sally who, though born in Lithuania, showed no traces of her origin. She emulated Rita Hayworth and Betty Grable whom she saw in the bioscope, elevating herself to four feet ten with her high cork sandals. Sometimes when a ship from America arrived, Mrs. Peker would send Sally to the harbour to lure the sailors over to her house for the benefit of her older sisters. Sally herself, who was scarcely fifteen, had already captured the heart of one of the wealthiest Jewish boys in Sea Point. "He's a Hollywood matinee idol, a Gary Cooper," Mrs. Peker boasted, "and his father has a prosperous scrap metal business."

Libka didn't understand why her mother tolerated Mrs. Peker. They were so different. Mrs. Peker had abandoned all traditions of the old country in her anxiety to climb in society, while Sara preferred to live modestly and preserve the customs of her homeland.

More than ever, Sara was now drawn to the traditions her mother had observed, making *kreplach* filled with meat for the chicken soup; *lokshen* pudding stuffed with raisins, apple and dried fruit; and stewing carrots, prunes and raisins for *tsimis,* which she served with fatty brisket. Dessert consisted of stewed prunes and apricots, and she simmered *taiglach* in honey. As she worked, she hummed Yiddish melodies from her girlhood. "The songs bring me closer to what I left behind," she would tell Libka. But she no longer made wine from the abundant grapes in the Cape, and the barrel Yosef had set up for this in the courtyard now stood empty, gathering moss.

· *four* ·

All afternoon Libka had been in her room and she forbade anyone from entering. If the family found her crying, she would feel disgraced, yet each time she tried to compose herself a new outburst overwhelmed her.

She had sat through the morning sessions at school, dreading the lunch bell when she would go into hiding to avoid being caught alone in the playground. Amid the chatter and excitement that arose the instant the bell rang, she fled from the classroom, heading for the toilet cubicles. This had been her sanctuary for many weeks. She chose a cubicle at the end and sat on the toilet seat, crossing her legs so that they would not be visible. As she unwrapped her sandwich of bread and mashed banana, she listened for any sounds.

Here she would sit for the duration of the lunch break, stiffening each time someone entered the toilet rooms, breathing in relief when the toilet was flushed and the intruder vacated.

When the first bell signalled the end of lunch, she would remain in place because often there would be an onrush of students at this last moment. When the second bell sounded, it was time to hurry, yet she dreaded her exit, imagining a clique of girls waiting outside the cubicles, ready to expose her.

Sometimes she attributed her state to her father's death. Perhaps it was the sadness in her face that drove people away. Sometimes she blamed her mother's European ways; but then she would ask herself why Beryl and Golda did not encounter the same rejection. How was it that they didn't have her troubles? Libka wondered bitterly. Their lunch was no different from hers, and they also came home to a mother who spoke in Yiddish and broken English. At times she wondered if it was her size, the fact that she was so much smaller than other girls of her age. She dreaded the march in line to the assembly hall, the smallest leading the way. When she travelled on trams and buses with her mother she still paid half fare. On seeing Golda and her, people always said to Golda, "You must be the older sister." And Golda never knew what to answer.

Yet why was it that Rebecca Weiss, who was even half an inch shorter than her, was the second most popular girl in school? And what about Sally Peker, who was fifteen already and measured only four foot nine? Was it the lightness in her eyes and the haughty manner that made her so popular?

But all that day Libka sensed that something would be different. She remained withdrawn in the classroom, averting her eyes from any contact with her classmates. And as she hurried to the toilet shed at the sound of the lunch bell, it was as though she knew what awaited her.

She had felt it building in the preceding days, a gnawing in her stomach with sudden tight pains.

Girls were washing their hands at the row of sinks as she entered the grey shed at the back of the playground. Toilets flushed as girls scuttled in and out. She slipped into the end cubicle, hoping no one she knew had noticed, and there she waited for the bustle to subside. Even when the sounds faded in the playground, she remained still as though to muster courage for this moment. And then she knew for sure when she saw the red stain on her bulky bloomers.

She had heard whispers of the beginning of womanhood and had seen her mother scrub similar stains from her own clothes, but she did not understand it and there was no one whom she could ask. She walked awkwardly, her breasts feeling heavier, and her legs could scarcely bear the weight of the oxfords.

She made it back to her class unnoticed, yet when school broke up and she found herself plodding through the grounds and out of the high gate, walking under the silver leaf trees towards the tram stop, tears began to well up. As always, she heard the chatter and laughter of the crowd and felt she could never belong.

As Libka stepped onto the tram heading for Green Point, she walked down the aisle as far as the whites could be permitted. Several coloured women and a few black men sat in their section in back.

Safely home in her room, she removed her tunic, relieved that the stain had not penetrated. She changed into black shorts and was in the midst of a crying spell when the door creaked open. She rushed to it, pushing against the intruder.

"Let me in," Golda begged through the door. "I left my sandals in your room."

"I'm busy. You can't come in."

"But I need my sandals."

"You'll have to wait."

"Mommy," she heard Golda cry, and Libka was hurt that her sister would tell on her. She always got the blame, whether she was guilty or not. When her father had been alive, he would come to her defence, and at night they would sit on the stoep and look at the sky, and he would tell her about the stars and the planets. She always felt he understood her more than anyone else did. Libka buried her face in the pillow and lost herself in longing for her father.

A few times during the afternoon her mother came to the door.

"Libka, open up. What is it with you?"

"Leave me alone."

"Come, have a glass of milk and some *imberlach*."

"Keep your bloody *imberlach*. Do you want me to break another tooth with your gooey carrot cake?"

"Uh! Goldie needs her shoes. She left them in your room by mistake."

"Too bad for her."

Libka would not relent. Her eyes were red and puffy, and if they saw her like this, they might take pity on her and make her cry even more.

Later Shneyer jiggled the door handle and pleaded, "Libka … Libka … Let me hide with you."

She longed to bring in her little brother, bury her face in his golden hair, allow him to cheer her with those wondrous blue eyes and cherubic face, but that would mean submission.

"Open up, you fool!" This was Beryl, who had made an appearance around suppertime. She could just picture him in his grey flannels and green blazer, with the green-and-gold tie and the school insignia. Though he hated school, he loved the uniform, as he loved all uniforms — his khaki army outfit, his Boy Scout uniform and especially his navy outfit with the sailor cap. How he liked to prance about in the white suit with the navy blue trimming and the cap tilted on his glossy black hair that he slicked down with Brylcreem.

"Dummy," he persisted. "Golda needs her sandals."

Libka braced herself against the door, but she was no match for him with his Charles Atlas bodybuilding training. In a single shove he flung the door open and stood glowering at her.

"Pull yourself together," he said. "What are you trying to prove?"

Libka could not contain herself and her face distorted as tears spurted from her eyes. At this, Beryl's expression softened and his voice became gentler.

"I guess you have your reasons," he said, backing out of the room and drawing the door partly closed, "but it's almost suppertime, anyway."

Her brother's reaction triggered a new flood of tears.

No one came to the door after that, and when Libka finally looked at the clock, she saw it was past six.

She had wanted to go to the bathroom for hours and now felt she would make a puddle on the floor. Her stomach rumbled and she worried about staining her shorts. She slid the door open and heard her mother talking in the kitchen. She wondered if the bathroom was clear. Then she heard her brother's voice coming from the kitchen. She crept out of the bedroom and slipped down the passageway to her refuge.

When she was done, she opened the bathroom door a crack. The precise diction of her brother rang out clearly.

"Anyway, don't bother me. I have to get going. But she's partly right too."

"What do you mean?" Sara retorted.

"We don't live like other people, and there's no excuse for it."

"So you want me to throw away this house and build you a mansion in Sea Point?"

"You could at least dress decently and talk in English," he said. "I can't even bring my friends here."

Beryl was rarely home. There was always Joyce down by the Sea Point Pavilion. She and Beryl would stroll along Beach Road holding hands, a striking dark figure in white with a golden-haired princess in chiffon pastels.

"Your father is dead not yet four months ..."

"You've always been this way."

She was slipping out of the bathroom just as Beryl stepped into the hallway.

"Your supper's cold," he said as he elbowed his way into the bathroom. "Listen, Libka, maybe your intentions are good, but you manage to make a mess of everything."

As the door closed behind him she heard him singing:

> If you were the only girl in the world
> And I were the only boy
> Nothing else would matter in the world today
> We could go on loving in the same old way.

· *five* ·

After school the Sea Point girls gathered at the pavilion, where they pranced around in their colourful swimming costumes and flirted with the boys. They sat in groups and gossiped about those who didn't fit into their circle.

Libka remembered when she was still allowed to have lunch with them in the playground. They would confidently open their decorative boxes containing overstuffed sandwiches. There would always be surprises — confectionery in tinsel wrappings, biscuits with rich creams and milk chocolate, and huge juicy grapes. And she would take out her bread and butter from the brown paper bag.

It was so embarrassing! There was no need for such skimpy lunches, she thought. Her family was wealthier than many of the girls who arrived at school in chauffeured limousines and had lunches heaped with meat and eggs and salmon, and the sumptuous fruits from the Malay merchant in the red hat who drove around in his tall wagon, tinkling a bell.

"How can I eat lunch with the other girls if all you give me is bread and butter?" she would complain to her mother.

"I have enough on my hands," Sara would reply, lifting a crying Dina.

"Why can't Elsie make the lunch? No mothers make lunch. Elsie wouldn't send me to school with bread and butter."

"Beryl and Goldie don't complain."

"I'm not going to school anymore."

"So don't go. You have always been a headache to me. One minute hot, the next like ice. If you like something there is no limit, but if ..."

"So what's wrong with liking something?"

"The madness! Remember in the Newlands the Russian doll that you sleep with every night? The servant's baby took a look at it and you gave it away."

"She liked it."

"Of course she liked it. You are just like Daddy. On the ship coming over he emptied his pockets to the *landsleit*. On every island where the ship dock the immigrants wanted everything their eyes could see. 'Yosef,' they said, 'in South Africa we will get rich and pay you back.' You think that happened? They got rich, yes, but we didn't see a penny back."

"So now you're criticizing Daddy!" Libka flared.

"I'm not criticizing, I'm just saying."

"Daddy never complained that people didn't pay back."

"Maybe he didn't, but in his heart he knew."

"Too bad you aren't like Daddy. Everybody loved him."

"Of course. He was such a patient and good man. Even with you, Libinka, he never criticized. With all your tantrums and moods, he always made excuses. He had a sister who was the same, a talented violinist who died of polio when she was twenty-two."

"He told me I'm just like her. And I'm named for her?"

"May your life only turn out better, *mein kind*."

"I don't like you criticizing Daddy. He was the only one who understood me."

Sara lifted her apron and brushed a tear away.

"Enough crying already!" Libka said as Shneyer wandered in. She took her brother by the hand. "I'm taking Shneyer to the Malay store for a treat."

It was after four o'clock by the time Libka and Shneyer returned, and Golda had still not come home from school. Shneyer was excited, showing off his lead soldiers. "Can I play war?" he asked his mother. "The man with the red hat gave me this."

"He's such a nice Malay man," said Libka, her mood lightened by the outing. "It costs sixpence and we only had a tickey but he gave the soldiers to Shneyer, anyway."

"I like that man," Shneyer agreed. "He always let me play with the fire engines and cars and soldiers and war machines."

Sara was attending Dina, who was running a high fever. "Have you seen Golda?" she asked.

Libka shrugged. "Maybe Beryl took her for an ice cream cone."

But Beryl was at rugby practice, and when he returned Golda still hadn't come home. Sara asked him to look for her. "It is not like Goldie to stay away and we don't know where."

"That's true," said Beryl. "So where do you think she is?"

"When she went off to school she didn't say she would be late."

"I'm sure she'll be home any minute."

"Libka, what do you think?" Sara asked. "Is it possible Golda went to Anya's house after school?"

"Maybe," Libka said, trying to hide her concern. She knew how careful her sister was to avoid worrying their mother.

"She always tell us if she will be late," Sara added. "And she didn't have a piano lesson today."

"Without telephones," interjected Beryl, "that's what you get. Joyce has had a telephone in her house for over a year."

"I wouldn't be surprised if she's at Anya's," Libka said, ignoring Beryl's comment. "That girl hangs onto Golda because no one else will associate with her. She's violent like her father."

"I could never understand what they have in common," said Beryl. "And isn't she three years older than Golda, anyway? She's even older than you, Libka. I guess Golda is simply too polite to discourage her."

"People take advantage of her," agreed Sara. "She can't refuse even if she don't want."

"That's true," said Beryl.

"So you think Golda is by Anya's house?" asked Sara, concern in her eyes. "Soon it will be dark."

Libka offered to go to Anya's house. It was a trip of almost an hour on the tram and it was not safe in that district after sundown.

"Be careful, my child," Sara cautioned. "Walk fast and don't get into trouble."

When Libka got off the tram the sun was setting. The ice cream stand was closed and the street vendor was gathering his wares for the night. A few coloured men crouched on the littered pavement amid the smell of urine, and there was the rattle of trams and lorries. Libka waited for the tram to pass, the overhead cables sending out sparks, and then she crossed to the other side, heading towards the mountain.

She followed the steep gravel street where shacks huddled together, much like the coloured district not far from her own home.

The small grey structure with the tin roof where Anya lived stood halfway up the hill, a gnarled tree hanging over it. Libka walked up the narrow cement path and knocked on the door. It opened a crack, and the woman who peered out cautiously seemed to match the bleakness of the surroundings.

"You must be looking for your sister," she said, smiling gently. "Don't worry, my dear, she's here with Anya."

The house was dim. Unpainted furniture stood about haphazardly, and the rug in the passageway was threadbare.

As Libka lingered in the entry, the large, bare-chested form of Anya's father loomed in a doorway, his black hair unruly and his face hostile. He held a glass in his hand and Russian music blasted in the background.

"What does she want?" he hissed at his wife.

"It's all right," the frail woman said apologetically. "She came to fetch her sister."

The man took a gulp from his glass and watched Libka suspiciously as his wife ushered her towards Anya's room. Then, with a grunt, he stomped back into his room and flung the door shut.

"They're in there," the woman whispered to Libka, gesturing at Anya's door. "Maybe I should knock."

When Libka entered, Golda was sitting on the floor beside Anya, who had a puffy black eye and bruises over her face. Books were strewn all over — *The Communist Manifesto* by Karl Heinrich Marx and other volumes with descriptions on the cover like "dictatorship of the proletariat, capitalism and exploitation."

"Since when are you welcome here?" Anya's eyes matched her father's.

"My mother was worried about my sister."

Golda reached for her satchel. "I was just planning to leave."

Riding home on the tram, Libka reprimanded her sister. "Don't disappear without telling Mommy. You know she has enough worries, and I can't waste hours looking for you."

"What was I supposed to do?" Golda's voice was shaky. "She was waiting for me outside my school gate and was afraid to go home alone. She didn't even attend classes today because of the way she looks."

"So her father beat her up again."

"He was drunk and he was hitting her mother and she tried to stop him."

"It's no wonder Anya's brothers and sisters left the minute they matriculated from high school. Does Anya ever hear from them?"

"She says they live in Durban and Johannesburg. I don't think they write much."

"The father probably used to beat them too."

"I think they're annoyed at the mother for staying with him."

"He's violent. I'm surprised he hasn't killed any of them yet. But why do you have to be involved with this? What do you have in common with Anya?"

"How can I refuse?" Golda said defensively. "Anyway, she won't be there much longer. I think she wants to leave South Africa."

"That makes two of us," said Libka. "Daddy also hated this country."

———•———

When they got home, Sara began fussing over Golda so Libka slipped off into her room. She felt increasingly restless these days. She rarely spoke to anyone at home without snapping at them, and at school she would find herself drifting off during class, thoughts of her father taking over her mind.

Though he was dead he seemed even more alive in her. She was constantly remembering things from long ago when she would sit with him on the stoep at night and watch the stars. He told her secrets he would share with no one else. One night he even spoke of his first love, the beautiful Nechama. He had been engaged to her for over seven years and they couldn't marry because of her older spinster sister. Finally, when he fell in love with Sara, he gave up on Nechama, but he never forgot her. And he would tell Libka the story of how he met Maputo when he opened his workshop soon after he arrived from Lithuania, and how they communicated without words because neither of them spoke the English language.

One day, after spending more than the usual time in the cubicles, she simply could not go home after school. She took the tram into town. She had wanted to sit on the upper deck so that she might look down on the streets, but she felt clumsy and self-conscious and the climb up the narrow staircase discouraged her. The lower storey was practically empty except for a group of coloureds who sat in their section in back.

When the tram reached Adderley Street, Libka got off on an impulse. She felt an urge to visit Newlands, the area where they had lived before buying the house in Green Point, and just then the bus to Newlands pulled up. For the first time since they had moved away, she was going back to her old surroundings. She wanted to see again the house where she spent her childhood years, where she had been happy with her father. She wanted to roam in the veld, cut through the tall grass by the bull pen and wander along the narrow, winding paths hidden beneath the ferns and palm trees. She wondered if her old playmate Wendy van Hutenbek still lived there. She longed to pick the berries that grew so abundantly, to pluck the pawpaws, mangos and pomegranates from the trees, and the juicy grapes from the vines. She remembered how she and Golda used to play catch with Kaffir watermelons.

As Libka sat on the bus, the familiar landscape took her back to those years.

The Newlands area was enveloped by forests and streams. Her parents said it reminded them of their youth in Lithuania, where groups of their comrades would gather in the forests and sing and rejoice. The Jews back there were friendly with their Gentile neighbours, many of whom understood the Yiddish language. Still, there had been undercurrents of hatred. Her mother once told her of a pogrom in her *shtetl* of Butrimantz when hooligans flung a Jewish boy to his death from an upper balcony.

When they first moved to Newlands from the little rooms above the workshop, the neighbourhood children came around. Libka played jump rope and hopscotch with Wendy van Hutenbek and Marie Schmidt and sometimes she trailed them to their houses, where the mothers spoke in a language she did not understand.

"*Hoeveel kinders het jou moeder?*" Mrs. van Hutenbek asked Libka as she stood in the doorway with her hair in pink curlers and her petticoat showing.

When Libka looked confused, Mrs. van Hutenbek pulled a face at her.

"I don't understand how she talks," Libka told her mother.

"It is called Afrikaans, the language the Boer people speak. When you start school you will learn it."

Beryl, who was now seven, would return home from school flaunting words in English and Afrikaans. He tried to come to Libka's rescue.

"When they talk to you in Afrikaans, just ask, '*Hoe gaan dit met jou?*' It means 'How are you?' And when they answer say, '*Dit gaan goed, dankie.*' He was proud of the new words, but Libka was even more confused.

Beryl found it easier to learn Afrikaans than English. "It's almost like Yiddish," he told his mother. "They have the same words for house and children and eggs."

"Yes, many Yiddish words are the same in German and Dutch."

Beryl even sang the South African national anthem that he learned at assembly, while he danced the *kazatska* in the kitchen.

"Why do you do a Russian dance when you sing the Afrikaans song?" Sara asked in Yiddish; but Beryl only hopped more fervently.

Libka and Golda would repeat the Afrikaans words that Beryl tried to teach them. "In this country you must learn this language also," Sara told them. "They require English and Afrikaans." She already knew several languages due to the constant changes of regime in her homeland. In addition to Yiddish, her mother tongue, she was fluent in Hebrew and Russian, and understood German, Lithuanian and Polish. Yet she could not put her mind to the new languages, overwhelmed by the demands of raising a family.

Often Libka's mother would take a hen from the hok, bind its legs and hurry through the path in the veld to the ritual slaughterer in nearby Claremont. Sometimes Libka would tag along. On such occasions they would stop off at the Shevah family, who had arrived in South Africa on the same boat. Over glasses of tea with raspberry jam they would talk of those they had left behind in Lithuania. Letters were coming less often from their homeland and there were rumours of increasing problems for the Jews. In one letter Sara's mother had written that they had no sugar to put in her grandchildren's tea. Yosef had filed applications for naturalization, with the hope of bringing over members of the family once he was legally established in the new land.

"At least in South Africa the Jews are safer," he would say. "We should be grateful that Prime Minister Smuts is against the Nazis. But the Afrikaners are not our friends. After all, our ship was the last one they allowed with our people from Europe."

—— · ——

As the bus came closer to the old house in Newlands, Libka thought for the first time in years of her friend Zelda Davinsky. Hers was the only other Jewish family in Newlands and they had befriended her parents soon after they moved to the district. Libka would play with Zelda, a wisp of a girl with piercing black eyes and a freckled nose. To get to Zelda's house Libka would cross the bridge over the brook and see the old white-bearded man with the bent stick. Would he still be there? she wondered. And what about Zelda with whom she used to play marbles and hopscotch and talk in Yiddish?

Sometimes Libka would invite Zelda to her house, where they would sit on the peaked red roof of the chicken hok. The rooster would crow, and it seemed that almost every day shells would crack open and wet little balls would stumble out of the incubator. By the following day their feathers would be ruffled and yellow, and they would peck under their mother's wing. Libka would mix their mash in the troughs and watch them gobble it up, giggling as each scampered to get the largest helping.

Zelda's father peddled needles and notions in the neighbourhood and the family was poor. Sara would sometimes offer them a few chickens, which Zelda's mother would take to the ritual slaughterer. In return she would bring Sara chopped herring, *gefilte* fish and apple strudel.

Beryl had developed an interest in birds and gradually they acquired a cage full of parrots in a myriad of colours. Their screeches from the sun room filled the house. Then there was Mickey the Monkey, devilish and loving, that Beryl had encountered in the forest. Mickey would swing from the branches of the trees in the back garden and nibble on mangos and grapes. Sometimes he would dangle from the washing line, pulling faces and performing like a trapeze artist. His favourite perch was Beryl's shoulder, where he munched on a banana, then flung the peels on Beryl's head. Libka and the other children loved to tease him. He would pretend to be sulking but then he would play a trick on them.

Libka never understood why things began to change. One day when she went to play with Wendy van Hutenbek, Wendy slammed the gate in her face.

"*Jood!*" she shouted, and her brother Piet spat at her.

It was soon thereafter that Scottie, the black-and-white dog that Beryl found limping in the veld, was run over by Mr. van Hutenbek's lorry. The man was always shouting at Beryl, "You keep that crippled dog out of my sight, *Jood*, or you'll find his bones in your yard!"

Other strange things began to happen. Mickey the Monkey was found dead in the back garden, and the children believed he had been poisoned. And then one day Beryl came home from school to find the door to the cage open and all the parrots had vanished.

When Beryl exploded in tears, Libka yelled at her mother. "It's your stupid Jewish. Everybody calls us *Jood* and hates us."

But Sara denied that the family was being sabotaged. "South Africa is a free country. Prime Minister Smuts is still a friend to our people. We are proud to be Jewish and can speak what language we want."

They had been good times until the end, thought Libka. Why had people changed like that? And then she shuddered. At home they rarely spoke of that day of the parade, but Libka remembered every moment. It had been a Saturday morning. Beryl was in Claremont, visiting his friend Itzhak Shevah, and Yosef had gone to the factory. Libka and Golda were playing jump rope in the garden.

For many months the Boer families in the district had been preparing for the Voortrekker march to commemorate the mass emigration of the frontier farmers in the Great Trek. For this centenary celebration the men had grown long beards and the women were sewing Dutch-style dresses and bonnets. And then came the day of the parade that all the children had awaited.

Bouncing in anticipation, Libka and Golda looked in the direction of the sounds. When they caught a glimpse of the spectacle far up on the hill by the bridge, Libka ran out into the street, Golda following. Men and women in Dutch attire were marching to the beat of drums and bugles.

> *O bring my t'rug na die ou Transvaal*
> *Daar waar my Sarie woon.*
> *Daar onder in die mielies*
> *By die groen doringboom*
> *Daar woon my Sarie Marais.*

The Afrikaans folk song grew louder, reverberating with the energy of the marching band. Children raced out of every house, running to meet the sound.

As the pageant passed over the bridge and descended the hill, the marchers sped up, and now women flourished their long skirts as the men stomped their boots.

But when the long beards of the Afrikaners came into view, the procession grew bolder, the drums louder. A black cloud seemed to obliterate the sun and Libka froze as the women's faces twisted into witchlike shapes. A woman whipped her skirt, unleashing the panic within Libka who seized Golda's hand and fled back towards the gate.

The gate was stuck and Libka pounded on it, the sounds of the parade growing louder, with jeers and menacing laughter. Then suddenly the gate bounced open and Libka tumbled through, her sister on her heels, as they fled to the back garden where their mother was hanging out the washing. "Mama!" Libka yelled, tearing at her mother's apron. "Mama!"

"*Sha!*" Sara shouted at the sight of Libka's blazing eyes.

"Mama, they're coming for us!"

"Stop! Don't make a drama!" Sara flicked a wet sheet on the line, but Libka could see that her mother's hands were trembling.

The parade had halted before their house and now they could hear howls and taunts. "*Joods ... Joods ...*" The chant was accompanied by a rhythmic pounding, then the shattering of glass.

Libka squeezed into the chicken hok with her mother and Golda, and they crouched there in terror until the sound of the parade rose up again and disappeared in the distance.

That night when Yosef came home and saw the shattered windows with the rocks scattered in the living room, he grew solemn.

"My family is not safe here," Libka heard him say under his breath. "In this Afrikaner district it is dangerous for a Jewish family to live. We will move. We will go where there are other people like us and where we will not be afraid to be Jewish."

———•———

As the bus entered her childhood world, Libka shook the memory from her head. She got off at a stop near her old street and strolled towards her house. All seemed different. Strange children played outside a tall gate, and the honeysuckles that used to dangle over the hedges were gone. The white house was now an ochre shade, though the awnings remained green, and a dog kennel had replaced the large sunflower in front. She went around to the back and rose on her toes to look over the stone fence. A garage now stood where the chicken hok had been. No Kaffir watermelons grew freely in back, and a brick promenade with white plastic furniture and metal toys covered the area where the fruit trees once stood and flowers used to sprout from the moist soil.

Libka glanced up the hill towards the bridge where the Voortrekker parade had passed. Beyond was the forest, thick with trees. When she was little she would enter through a high gate in an iron fence. Strange bird calls sounded there, and often she sensed that the trees were communing with each other. Libka used to wander deep into the forest where rarely a figure was seen, nestle under an ancient tree and take out her diary where she wrote things she would reveal to no one — poems unloading her feelings and dreams.

"*Waar woon jy?*"

Startled from her recollections, Libka found herself confronted by a flaxen-haired boy surrounded by a group of children.

"*Ek het hier gewoon lank gelede,*" she answered in Afrikaans, explaining that she had lived here a long time ago. It was so rare that she used this language outside of the classroom and the words seemed alien on her tongue.

The boy eyed her dark hair suspiciously.

"*Hier woon my moeder en my vader en my ouma en my oupa en my broers en my susters!*" The snotty-nosed boy recited the members of his family who lived in the house as he flung his bicycle to the ground and stepped forward. He did not believe she had ever lived here.

Sensing the boy's arrogance, the other children rolled up their tricycles, tractors and carts, joining in the protest. An emaciated black dog barked fiercely, charging forward and cornering Libka.

Masking her fear, she extricated herself from the group and crossed the street to the path that would take her into the veld. No palms or fern trees reached out to encircle her, and she wondered if they had ever been here. The land was flat and dry, and the bulls looked angry enclosed in their wire pens. Sometimes she used to come here with Zelda and they would shiver in terror when the yellow-faced woman appeared at the window of the bleak cottage, flattening her nose against the glass. But now the house was barred up, the soiled windows cracked.

As she reached the brook, she followed the steep mud path that took her under the bridge. The water sparkled and lapped against the fertile soil and the tadpoles frolicked. The sounds of cars were muffled from here.

"*Meisie.*" Libka jumped at the sound of an eerie voice.

The waters that had looked so pristine a moment before now mirrored a threatening form.

"*Wat jou naam, meisie?*"

The shadow fleeted across the waters, and then she saw the sallow face.

"*Doodskrik?*"

He was asking if he scared her to death. One look at the yellow-skinned man with bloodshot eyes and she panicked. He held out a sixpence to tempt her. Should she run, or was it better to hide her terror?

At that moment a rock from high up on the bridge splashed into the water. Libka seized the opportunity.

"*My broer!*" She jumped up and looked in the direction from which the rock had fallen. "Coming, Beryl!" she shouted, pretending her brother was there.

She clambered up the muddy path to the bridge and then began to run.

When she finally reached the road the sun was beginning to set. The street was almost empty except for two men who hurried by, talking in Afrikaans.

She found a bus stop and waited for what seemed like hours, worrying that she had missed the last bus. Shaken from the encounter with the intruder under the bridge, she dreaded the thought of having to sleep in the veld. She sat down on the step of a general store, which was closed at this hour, and considered what she should do. If she did not come home that night, her family would likely call the police.

She was ready to give up when a bus appeared. She waved desperately to the driver and breathed a prayer in relief when it slowed down and stopped. The bus was empty except for a boy who got on a short distance from the centre of town. They both stepped off at Adderley Street and the bus veered away. Closer to home, she relaxed and waited for the tram that would take her to Main and York Road.

· *six* ·

As Libka hurried up the hill towards her house, she was still wondering how she had managed to escape. If someone on the bridge had not thrown a rock into the water, she might never have gotten away. The man's eyes were bloodshot and his breath had emitted a strange odour, signs that he was intoxicated with dagga, which was known to drive men to madness.

Darkness was coming fast as she neared her house, and the street lanterns were turning on. Light flickered from some of the houses, but soon the shutters would be drawn, and any white man or woman would hesitate before venturing into those streets.

"Stupid ass!" Beryl blurted as Libka entered the house. "Mom was ready to call the police!"

Elsie came running. "You had your poor mother worried sick. What is it with you, coming from school at dark?"

"Leave me alone."

"A white girl out in the streets after dark! Where you been?"

"Just looking around for trouble," Beryl chimed in.

Libka rushed past them and into her room, but stopped in bewilderment. In the centre where her bed had stood was a chest, and another bed had been placed against the far wall. On that bed sat Golda.

"What's this?"

"Mommy said we have to share a room."

"The house isn't big enough? I'm not sharing a room with you!"

"We have to rent out rooms."

Now when more than ever she needed to be alone, when these strange new things were happening in her body, and her mind seemed so confused, her sister had been thrust in with her!

She clutched at her head. "Why are all these things happening? Why does she have to rent out rooms?"

"You know," said Golda. She hunched her shoulders and escaped into her arithmetic book.

Libka stood over her. "Take your face out of that book!"

"Mommy has to," her sister protested. "She says money goes and now with nobody ..."

"Daddy left us a factory. We're not paupers."

"You know the trouble we're having in the factory. There's no one to manage it."

"If Beryl wasn't such a lazy show-off, he could go in once in a while. But he's too high and mighty to go down to Sir Lowry Road. What would the Sea Point girls think!"

"What could he do, anyway? He's only in school."

"He's fifteen, isn't he?"

"But you know Beryl. Besides, he's not an engineer. What does he know about machines?"

"He's useless. Just wants to be the rugby star and flirt with girls. And he gets so excited when he sees the hundreds of soldiers marching in formation. Stands around and throws them oranges. I bet if he was old enough he'd fight in the war, if for nothing more than to wear the uniform."

"Shh," pleaded Golda. "There's something else." Her voice trembled. "It's about Maputo. Mommy had to let him go."

A sick feeling ran through Libka's body. "Maputo is gone?"

Golda hid her face in the book again, but Libka pulled it from her sister's hands.

"Mommy couldn't afford a bowl of mealie-meal? Have you forgotten that Maputo was in our family before you were born?"

"Give me back my book!"

"Not before you tell me everything! I step out and this is what happens."

"It's not Mommy's fault," Golda wept. "Elsie said he was stealing."

"Stealing! Maputo stealing? If he'd be starving to death, he wouldn't take a mealie unless Mommy gave it to him."

"Well, the silver set that our grandmother gave Mommy is missing."

Libka felt dazed. The set had been in the display cabinet in the dining room ever since she could remember. It was not possible that it could be missing. The only one who had eyes on it was Mrs. Peker, but Libka could not imagine that she would have taken it.

"We found one of the goblets in Maputo's room. He must have sold the rest."

"Something is wrong," said Libka. "And I can assure you that it has nothing to do with Maputo. Where is he now?"

"I don't know. Just give me back my book."

"Cry!" stormed Libka. "Cry over a stupid arithmetic book. But the person Daddy and I loved most in the world is gone, and you don't give a damn about it!"

She flung Golda's book across the floor. Thinking she would burst, she looked about the cluttered room, the unmade beds, the dusty dressers, clothes and books strewn all over. Once, Elsie had kept the rooms neat and she would fuss over the beds and dressers. Now she hardly ever changed the sheets or did the laundry, and yelled even if nothing was asked of her. She shouted at Shneyer and hit the baby, and often lost her temper with Sara.

Libka no longer felt safe in this house and feared what might happen next.

———•———

Sara, Beryl and Golda were sitting around the dining-room table while Libka lurked in the passageway, glued to every word.

"Naturally, it can't go on like this," Sara was saying. "She was never a normal child, but since Daddy died she's out of control."

"It can only be for the best that Maputo is gone," Beryl said, pouring vinegar over his potato chips. "Particularly so if it turns out that he's a thief. I must confess, though, that it's hard to believe, but why would Elsie lie?"

"Who knows?" said Sara.

"Wasn't that the silver set your mother gave you for a wedding present? And I seem to recall you told us our great-grandfather made it."

"Yes." Sara brushed a tear away.

"Anyway," said Beryl, "don't start crying again. I think on the whole it's good that Maputo is gone, with the way Libka was so chummy with him. It's one thing to be civil, quite another to socialize with a Kaffir."

How could anyone who talked like that be in her family? thought Libka. No wonder he fit in so well with the Sea Point crowd.

"I don't want any more snoek." Golda pushed her plate away. "I have such a terrible headache."

Beryl's eyes brightened. "Can I have it?" He stuck his fork into the fish on Golda's plate.

"I wouldn't be happy to break up the family," Sara sighed, "but what else can I do?"

"Didn't you say it's very expensive at that boarding school?"

"The school in The Gardens is very expensive. But there is another place Mrs. Peker mentioned. It is far from Green Point and she don't think many Jewish girls go there, but she claim it will do Libka good."

"Her recommendations aren't the best," said Beryl, "but I guess you've got to do something."

"I would like to send Libka to a place with other Jewish girls, but I have to be careful with the money with five children still to educate."

"Okay, okay, I'm not interested in your education."

"It is important, Beryl. Education is the most important thing, especially for young people."

"I don't see what I get out of it."

"If you would concentrate more on your studies and less on the girls and your weight lifting, maybe you would do better in school."

"Don't tell me how to run my life." Beryl got up from the table, almost capsizing his chair.

"Stop," pleaded Golda, "my head is splitting."

"But it's true," said Sara, "Maputo was a good servant, devoted like a dog. And with Elsie it's not so easy, such a fussy lady. It don't suit her to do the heavy work. And mealies and porridge she don't like. Fresh orange juice and eggs and milk and fish. Only the best. Ugh!"

"These coloureds," said Beryl, "they have to be kept in their place. I agree with you about Elsie. She's been acting as though we have to serve her. Let's face it, what would these coloureds do without us! We give her a room, we give her meals and four pounds two shillings a month."

"Yes, Elsie is not the same. In the months when Daddy was sick and we had heavy expenses, she told me, 'Missus, I'm sorry if I argue about the wages. You can pay me as much as you want.' Of course I didn't reduce her wages."

"She sure has a different attitude now. She even neglects to polish my shoes. Says that's Kaffir work."

"That's what happens when a father dies," said Sara. "Everybody takes advantage."

"Suddenly they all start acting like white kings," said Beryl, reaching for another chip. "And she doesn't seem to be around much anymore. Gets dressed up in those bright outfits and trots off through the front door without an explanation."

"She tell me the coloured people like dancing and music and in the house she hear only crying. She take the day off whenever she want, and the truth is I don't care."

"Do you think it's true, Mommy," Golda asked, "what she said about Maputo?"

Sara shrugged. "I would never believe that Maputo would steal, but why would Elsie make up such a thing? Also, she find the silver goblet in his room. She show me."

"Libka doesn't believe that's true. She said he would rather starve than take even a mealie."

"She tends to be overly dramatic," said Beryl, "but I confess it seems strange. After all, he's been in our household all these years and nothing like that ever happened."

Libka, still lingering in the passageway, drew closer.

"Was he sad, Mommy," Golda asked, "when you told him he had to leave? I just saw him walk off with his blanket and that torn old canvas sack."

"Are you going to start crying over him too?" asked Beryl.

"I didn't tell him to leave, Goldala. Beryl and I only tell him what Elsie say. He listen quietly, then said he don't want to make more problems in the house, so he will go away."

"I must say he conducted himself in a most dignified way," commented Beryl. "He went into the yard, slung his old blanket over his shoulder and slipped out of the rear exit."

"And we still owed him for almost a month's wages," said Sara. "I was ready to give him an extra crown, but he went before I could pay him."

"Fancy that, going off without his wages," said Beryl. "Well, at least he has his blanket, which is his most prized possession. He'll likely return to the Transvaal where he came from."

Heartsick, Libka tiptoed out onto the stoep. Evening was coming and darkness comforted her. She nestled into the leather armchair where she used to sit with her father. He wouldn't have let this happen to Maputo.

She remembered the story he had told her of how he found Maputo even before she was born. Her father had arrived on the ship from Lithuania only two months earlier and opened his workshop in the industrial district around Sir Lowry Road. One day he sensed someone hovering in the doorway and turned to see the tall figure of Maputo. He was soaked from the rain and had no shoes on his feet. All he carried was a torn grey blanket. Neither her father nor Maputo could speak English but her father knew instinctively that Maputo could be trusted. He led him into the workshop and brought down a cot from their small quarters upstairs, and Sara prepared a bowl of mealie-meal. They later learned that he had come from the Transvaal, where his family was wiped out by an epidemic, and had been wandering through the townships and shanty towns, where he slept in squatter camps. Maputo would always say that her father had saved his life.

A flood of light struck Libka from the passageway as Beryl appeared in his Boy Scout outfit. "Your supper's cold."

She did not answer, embarrassed to be found in the dark, snuggling in her father's chair.

"Seriously, Libka," her brother said, "for your own good, start behaving properly."

She sat unmoving, determined to maintain her composure.

Seeing her strangely fixed stare, Beryl grew nervous. He stuck his hand into the pocket of his khaki shorts and produced a small packet of chewing gum. He rattled it and held it out to her. "Here, have a chiclet. A sailor from America gave it to me."

Although Libka loved the candy-coated gum, she ignored him.

"Go on. Take two if you want." He rattled the box again.

"Just don't interfere in my life," Libka blurted out, ashamed at the emotion in her voice.

"You'll thank us for it," said Beryl. "I can understand partly how you feel about Maputo," he continued. "It's true he was like a member of the family. But, Libka, what did you have in common with him? After all, he's not of our class. You can't get away with that kind of behaviour around here. Didn't you hear recently over the wireless that a white woman was arrested for a similar offence?"

"Offence! What do you mean?"

"You know bloody well you used to socialize with Maputo way beyond the call of duty."

"I'll socialize with anyone I please, and it doesn't matter what colour they are."

"You know where radicals like you end up in this country."

"Then I'll proudly go to jail."

"Don't be so smart!"

Libka jumped up from the armchair and headed for the entrance, but her brother stopped her. "I might as well tell you, everyone's ridiculing you. What's this about your spending lunch break in the toilet cubicles?"

His words were too horrible. How did he know?

"It's no secret, Libka," he said. "Everybody's talking. Joyce even told me."

Joyce! The beauty queen at the Sea Point Pavilion! Was she Beryl's spy now? They made a pair, Joyce and her brother. Just all show!

"You bring Joyce to this house again," she fumed, "and I'll ..."

She dodged past him, rushing for her room, but there on the bed lay Golda, destroying any hope of privacy.

seven

As Sara would sit in the kitchen late into the night, Libka would often lie awake in bed, rigid lest the springs of the mattress give her away. In these quiet hours compassion would well up in her. The tension and anger that so possessed her during the waking hours would give way to tenderness, and many times tears would drench her pillow. She would listen for sounds that sometimes escaped from her mother — a sudden exclamation, *"Ver vais!"* or a stream of Yiddish words rambled off so rapidly that Libka couldn't grasp them, even though she often spoke in Yiddish with her mother. And still there would be songs, old European melodies that her mother sang as a girl. She would also recite from the Russian poets, one of her favourites being Mikhail Lermontov:

> Marvellous and solemn are the heavens
> And the earth is sleeping in a pale blue light.
> Then why am I so troubled and so heartsick
> Do I still hope or do I feel regret?
> Do I still hope or do I feel regret?

One night the sounds coming from the kitchen were so harsh that Libka became afraid. There had been a letter from her mother's brother Meyer in America in which he wrote that the Nazis were determined to murder all the Jews of Europe. Sara had been strange all day. And now, was she going mad, talking to herself so heatedly? Her words became more intense, with exclamations followed by weeping, and Libka decided she had to stop this.

She turned on the hall light, then called "Mommy" before entering the kitchen.

"Aw, Libkala, how come you are up?"

"How can anybody sleep with your endless chatter?"

"Me? I was just reading."

Libka lifted the Yiddish book lying beside her mother. "All your books are in Jewish. Can't you start reading in English for a change?"

Sara fingered the book reverently. "It is by a great Russian writer, Anton Chekhov. I even act in a play by him when I was a girl in Europe — *The Three Sisters*, like my three daughters."

"Oh, stop. So who were you talking to all night? I couldn't even sleep."

"Ugh, come on," Sara tried to humour her. "Maybe you'll have a glass of milk, warm with Hershey's chocolate syrup?"

"Put plenty of chocolate in this time."

Cheerfully Sara went to the refrigerator, removed a large container and poured milk into the pot. Then she put it on the stove to heat.

"You know, Libkala," she said, "I was thinking tonight, in fact more than usual I was thinking ..."

"You mean more than usual you were talking!"

"Don't watch me like a prisoner. Really, I must say, you are a wonderful child."

"Muzeltov!"

"No, no, I mean it. Aw right, so you fight, you argue, but in your heart is good. Like Daddy."

"I didn't come here to listen to this."

"No, hear me out." Sara rose and moved to the stove. "Aw, wait. I better check the milk. The cream shouldn't boil over. Is it all right only lukewarm?"

"Don't be stingy with the chocolate."

"Here. I give you the jar and do yourself."

Sara put a glass of warm milk beside Libka, then she hurried to the refrigerator and removed the jar of chocolate syrup.

Libka tried to open the container but it was stuck.

"You give me a jar that doesn't open."

"I will put a little warm water on the rim and it will open. Come, I will show." Proudly she demonstrated. "See? Magic!"

Sara sat down opposite Libka, watching as she dug the spoon into the syrup and let it dribble into the glass. Once ... twice ... but when the spoon entered the jar for the third time, Sara exclaimed, *"Oy!"*

"I thought you said I could have all I want."

"Ugh, don't be mad."

Libka licked the spoon from every direction.

"You put on the act, you get dramatic, but I must tell you — Beryl, Golda, they are good children, but they are more interested in themselves. Beryl always dress up and fuss and run with girls and want that the house should be a palace in case the fancy Joyce will come to inspect. And always the best meals he demands, everything on time! And God forbid if a fork is missing from the table. Of course I'm not complaining — he is like all the boys. Listen, and why not? A handsome boy, popular, sociable. And Golda we know, a good child, agreeable. Whatever you give her is good."

"Shush already!" Libka stirred the chocolate at the bottom of the glass, slowly funnelling it upwards.

"And you, my Libinka, you are a troublemaker, we know that. But I tell you really that you sacrifice more than anybody else. After all, you are already a young lady."

"What do you mean, lady?"

"All right, you *are* a lady. Of course! So why shouldn't you dress up nice sometimes and go out and have fun and play?"

"You go have fun."

"Always in the old black *shmate*, barefoot, hair in your eyes. And I'll tell you, you can even put on a little lipstick."

"I don't need your permission."

"Of course I understand we are still in mourning, but, Libinka, it would be better for you also if you took more interest in yourself ... not always just in the house, worrying about Dina and Shneyer ... and how you eat yourself up over Maputo."

"You have no heart!"

"I know Maputo was a devoted —"

"How could you! After so many years! Wasn't he in the family even before Beryl was born?"

"*Sha!* He will be better off in the Transvaal with his own people. What do you think, with Daddy dead, this was such a paradise for him? Always singing the sad African songs and the eyes big and watery."

"Quiet!"

"And it will be better for you too. A white girl ... it is not normal to be so attached to a servant."

Libka guzzled down the chocolate syrup.

"*Mein kind,* look after yourself. And don't worry so much about everything in the house. If you will be happy, we will all be happy."

"What should I do, go down to the docks and pick up a sailor? Like Mrs. Peker's daughters, like her Sally?"

"Who talk about sailors? But what was wrong with Dr. Lerman's son, the boy who used to come sometimes here?"

"You mean Beryl's friend?"

"Don't tell me Beryl's friend. We know he come to see you. He also like poetry and books."

"So you get chummy with him."

"Ugh, it is impossible to talk to you. And what with Sheila Lipstein? Why she haven't come to the house now for months?"

"Because she's too fat."

"Ugh, who can talk to you!"

"And I can't stand fat people." Libka opened the jar of syrup and removed another heaping spoonful.

"If you can't stand fat people, maybe you shouldn't eat so much the rich chocolate."

Libka slurped the syrup into her mouth. "Mmm ... mmm ..."

Sara waved her hand in resignation. "Go back to sleep. What's the use?"

"You can't wait to talk to the mice again?"

"The mice give me less trouble than you."

· *eight* ·

One Saturday afternoon Sara was supervising the children's bath before going downtown to Adderley Street to check the Jewish Agency for possible survivors in Lithuania when a car pulled up in front of the house and deposited Mrs. Peker. She made her way up the steps, studying them for glossiness. Outfitted in a floral dress with a veiled summer hat and white gloves, she might have been going to a garden party. Sara sighed. Mrs. Peker hadn't been visiting so much lately, and Sara preferred it that way.

"Sorry to barge in like this, my good Sara, but we need to talk." She stopped short when she saw Golda wrapped in a towel. The girls had just had their turn in the bath and Sara was bathing the two younger children.

"There isn't enough hot water in Cape Town?" Mrs. Peker declared. "The whole family bathes in the same water?"

Sara motioned to Golda to finish up with the little ones, and ushered Mrs. Peker from the room.

Passing the dining room she caught sight of a freshly scrubbed Libka sitting at the table studying a sepia photograph of a wrinkled old woman wrapped in a shawl with two little girls in matching frocks and high laced boots.

"Oh, can I look?" Lifting her veil, she tugged the photo from Libka's hands and scrutinized it. "Your *boba!* And these must be your cousins." She turned to Sara. "Where did you get this picture?"

"I received yesterday a letter from my brother Meyer in America and he send the picture of my mother and Shleymi's daughters. Libka was always asking how her *boba* looks. The picture was taken in 1939. The last letter I received from Shleymi was in May 1940. Who knows if they are still alive. Meyer think maybe the whole family in Europe is dead."

Mrs. Peker removed her gloves and rested in a chair, for once at a loss for words. She fiddled with the picture. "Your mother looks so old and worn out. Terrible!" She dropped the photo onto the table.

Libka snatched it and fled the room, appalled at the woman's tactlessness, but Sara merely sighed.

"Of course, wartime."

"So what else does your brother write?"

"He would like us to consider immigrating."

"To America?"

"Well, with Yosef dead, we don't have anybody left. I would like to be closer to Meyer and it would be good for the children to have cousins."

Mrs. Peker waved a warning finger. "You know the story about Malka Garbovsky and her family who went to America. In two months they came back. Listen, in America the life is not easy. Here your Libka, if she straightens out and gets married, can have three servants, four if she wants. But in America she'd be lucky if she had one servant."

"Servants are not everything," said Sara.

"Don't fool yourself!"

Dina crawled in, reminding Sara she must prepare the pram for the trip into town.

"If you will excuse me for a minute," she said.

"This chair is very uncomfortable," Mrs. Peker complained, moving to the sitting room where she spread out on the mauve settee and hoisted her puffy legs onto the footstool.

"Come on, Sara, I don't have time, so I'll get right to the point."

Sara wheeled in the pram, placing a fluffy pillow inside it.

"Sit, sit, what's the rush? And listen carefully, Sara. You want that your children, God forbid, should be ousted from the Sea Point community? You already ran away from Newlands."

"I don't understand what you are saying," said Sara, sitting down on the edge of a chair.

"Who but an old friend would come to talk to you like this? If I can't speak plainly, who can? And it's not even surprising what my Sally tells me about your Libka. How can you expect a girl to have any self-respect under the circumstances? God forbid, next you'll be getting down on your hands and knees to scrub the floors."

Shneyer toddled in, pulling at his mother as Dina tugged at his feet.

"Riva, I must go now," Sara said firmly, but Mrs. Peker remained undeterred.

"You think it's easy for me to talk like this? But my Sally come home from school yesterday, and I'll tell you plainly, she shook me up. Funny rumours are spreading around the school about your Libka."

"Rumours?"

"In plain English, your daughter is eating lunch on the potty."

"Potty?"

"Potty potty. Lavatory! She eats her lunch in the lavatory!"

"Ugh," said Sara, "what girls talk."

Shneyer pushed Dina away and she began howling.

"Shh, shh ..." said Mrs. Peker. "I know it's a terrible thing to lose a husband. Such a respected man. But for your own children, you got to go on. You got to maintain the proper front. And what's this I hear about your planning to rent out rooms? When my Mishka told me this, I almost got a blackout."

Sara tried to calm the infant.

"How will it look to other people?" Mrs. Peker persisted. "So it will bring in a few pounds. Is it worth it? I'm a liberal person, but what class of people could you get? A *menchisdika* person don't look for a room. You'll attract the lowest element! Will this be a suitable influence for your children?"

"In my position," Sara explained, "I have to be practical. I have five young children to bring up and educate."

"Your husband, may he rest in peace, left you a prosperous factory. And what about the sawmill where Yosef was a sleeping partner? Those two brothers didn't treat you right?"

"After Yosef died they tried to make that it wasn't worth anything. I didn't get much from it."

"Well, you don't want the same thing to happen with the engineering factory. What you need is a good manager. Motel Shmerl from Wynberg, he's still interested?"

Shneyer and Dina were rolling on the floor, playing and fighting, Dina's diaper soggy.

"Your children, they can be a goldmine to you," Mrs. Peker continued, oblivious to the commotion. "The years go by, they go by fast. And before you know it, in another three years your Libka will be sixteen. If you play your cards right, you can marry her off to a rich South African. But, Sara, not the way it's going. What young man will look at her, showing up for services on *Shabbes* in the same black *shmate*. And still the rip in the collar."

"She is in mourning for her father."

"When you're young, you're young. And a normal girl don't act that way. A normal girl don't eat her lunch on the potty. Listen, I'm not saying every girl has to be like my daughters, God bless them. The sailors shower them, shiploads from America they shower on them. The Wrigley's chewing gum, American sweets, fancy film star magazines with fashion models and starlets ... And they even send love letters. I have evidence."

"Libka is a different sort," Sara said, "more serious."

"So that's smart, for a girl to be serious? The best marks in school won't buy her a husband. A boy can be a scholar, but a girl should plug up her brains with all this nonsense? It's more important to look pretty. The simpler she is, the better catch she makes."

· *nine* ·

When Libka came home from school that day she sensed, even as she walked down the passageway, that there was a beacon on the horizon for her family. The house was unusually quiet, and she spotted Dina tottering happily along. When the infant caught sight of Libka, she ran towards her. She circled her pudgy arms around Libka's leg and tilted backward, looking up and laughing gleefully.

Libka flung the satchel from her back and lifted her sister into the air. She twirled her around and then put her down gently. Dina sat dazed for several seconds; but when Libka moved on, she crawled after her, babbling for more.

Libka found her mother in the dining room sorting through papers on the table. She was humming a cheerful tune. When Libka entered, she ran to greet her with a smile.

"Good. You came straight from school."

Libka could not believe the change in her mother. Sara wore a floral dress with a magenta brooch, high heels and silk stockings, and her dark hair was neatly arranged in a bun with a pearl decoration. Libka noticed she even wore lipstick. Since her father's death, Libka had not seen her mother look so vibrant.

"How come you're so togged up?" she asked.

Sara dismissed it with a chuckle. "Just a little respectable, that's all."

"It's about time, but what's the occasion?"

"Oh, stop that nonsense. Should I dress up all the time at home?"

Libka glanced at the papers on the table. "What are these?"

"Wait," Sara said. "Change from the school uniform and we will talk. A glass of chocolate milk and a *taigel*?"

"Oh, you made *taiglach*?"

Dina pattered in, saliva bubbles over her face.

"What a *popke!*" Libka tickled the baby's belly. This made Dina laugh so much she almost choked.

"Enough already," said Sara. "Don't get wild."

Libka retrieved her school bag from the passageway and headed towards her room, Dina scurrying after her.

A few minutes later when Libka came into the kitchen dressed in yellow pedal pushers and a white capped-sleeve blouse, Sara was scooping tarts out of a pot of honey and placing them on a platter. Libka reached for a gooey tart.

"Wait, wait," Sara reprimanded, "don't burn your fingers with the *taiglach*."

Libka blew on the hot tart, then stuck it in her mouth, moaning with pleasure.

"Sit down like a *mench* and eat with a glass of milk."

Elsie dashed in and headed for the dishes in the sink. "Is she causing you problems again, missus?" the maid asked. She too was in a festive mood.

"You know how she is when something comes fresh out from the pot."

"I reckon I do." Elsie straightened Libka's messy hair. "Now scoot, child. I'll bring out the refreshments in the dining room, and you'll sit at the table like a proper young lady."

"Proper young lady," scoffed Libka.

"Yes indeed." Elsie waved the dish towel at her. "And why not?"

"Who wants to be a proper young lady?" Libka reached for another *taigel* as Elsie pushed her out of the kitchen.

"And put on shoes," the woman added, "or you'll make footprints on those darned floors. There's no Maputo no more to shine them up."

Libka clamped her mouth and left Elsie and her mother chatting in the kitchen.

She was on the stoep, her bare feet dangling over the ledge, when she heard Elsie's voice, "Refreshments on the dining-room table."

Libka bounced up in excitement.

"That child," Elsie mumbled as she patted Libka's behind. "You are a terror if the truth be known."

In the dining room Sara was spooning raspberry preserves into a glass of tea, and a mug of chocolate milk with a plate containing two *taiglach* stood at Libka's place.

"What happened to the rest?" Libka stuffed a tart into her mouth.

"*Sha!*" said Sara. "The other children also like the *taiglach*."

"So what are those papers all about?"

"Mr. Shmerl was here this morning," Sara said earnestly, stirring the preserves in her tea. "We are thinking of making an arrangement for him to run the factory."

Libka was startled. Mr. Shmerl was a *landsman* who had come to South Africa on the same ship as her parents. He was a ruddy-faced man with a gleam in his eye that Libka never trusted. His wife was a timid woman whose stomach always bulged. They had at least nine children.

Libka remembered what she had overheard at the time of her father's funeral, about him pinching someone's behind and his wife having no teeth because he wouldn't pay to fix them. As far as she could see, Mr. Shmerl was someone to avoid.

"Motel Shmerl sees that I am a widow with five small children and he had the greatest respect for Daddy. He is a qualified mechanical engineer. In Durban he worked for the railroad, but I don't know what happened. Since they came back to Cape Town they're struggling with their variety shop in Wynberg so he's ready to make a change."

"Hmm, hmm ..." Libka sipped her chocolate milk.

"You have something against him?" Sara inquired.

"I'm just listening."

"He will go down to the factory and inspect. Right now there is nobody to manage it. Fortune is a loyal foreman, but he is not a engineer. I think it would be a good thing for us and also for Mr. Shmerl."

Sara spoke with such optimism that Libka restrained herself, despite her doubts.

"It's true in Europe Mr. Shmerl was considered unstable," Sara continued, "but his wife Masha straightened him out."

"So you're thinking of making him a partner?"

"Not a partner. He doesn't have money to invest, but we can make an arrangement for him to manage the firm. He is, after all, a *landsman* and a qualified engineer."

Since Yosef's death, the United Engineering Works had been without a manager. Mr. Adelson, the accountant, checked in a few times a week strictly out of friendship, refusing to accept compensation, but he had his own accounting firm to manage. A consulting engineer came in periodically to resolve mechanical problems, but he remained detached from the daily operation of the firm. A skilled engineer was needed to run the business.

"So when will Mr. Shmerl start?" Libka asked.

"We have to sign the papers. His oldest boy Chaim will run their variety store in Wynberg. Mr. Shmerl is thinking of closing the shop anyway, so he is ready to start in the factory right away."

· *ten* ·

The clang of the school bell announcing the lunch break continued to unsettle Libka. It was the time that exposed her aloneness. Sick of the cramped toilet cubicles, for a while she found shelter behind a bent old tree in the rear of the playground, and on rainy days she sometimes hid in the cloakroom. But when Sally Peker and a few of her friends caught her, she abandoned these sites and searched out others. Hiding behind the caretaker's tool shed one day, her Afrikaans teacher found her.

"What are you doing here?" she demanded in Afrikaans.

"Practising ..." Libka held up her calligraphy book and fountain pen.

"But, child, the ground smells of manure. Brush the mud off your tunic and go wash up."

The toilet shed offered the least threat. Here she would wait out the hour until the second bell struck for class.

One afternoon as Libka came out of the shed she sensed someone behind her. She was in her white gym suit and felt self-conscious, so she sped up her pace and walked down the hill without looking back. The second bell had sounded, and she must hurry to make her gym class in time.

The footsteps behind her persisted; and when she walked faster, the steps kept up.

"Toodly too!" came a familiar voice.

Libka threw her empty lunch bag into the bin and continued on.

"Poodly boo!"

The voice sounded like Anya. Maybe if she didn't respond, she would be discouraged.

"Yoodly poo!"

Just as she passed the caretaker's shed, her pursuer jumped ahead and stood radiant in the sunlight.

"Stay away from me, Anya!"

"How does it feel," the girl mocked, "listening to everyone make doody?"

"Scram!" shouted Libka. She tried to escape but the other blocked her way.

"Come on, tell me."

"The second bell's gone," said Libka. "Let me go."

Anya remained calm. "What do you do, pray on the toilet for your father?"

Libka glared at her. "I see you have another black eye. I wonder how you got that. I guess my sister hasn't stayed over your house lately, huh?"

"Starting up again, little twit?"

"I wouldn't waste my energy." Libka shouldered past her.

"Hey," shouted Anya, "the twit's got something on her gym shorts."

The taunt in Anya's voice alarmed Lipka.

"Hey! Don't you want to know?"

With dread in her heart Libka continued to move towards the school entrance, Anya jogging along behind her.

"Here, let me show you."

When Anya reached towards her, Libka flared up. "Go away!"

"It's only your period," squealed Anya.

Libka turned to her, frozen.

"Don't be mad at me. I didn't do it," said Anya, her eyes twinkling with laughter.

Libka had no choice but to turn back towards the toilet rooms. Anya continued her pursuit. Sauntering behind Libka, she called, "Toodly too! Poodly boo!"

Finally Libka exploded. "Drunkard's daughter!" she yelled.

They flung each other to the ground, and an excited crowd had gathered by the time strong hands intervened.

——•——

Two days later Sara received a letter from Miss Bloemfontein, the head-mistress of Promenade High.

> We are sorry to notify you that your daughter Libka has been the cause of a serious problem at our school. For some time we have had reports of unusual behaviour, and on the afternoon of April 9 she attacked a schoolmate in the playground. Due to these circumstances we consider her a hazard in the school and have no recourse but to suspend her from further classes. Should you wish to discuss this most unfortunate situation in greater detail, I shall be delighted to do so.

Sara went to see the headmistress right away. A stern-looking woman with a silver bun, Miss Bloemfontein nonetheless greeted her cordially, though she was insistent about the decision. This was based, she explained, on reports from reputable students who had observed

Libka's behaviour and the remarks of a particular teacher who had discovered her eating her lunch in a manure patch.

"What you recommend I should do, Miss Bloemfontein?" Sara appealed to her. "You consider she is a danger to the school?"

"This is our conclusion," the headmistress said. "When a student's behaviour shows evident signs of a curious nature, and is confirmed by a display of violence, what do you expect us to think, Mrs. Hoffman?"

"This girl she fight with," Sara said, "they are friends but they always argue and play together."

"When such an occurrence takes place outside the confines of the school grounds, we have little authority in the matter. However, when an outright display of violence is thrust before us, is it not our duty to protect innocent pupils?"

Sara groped for words. "Miss Bloemfontein, you say her behaviour is not right. Can you give me a example?"

"I've already mentioned several instances to you, Mrs. Hoffman. Her Afrikaans teacher was the first to bring the matter to my attention. She found it distressing that your daughter would spend the lunch break in a smelly part of the playground behind the caretaker's shed. When confronted, her reaction was hostile. Naturally, I did not wish to be rash, but thereafter I alerted my faculty to keep watch upon your daughter. I am sorry to have to tell you, Mrs. Hoffman, that when a girl spends day after day hiding out in a lavatory, we do not consider this acceptable behaviour."

The headmistress fingered a black fountain pen and peered at Sara from over her glasses.

"Though we cannot make any assumption," Miss Bloemfontein went on, "it seems that this is a case of an emotional disorder. Your daughter unquestionably needs a psychiatric evaluation. I urge you, my dear woman, to tend to the matter without delay."

————•————

For several days after her session with Miss Bloemfontein Sara was silent. She could speak to no one of this misfortune, for she believed that such an admission could ruin the lives of her entire family. This kind of sickness was unmentionable. She could not believe that such a curse had befallen her. She recalled cases of madness in Europe. People would whisper, and the family of the cursed one was forever doomed.

It was to Beryl that Sara finally vented her feelings.

"I will not start up with doctors," she insisted. "I already know from the experience with Daddy. He was not so sick in the beginning, but then when we start with Groote Schuur Hospital and the operations and specialists from all over South Africa, even England, they finish him off. Cutting him open, sewing him up and then cutting open again. I'm sorry, but to me it looks like a healthy person can get sick when they start with the doctors."

"But if the headmistress said so, wouldn't she know?"

"It is easy for people to talk. One little thing a child do different and right away she is not normal. You know already about Anya Steinberg — a wild animal, just like the father. So is it so criminal for two girls to argue?"

"But what about the other thing," said Beryl, "her hanging around the toilets?"

"Not everybody is a social butterfly," Sara flashed. "Daddy was also not a big mixer, and she take after Daddy. So what, everybody has to talk and laugh every minute? And her marks! All A's and Excellent and 'Libka is exceptionally gifted,' the English teacher wrote."

Beryl hesitated. He would have liked to believe his mother, but other feelings persisted. "But Joyce even said ..."

"Never mind what Joyce say," Sara cut in. "Libka will never be that sort, with the fancy nonsense and the big airs."

"What d'you mean!"

"When girls get together they talk and spread all kinds of rumours. Who knows if it is even true. So Libka is not a sociable child, but she isn't mad, that I can guarantee you. Besides, she is calmer these days. She saw the letter from the headmistress and she didn't throw or break anything. So she won't go to school the rest of the term. She will make it up. I'm not worried. But I don't have to call doctors for such a crime."

—•—

To Libka news of her expulsion from Promenade High seemed natural and inevitable. She was relieved things had turned out this way.

She hated school and there was so much happening in the house that demanded her presence.

Strange people were coming and going, inspecting the rooms, talking with her mother in the sitting room. One man in a soldier's uniform stayed longer than the others, then he wrote out a cheque and ruffled Shneyer's curls. "Nice little chap."

Two days later, as Libka was coming home from a swim in Three Anchor Bay, a lorry pulled up in front of the house. The man who jumped out was dressed in orange shorts and sandals and his open shirt exposed a hairy chest. He was hardly recognizable as the same person who had rented the rooms. Flaunting his muscles, he growled in Afrikaans as two black men appeared from the rear of the lorry. He shouted orders as they struggled up the steps, breathing heavily against the weight of the chipped cabinets and rusty bed.

"*Aantrek! Aantrek!*" he yelled from his position on the stoep, ordering the workers to move faster. "*Domkop!*" he barked as they stumbled.

The men staggered up and down the steps while the white man's mouth circled a thick cigar.

"*Jy woon hier?*" he asked Libka.

What a foolish question, she thought, asking if she lived here.

"I don't understand Afrikaans," she lied.

He eyed her suspiciously and broke into crude English. "I saw one baby crawling around there in the back, another messing in the passage. Don't tell me there're more of you!"

"There are five of us," Libka said proudly, "three girls and two boys."

"Five! Then your mother lied to me. Where is she?"

Sara had gone downtown on her weekly trip to check if any survivors had appeared on the Red Cross list or the Jewish Agency.

"My mother's not home."

The man stomped through the house, inspecting every corner, and even peered into rooms where the door had been closed.

When he finally disappeared into the rented rooms, Shneyer came out on the stoep. He looked up at Libka. "Who's that man?"

"He's going to live here."

"Is he somebody's daddy?"

"I don't know."

Shneyer's eyes flitted to the stranger's rooms, then he pressed himself against Libka. "Did he come to be our daddy?"

"Nobody else will be our daddy," said Libka. "Our daddy is dead."

"Who's dead?" Elsie's voice cut in as she eyed the passageway in disgust. She flapped a rag at Libka. "You drag in all the dirt from Three Anchor Bay. Why you don't go to swim at the white pavilion like all the girls?"

"I don't like the Sea Point Pavilion."

"You strut in here with the filthy towels and there's no Maputo to clean up after you!"

"I miss him. I wish he were still living with us." Libka rolled up her damp towel.

"Don't you mention his name to me," flashed Elsie. "These Kaffirs! Imagine stealing your mother's silverware."

"I still don't believe he took it."

"Didn't you see the goblet I found in his room? Who else would do such a thing?"

"I wonder where he went."

"Now listen here, Miss Libka. I tell you once and I tell you again, I don' want you bringin' up his name. Imagine, a white girl behaving in that fashion with a Kaffir!"

"He's my friend, Elsie."

"You watch yourself or you'll end up in jail. But one thing I tells your mother yesterday, and she's to get this straight: I been hired to be the housekeeper. I tend the children, I make up the beds and I do the dustin'. But you not to see Elsie stoopin' down on her hands and knees and scrubbing them floors like a Kaffir. And it's not enough I have six in the house to tend to. Now comes down this soldier with his woman and an infant and one yet unborn. This soldier's woman will be in the washtub half the day, cleaning up them diapers and leaving a filthy mess for me!"

"I'll help you, Elsie. I don't mind."

Elsie burst into laughter. "Is no strange thing they take you out from school. Any white girl behaving this way is nothing but daft."

———•———

Sara was often stooped on the floor, scrubbing the hard surface, while Elsie sat in the kitchen and munched on a late breakfast of freshly squeezed orange juice, scrambled eggs and crumpets, with sometimes a wedge of crab fish on the side. She refused Sara's potato *knishes*, dumplings and *lokshen* pudding and instead prepared meals for herself. Before Sara went shopping, Elsie would remind her to bring back the special items that were part of her diet.

Sara enjoyed the cooking and housework. She might have done without servants were it not for the pressures of South African society. She found release in the work, and it seemed to heal her sorrow. Dina too seemed happier, crawling around near her mother, gurgling and laughing.

Libka helped with the housework, and now that she was home all day, she felt a growing concern for the younger children.

"Dere's only three goldfish left," Shneyer told Libka one day. "Will Beryl be mad?"

He led her into the playroom where Beryl's goldfish were kept in a round bowl. Then he pointed a finger at a pink-nosed mouse that played in the wire cage nearby. "He ate them."

"The white mouse ate up three fish?"

Shneyer nodded emphatically.

Later that day Libka found the dead fish in a jar in which Shneyer collected ladybirds and chameleons.

Libka worried about her brother and wondered how badly their father's death had affected him. She began taking him along on her daily excursions. Sometimes they would go up to the mountain and pick the wild purple and yellow flowers, and Shneyer would always bring a large bouquet home for their mother. But most often they went down the hill until they came to Main Street. Here they crossed to the Green Point Commons where running games were played, and they cut through the fields until they reached Three Anchor Bay. It was Libka's favourite swimming spot. They would undress down to their swimming costumes and clamber on the gleaming black rocks that enclosed the bay. Few people came here, but Libka would sometimes see a boy sitting on a rock, looking out to sea. She remembered him from the Malay shop. He would usually sit in the back of the shop, holding a book in his hands just as he did here. Once she walked close to the rock to see what he was reading, and made out the name Dostoyevsky on the cover. She recognized it as an author her father used to read. She was fascinated with the boy's dreamy eyes and serene expression. She sensed he looked at her sometimes, yet when she turned in his direction their eyes never met.

She felt awkward swimming while the boy was there, but after a few days, Libka resolved to overcome her shyness. She dove into the water with pure joy and helped Shneyer off the edge of the rock and swam along with him. Her limbs were strong and golden from the sea and the sun, and she displayed grace and vigour in the water. She knew the power of each part of her body, and she relished in it. She was among the finest swimmers in Cape Town and had won blue ribbons and trophies.

No matter what gloom overcame her, the sea seemed to bring renewal. The moment she touched the water, diving into the depths, then rising to the surface to relish in the sun, she felt there was no problem she could not conquer.

She always felt buoyant after her swim, and she and Shneyer would wander along the shore to a private spot where a rock shielded them from view. Libka would dry her glistening body and change into shorts and a top. Then she would dress Shneyer in his blue terrycloth outfit that Sara had made on the sewing machine, and roll the swimming costumes into the damp towels.

One afternoon Libka noticed that the Malay boy had come down from his rock and was sitting on the sand nearby, engrossed in a book, his clothes and a knapsack beside him. When she and Shneyer passed by on their way to the field that would take them back to the Commons, she found herself willing him to look up, but he did not respond.

"Can we go to the Malay shop?" Shneyer asked eagerly. She wondered if he had recognized the boy from the store.

By the time they approached Main Street, the sun had dried their hair.

They stopped to watch boys running three-legged races on the Commons, and then Shneyer's eyes filled with excitement as he glimpsed the Malay store across the way. Libka took his hand before he could run into the busy thoroughfare.

"Stop that!" she teased. "You won't get it any faster."

Shneyer laughed, now sure of his treat.

"Pick anything you like," she told her brother as he explored the displays of sweets and toys. "Anything up to a tickey."

"How much is a tickey?"

"Three pennies."

"Is this for a tickey?"

"That's sixpence."

"This?"

"That's a shilling."

The Malay man recognized them and smiled at Shneyer's excitement. Seeing the damp towels Libka held, he asked, "You been swimming there by Three Anchor Bay?"

When she nodded, he said, "My grandson goes there. He's on school holiday from London. He's a good boy but his eyes are always lost in a book. He wants to be a barrister."

Libka wanted to know more but she was shy and couldn't find the words. Shneyer came running with a fire engine. "Is this for a tickey?"

"No," said Libka.

"If you like it," the man said, stroking Shneyer's hair, "you can have it. You look like a good little fellow."

Knowing it was too expensive, Libka returned it to the shelf and selected a vanilla toffee on a stick.

As they strolled up the street towards their house, Libka wished she could talk to the Malay boy.

When she got home, energy burst from her body. She would stay outside in the sunshine and polish the steps.

Just as Maputo had done in times before, Libka applied the heavy wax. Covering each step with a thick coating, she buffed with a dry cloth until the red stone gleamed. As she worked, she forgot her worries, and her mind reached to new horizons. She dreamed of other lands, of America and her relatives there, and she had a flash of herself as a grown woman, glamorous and confident. And as these thoughts soared, they evolved into poems in her mind, words of love and loss and loneliness.

"Out of the way!"

Startled from her reverie, she turned to see Beryl with Joyce beside him. Her brother wore his sailor suit with the navy blue collar, and Joyce was bedecked in lavender organdie and pearls. She seemed fragile as a china doll with her golden hair and ivory skin.

"Oh, I'm sorry!" Libka darted aside.

Beryl leaped up the steps and Joyce's dainty white sandals followed.

They stayed only a short while, and then Libka heard them leave through the rear door.

Late in the afternoon, when Libka was gathering the rags, her brother stormed up to her.

"It's finished! It's all finished!" His face was pale and his eyes were bloodshot, as though he had been crying.

"You did it!" he shouted. "You ruined it!"

She rose from her stooped position. "Can't I polish the steps?" she defended herself. "Weren't you the one who wanted Maputo to go?"

"It's a disgrace," said Beryl. "I can just imagine what Joyce will have to say. The whole of Sea Point will be talking."

"Let them."

Beryl grabbed Libka as she leaned down to pick up a rag. "Maybe you don't care, but do you realize what this is doing to us!"

"Dirty steps can't improve our reputation either," Libka retorted, pulling away from his grip.

"With this kind of behaviour, even Elsie will spit in your face. How do you expect her to serve us with respect if this is the example you set?"

"Do you know what I think?" flared Libka, facing her brother. "You're a pompous fool."

Just then a neighbourhood cat jumped onto the steps. Beryl scooped the creature up and flung it at Libka. "There!"

The cat's claws slid down Libka's flesh. She watched in horror and fascination as thick clots of blood formed on her shoulder.

"That's what you get for disgracing us!" Crying openly, Beryl ran into the house.

———•———

Hovering in the passageway at suppertime, Libka overheard her mother.

"It isn't a crime to polish the steps."

"But why this afternoon? I wanted Joyce to see how I papered my room. Libka must have known I was bringing her."

"She didn't know. How could she know?"

"Can't you see what she's doing to us? She's disgracing us for the whole of Sea Point!"

"*Sha,* Beryl, calm yourself. She is not such a bargain, the girl Joyce. There is plenty pretty girls."

"It's not even that," said Beryl. "It's what she's doing to us. Do you know that Joyce said they have six servants? Imagine, six!"

"Let them have a dozen," said Sara. "I don't consider them such high-class people. These kind, who came to South Africa without a penny, they became kings here. Sometimes I even think the Afrikaner is right to hate this kind of people."

"You mean, to hate the Jews?" Beryl asked, aghast.

"*Sha, sha!* Take Mrs. Peker, what was she in Europe? A servant in my mother's inn, scrubbing the floors, emptying the bed pans ... And here she gives orders to her servants and nothing is good enough."

"Believe me," said Beryl, "you can learn from her. They may live in Green Point, but they know how to conduct themselves."

"Wonderful. Her husband pedals on a bicycle and delivers milk when it is still dark, and their boy Sheldon didn't finish high school and works at three jobs, but she sits on her fat *hinten* like a queen. In Europe we didn't had to put on such airs. If I wanted to scrub a floor, nobody would put me in jail."

"Good for you," said Beryl, "but you aren't in Lithuania now. If you live in a country, you have to act accordingly."

"I will tell you, Beryl," Sara said gravely, "to me this country is not such a dream. Maybe for people who want to live in high style and don't want to lift a finger — and who like to treat the black and coloured people like dogs — maybe for them it is a ... paradise. But this country to me is not a goldmine."

"So maybe we shouldn't live here," said Beryl. "What about America? Perhaps you should consider our uncle's offer."

"You think it is easy," Sara said grimly, "to move to a new country with five small children?"

"Damn it," said Beryl, "meanwhile Libka has managed to mess up our lives!"

"Enough already. You will upset her more."

Sara went into the bedroom and found Libka crying.

"Stop already, *mein kind,*" she pleaded. "You also have bad luck. For everything that happens, we blame you."

"Get out!" Libka ordered.

"*Sha,* Libkala, don't eat yourself up. It wasn't your fault. Let me look at the shoulder where the cat scratch."

As Sara touched her, Libka broke away. "Get your hands off me!"

"Don't be wild. We have to wash out the wound. After all, a cat ..."

"Go!" Libka pushed her mother out and slammed the door.

As though in reply, she heard the soldier's voice in the passageway.

"What's going on here!" he shouted at Sara. "My wife and I can't have any peace. Why didn't you tell me, woman, that you breed children like rats?"

"It is my house," Sara said firmly, "and my children can do what they like in my house."

"*Ja?* Is that what you think?"

"If it don't suit you, mister," she said, "you are welcome to leave without any obligation."

"*Ja?* And what if I demand quiet and peace?"

"Demand."

"You speak too sharply, woman. And, by the way, my wife complained there was no hot water this morning. What do you do, shut it off?"

"Like I told you, Mr. Smit, if you are not satisfied, you know what you can do." She walked back into the kitchen.

The soldier stood in the hallway, uttering low curses, then he went into his rooms and banged the door shut.

That night when Elsie served dinner, she slammed the plates down, anger boiling on her face. Dina was gurgling on the high chair and Shneyer was spinning a top on the table. Libka was still in the bedroom.

"He's a bad man," said Shneyer. "He make funny faces when I go on the stoep." He pulled his eyes to distort them. "Like this."

"The stoep is our property," said Sara. "You can go where you want. It is still our house."

"We really ought to get him out," said Beryl. "He's taken over the whole house. I haven't heard Golda practise piano for weeks ... since the last time he yelled at her."

"I practise," she said softly.

"Where? Not here you don't. Aren't you falling behind in your musical studies?" Beryl asked her.

"Well, I guess I should practise more."

"There you go," he said. "He's lousing up everything. But, Mom, you should have known better than to take in an Afrikaner. Didn't we have enough of a lesson when they threw rocks at our house in Newlands? With a name like Smit you should have known."

"Not everybody is a tyrant. Prime Minister Smuts is also a Afrikaner and he is a good man. And the boarder talk to me in nice English."

"I wouldn't call his English nice. It's guttural."

"Huh?"

"I could have told you in two seconds that he's a Boer. Anyway, we've got to get rid of him."

"You are absolutely right, Beryl," said Sara, "but you think it is so easy to get him out? There is a shortage of space in Cape Town and the law is not on the landlord's side. Many people are returning from war and living in garages. As you know, we weren't allowed to ask any questions ... if he got a family, if he got children, nothing. He come down one day, a young man in a soldier uniform, and right away he pay for a month in advance. So I thought it was just for himself. Who would think he would make such an invasion?"

Late that night when the children were asleep and Sara sat in the kitchen, Smit loomed before her. He peered at the Yiddish books lying on the table.

"Watch out, *Jood*," he sneered, "your mouth's too sharp for your own good."

· *eleven* ·

Now that she was no longer at school, Libka had more time to read books of her own choice. Strolling down York Road on the way to catch the tram to the library, she passed the shanties of the coloured people. She felt comfortable in this area, despite Beryl's warnings. Coloured children played in the gutter, and people sat on orange crates in the alleys or stared out of foggy windows.

As she neared Main Street and approached the tavern with the sign "No Dogs No Jews," she sensed movement in an alleyway between the shacks. Turning, she glimpsed what seemed like a mirage. She looked again. Could that be Maputo? She had resigned herself to accept that he had returned to the Transvaal. The large man had his back to her and for a moment she stood frozen; but the instant he turned sideways, she knew for sure it was Maputo. Their eyes met and then she rushed to him and flung her arms around him.

Wrapped in the comfort of his grasp, Libka was transported back to her father's workshop on Sir Lowry Road, a child protected by her two most beloved people.

When she finally released him his eyes were set on her.

"I thought you went back to the Transvaal," she said.

"It is a long story."

"Please tell me. I want to know everything."

She knelt on the tattered blanket spread on the ground, motioning for him to join her.

"It is not wise for you to sit here," Maputo said.

"I must know everything."

Dropping to his knees beside her, he told her how he had roamed for many weeks, sleeping wherever night found him in the veld. With his blanket and knapsack and two shillings and sixpence in his pocket, he could not get far. He would climb a *kopje* to scan the surroundings for a settlement and find a few days' work whenever he reached a *dorp* of tin-roofed dwellings. One day Maputo came upon a site where they were constructing a tall building, and the *baas* gave him work hoisting bricks on his head.

"It was my dream to go back to the Transvaal," he told Libka. "There where my family once lived."

"My father told me they died in the epidemic."

"Much sadness lies in my homeland and for these many years I have tried to dispel from my mind the good wife and children who perished. It was this that brought me to the Cape Province, Miss Libka — the wish to forget."

Libka reached for Maputo's hand and held it tightly.

"But you had a home with us, Maputo. You should never have left."

Gently he extricated himself from Libka's grasp.

"It was your father's voice that brought me back."

Libka stared at him. "You heard my father's voice?" she whispered.

Maputo recounted that as he finished hoisting the bricks, his master's voice had come to him loud and clear. Somewhere from the heavens the voice filled him, and he knew what he must do. He slung his blanket over his back and turned in the direction from which he had come. It was a long trek through the veld and the shanty townships where he slept in squatter camps constructed of cardboard, but Maputo's path was clear. He must shield his master's home and watch over the family.

On his return to Green Point he slept in the Commons and roamed up and down York Road, but the coloured people were not hospitable. Then one night he collapsed in an alley. Next morning when he opened his eyes, an old woman was staring down at him. She motioned him to lie down, then went into her shack and returned with a bowl of mealie-meal.

"She gave me back my life, Miss Libka, just as the good *baas* did so many years ago."

He told her that from the alley he could see those who passed down York Road on the way to Main Street, and he would sometimes see his young master Beryl hurrying towards the tram stop. Once he saw the missus wheeling Dina in the pram, with Shneyer at her side. Perhaps they were going to Adderley Street to check if any of their brethren from Europe had managed to escape. He knew how it preyed on his missus's mind.

Maputo confessed that sometimes late at night he would creep along York Road to the point where he could glimpse his master's house. He knew he could be arrested for prowling through the district at night without a passbook, but he could not restrain his longing to be close to this cherished home.

"I was sad to see the steps to my master's house trodden with mud and no one to shine the brass plate on the gate."

Libka shifted on the blanket and crossed her legs.

"Do you live here now?"

"The kind lady permit me to stay."

Libka glanced at the shack beside the alley and saw an old yellow-skinned woman peering out of the window.

"It would be better if you go," Maputo said. "It is not wise for you to be here."

"Now that I found you, Maputo, I won't let you go."

There was so much to tell him, so much to share. It was as though he had returned from the dead.

"If they want to put me in jail," she said, "I don't care."

"No, my young missus, you must not speak like that. Is this not the hour you should be in the Sea Point school?"

"Maputo, so many things have happened since you left. Everything is different."

"It is right that I went away. Is your home more peaceful with Elsie?"

"I think she was jealous of you, Maputo."

He rolled his luminous eyes. "No mortal should envy another. Elsie is a good woman."

"Everybody is good in your eyes, Maputo. Don't you even feel bad about what happened?"

"My wish is that my good *baas's* family should be safe."

"Well, we're not safe, Maputo. There is an evil man living in our house. He calls us *Jood* and threatens my mother."

"I recall what my *baas's* family endured in that district of Newlands where the Hebrew people were not welcome. Then why is this man in your house?"

"My mother was worried about money so she rented out the two rooms near the rabbit hok."

The woman who had been peering from the window shuffled out and came towards them.

"This is the good lady. To her I give thanks."

The woman moved close and eyed Libka as she sat on the blanket beside Maputo.

"She my *baas's* daughter," Maputo explained. "She live in Green Point not far. I tell her she shouldn't be here."

The woman nodded, her eyes riveted on Libka. Then, seeming to sense she may be intruding, she went back into her shack.

"She a good soul. Like the *baas's* family."

"It isn't right, Maputo, that you don't live with us anymore. And I don't believe what Elsie said."

"We must not question our destiny, for the good Lord will preside over us. Now you run along, my young missus. Why are you not in school today?"

"I don't go to school anymore. I got into trouble and they threw me out."

Maputo set his eyes on Libka. "Then a brighter ray on the horizon awaits you."

———— • ————

Libka could not disclose Maputo's whereabouts to her family. It was a secret she kept within her. She knew it could be dangerous for him if he were seen with a white girl, so she held back from visiting him. But she would find herself going down York Road more often, peering into the alley to see if he was there. Usually there would only be his blanket, but sometimes she'd see the old woman looking out of the window.

Libka started sneaking food from her pantry, leaving it beside Maputo's blanket. She would attach a piece of paper with a picture of a smiling face, knowing he would guess it was from her. Once she snatched a fluffy pillow from the top of the closet, hoping her mother would not miss it. It was stuffed with chicken feathers and her parents had brought it from Lithuania. If Maputo could rest his head on the soft pillow, it might bring him comfort, as it had brought her father, especially during the months before he died. She also left a piece of biltong, for she remembered how Maputo loved the spicy meat.

She wondered where he was during the daytime. Perhaps he had found work hoisting bricks on a construction site. He could balance a load of bricks on his head, and his arms were powerful.

One day as she was passing the shack she noticed the crazy lady from the mansion near the tram stop. The woman bounced along York Road, talking to herself, carrying two huge shopping bags. At her approach, women and children appeared at the doors of the shacks. She would stop beside them, remove goods from her bags and continue on, smiling. Libka lingered beside the tavern on the corner and saw the woman stride down Maputo's alley and deposit a bundle on his blanket.

When she got home, Libka found Anya sitting on the stoep.

"Don't think I'm here to see you," Anya said. "Where's Golda?"

"I guess she's not home from her music lesson. Or maybe she went to Hebrew school."

"Now that I got you thrown out of school, I thought you'd be swimming at Three Anchor Bay. Isn't that your favourite haunt?"

"I go there," said Libka.

"You don't have to talk to me while I wait for Golda."

But Libka no longer felt anger towards Anya. She herself might have instigated the fight when she said terrible things about Anya's father. She knew how she would have felt if anyone dared to say a word against her father. Libka could not imagine living with a father whom one did not love. It was almost worse than if he were dead; at least then you could remember happy times. Anya must always be in terror of her father's violence.

"I don't mind. You can talk to me," Libka said, following Anya to the side of the garden near the primrose trellis. She remembered how Anya had swung on this trellis at her father's death, but now she only sniffed a flower.

"I'm not mad at you anymore," Libka said as she hovered around the trellis and plucked a petal.

"You should be furious with the mess I made of your life."

"Why, because I don't go to that school anymore? Are you learning anything there?"

"The only place I learn anything of value is in my room with the books I select myself. When I'm in the classroom I barricade my mind to all the so-called facts and dates they try to stuff into it. The great virtues of the Afrikaners whose country this rightfully is! I've shut it out. But why should I have to tolerate it and pretend? You know, Libka, I envy you."

"I have to admit I'm excited about the books I find in the library, and I think I've learned a lot since leaving Promenade High."

"Are you reading Lenin, Marx?"

"I found books that my parents read in Russian, by Dostoyevsky, Tolstoy and Chekhov. The library on Adderley Street has them in English, and there's a nice lady, Miss Higgins, who helps me find things."

"Right now I'm more involved in politics than literature and philosophy. I think this country is so mixed up. How can it be right for people to be judged by their colour? Do you think it's fair that someone with black or yellow skin has to call the whites *baas* and master and missus?"

Anya's question comforted Libka. She was voicing Libka's own doubts, and it freed her to unload her heart.

"There's no one I could love as much as Maputo," Libka confided. "People condemn me for it, but I think he understands more than any white person."

"Golda said you miss him."

Libka then decided to share her discovery of Maputo in the alley.

Anya listened keenly. "I admire you for socializing with him, Libka. I would do the same. I don't care what they do to me for the way I feel, and I'll accept the consequences."

"Maybe we'll both end up in jail."

"That would be fine, except what could we accomplish from there?"

When Golda returned home, she was startled to find her sister and Anya sitting beneath the primrose trellis, their shoulders touching.

· twelve ·

Though Libka had no longing to return to school, time often hung heavy on her and she wondered what her future might be. She could not foresee ever finding her place in this country. At such times fantasies of distant places entered her mind. It was only somewhere far off and unknown that held out any hope.

She wondered if her mother had felt the same way when she left her home in Lithuania.

"Mommy," she said one night when she found her staring into space in the kitchen, "I know it was Daddy's idea to come to South Africa. He told me you would have preferred going to Palestine."

Sara was surprised at Libka's friendly tone. "Libinka, when I was a girl in Lithuania I was deeply involved in the Zionist movement, and my friends and I dreamed of building up the Jewish homeland."

"And you didn't really want to come to South Africa?"

"I left it up to your daddy."

"Are you sorry you came here, Mommy?"

"It was hard to leave my mother and brothers and all our family and friends because we wondered if we would ever meet again."

Sara told Libka how she had begged her own mother to come along, but she was too worn out to make a change. At the age of twenty-three she had lost a husband and was left with three babies. And five years later when she married again, this time the rabbi who was to become

Sara's father, it had also been of short duration. By the time Sara was seven he had died ... and she remembered the last weeks when, struck with a raging fever, he would jump out of bed in the middle of the night and stumble through the streets. Burning up, he would roll in the snow. Sara would run out with her mother and little brothers and they would drag him back into the house, and her mother would apply cold compresses to his forehead. Finally he died of blood poisoning.

"After my father died," Sara said, "my mother was not the same person, always sitting in the kitchen by the kerosene lamp, rocking herself like a old lady and singing the sad songs."

"That sounds just like you, Mommy."

"Ugh, stop it. You want to hear or not?"

Sara told Libka how regimes in Lithuania changed and she and her brothers had to sneak past guards when they went to the next village for sugar or flour or tea; the false documents they had to produce; the charm and wit she had to muster when confronted by the Polish guards. And the time when she and her brother Shleymi escaped a shower of bullets as they dove into the forest with the produce they hid.

"But families were close and we enjoyed a simple meal and getting together in the evenings, friends and neighbours singing, grateful we survived."

"And now you don't even know if your mother and brothers are alive, Mommy."

Sara shrugged. Rumours had been filtering into Cape Town about the fate of the Jews in Eastern Europe, but they had received no news of the family. Some of the *landsleit* spoke of ghettos, concentration camps and mass graves.

Libka thought of how every time the postman came, her mother would run to the door, hoping there would be mail from Europe, though it had been over four years since the last letter had arrived from her mother's eldest brother, Shleymi. He had two daughters, Rochel and Berta, who were the same age as Libka and Golda; and when last heard from, they had still been living in the family inn.

Shleymi's letter had only brought fear and doubt. It arrived in May 1940 smudged with strange marks and damaged and torn after months of travel, and Sara's hands trembled when she tore open the mutilated envelope. She wondered why it had not been her mother who wrote. It was always her mother who sent letters full of news about her brothers and cousins and aunts and uncles and the friends that she and Yosef had left behind when they journeyed to South Africa.

Shleymi's letter, in shaky Yiddish handwriting, had only brought grim news:

> *They are not giving Jews permits for business. The authorities are ordering us to close down the inn. There are Christians who want to take it over. They won't be subjected to any hardship. Please take steps to bring us over and I beg you not to postpone.*

"And of course Daddy also left behind his widowed mother, two sisters and five brothers. Two of his brothers were Zionists and immigrated to Palestine in the mid-1930s, but the others stayed behind in the *shtetl*."

"Mommy," Libka dared to ask, "do you think Daddy died of a broken heart?"

"Why do you say that, Libka? You know he was sick for a long time."

"People can die of a broken heart. He used to tell me that he blamed himself for waiting so long to file the application for British citizenship. He thought if he had filed the papers sooner there might have been time to sponsor the families from Europe."

"It's true, by the time the documents came, the borders were already closed."

"I don't think he ever got over that, Mommy. Even a few days before he died, when he was in a fever, I heard him mumble, 'We still don't have the papers. What will we do?' and he began to cry like a baby."

· *thirteen* ·

One night Libka tossed and turned sleeplessly, and each time she opened her eyes the light still burned in the kitchen. Did strange demons possess her mother in these hours when she sat reading the old Yiddish and Russian books from Lithuania?

On this night she did not enter her mother's private world, but when five o'clock came there was darkness in the kitchen. She arose and began to dress quietly so as not to disturb Golda asleep in the bed beside hers.

Possessed by an urge for space and silence, Libka decided that she would go up to the mountain, which seemed to loom so close behind her house. She pulled on her pedal pushers, stuck her feet into her sandals and did not bother to comb out the knots in her hair. She was about to sneak out the back door when she remembered and ran back for a piece of paper. "I went for a walk with a miserable black hawk," she wrote, smiling to herself. "I'll be back for breakfast." Putting the note on the kitchen table, she crept out into the courtyard, removing her sandals so as not to make a sound on the cement floor as she made her way past the quarters where Elsie slept. Once she shut the green wooden door and was out in the street, she breathed freely, full of exhilaration. She decided that she would go barefooted and linked her sandals together to string them over her shoulder.

She strolled up the steep cobblestone street. The shutters in the houses were barred. The air was cool and the breeze came down from the mountain, fanning her hair and cheeks. Feeling liberated, she asked herself: Am I my own prisoner? Perhaps what her mother had said was true, that she should build her own life and not be consumed by the burdens of the family.

As she proceeded up High Level Road she passed the sleeping houses with the vines dangling over the walls. Here lived the Vorsters, the Vandermerves, the Bothas, the Verwoerds ... How was it different from the Newlands? They had escaped after the march of the Voortrekkers, but her parents hadn't realized that they'd once again be surrounded by the Boers.

The children she had encountered on moving to Green Point seemed much like the ones from the old district. Hans, Willem, Jacobus and Geerte spoke to each other in Afrikaans. Once when Libka and her mother were going to the ritual slaughterer with a squawking chicken tied at the legs, Hans jeered at the sight as his mother looked on. And the next time he played hide-and-seek with Libka and Golda, he hissed *"Jood!"* and tried to trip them while the other children laughed.

"You're Jews," Jacobus Verwoerd said to Libka one day. "My *ouma* says you're Jews. She can tell by your funny names and the funny way your mother talks."

"Yes, we're Jews," said Libka. "What about it?"

"You're dirty and smelly, and who said you could come to our country?"

"It's my country as much as your country."

"Ja? My *ouma* and *oupa* were here, and their *oumas* and *oupas* — hundreds and hundreds of years they were here. See those pawpaw trees? See the mangos and the loquats and everything! Even the silver leaf trees! We planted everything that grows. And then you come and you eat it and just make trouble."

"Are those the stories your *ouma* tells you?"

"She tells lots more. The Bantus are no good too, and the coloureds. But you can whip them with the *sjambok*."

"Your *ouma* tells you very nice stories," said Libka. "Maybe one of these days the Bantus will whip her."

"I'm going to tell! I'm going to tell on you, *Jood!"* shouted Jacobus. "Jew! Jew! Dirty Jew!"

As she passed the Christian Brothers' tower and proceeded towards the mountain, Libka now wondered: Was there not enough hostility among her people? What about Joyce and Ruth Freedman and Sally Peker? Who had their parents been when they arrived from Europe? And now they scorned those who were not as showy as they were. She observed too from what her mother had told her that the less they had in the old country, the greedier they became in this new land.

The hill leading to the mountain grew steeper as she neared the stone steps that would take her up to the crest of the cliff. Now there was only the sky and the mountain and the daisies and wild flowers ... and the feeling of immense space.

It was here that Beryl used to come to get a view of the harbour and watch the ships as they rounded the Cape of Good Hope. Sometimes he'd come home bouncing in excitement because a large vessel had pulled in with dozens of small boats delivering soldiers to the shore where they marched in formation. The ships, carrying soldiers from Australia and New Zealand, stopped to load up with supplies on their way to the battlefields. He also believed there were German submarines prowling the waters. "Zip your lip," he'd often recite, the code for being secretive.

Libka roamed up the mountain, listening for the sounds of the birds and other strange calls. She had seen porcupines here and once she spotted a few baboons. She and Shneyer sometimes came here to pick wild flowers; but it was different being all alone with her thoughts.

She spied something in the distance and thought it was a springbok in flight; but then the form was lost to view, and when she looked again she saw that it was a human figure. At first she was afraid, but then she noticed a hand waving, and recognized that the form was that of a girl.

Libka sat down on the dry grass, tugging at the purple and yellow flowers, waiting for her pursuer to come into focus. And when at last she recognized Anya, joy raced through her; for despite the tensions that often erupted between them, she had always felt a peculiar link with this girl. She knew that if they could shed their defences, the bond would be strong.

When Anya reached her, they burst out laughing.

"I guess we had the same idea," chuckled Libka.

"So you mean we have more in common than we thought?" Anya flopped down on the grass beside Libka. "We're both nuts, huh?" Her eyes gleamed with mischief. "Who else would be crazy enough to come here at this hour? Haven't you read the *Cape Argus* lately?"

"I don't read the newspapers," said Libka.

"You should, even though it's often a waste of time."

"I prefer books these days."

"You know," Anya said after a moment, "I've been thinking of what you told me about Maputo. Why do you suppose he's hanging around there on York Road so close to your house?"

"I'm also wondering the same thing. But he told me that when he was far away he heard my father's voice."

Anya seemed to believe this.

"You know my father found him over fifteen years ago, just after my parents arrived from Lithuania."

"That was a long time ago. He must miss your dad terribly."

"It would break my father's heart to know Maputo isn't living with us anymore."

"Maybe you loved Maputo so much because your father loved him."

"He was there when I was born, when we lived in the little rooms above our workshop on Sir Lowry Road. I remember when I'd tiptoe behind him as he worked at the big machines, and when he'd discover me he'd lift me high up into the air and smile up at me. It was like going to heaven."

"I guess you lost two of the people that you loved most in the world," said Anya. "Would you have given your life for them?"

"I think I would, but how do I really know?"

"Let's say you were living in Lithuania and the Nazis attacked your village. Would you give your life to save someone in your family?"

Libka thought a while. "I'd like to believe I would, but I imagine people can go crazy in such times."

"Do you have nightmares about what happened to the Jews in Eastern Europe?"

"I'm sure my mother does. Maybe that's why she never sleeps at night and sits in the kitchen chanting those tragic Jewish songs. And you know, Anya, sometimes I think my father died of heartache. He left behind his mother, two sisters and five brothers, and his mother used to write him the most loving letters. He would translate the Hebrew letters for me to introduce me to my *boba*. And then all those letters from Europe stopped. The last one we ever got was in 1940 from my Uncle Shleymi, begging my parents to try to bring them over. And when those rumours started about concentration camps and ghettos in Europe, my father blamed himself for waiting so long to get his British naturalization papers. He rushed to get them so he could sponsor our families, but by the time the documents arrived it was too late."

"You mean the borders were closed?"

"My mother doesn't believe what I think about a broken heart, but my father was always such a healthy man. He swam the Black Sea and was a hero in the First World War. So why did he get sick and die when he was forty-six? Don't lots of people live to sixty and even more? Maybe my father lost the will to live.".

"I remember when I used to visit your house how sick he was, just lying there in that dark room."

"I used to run home from school in terror, afraid he wouldn't be alive anymore."

"He was sick for a long time, wasn't he, Libka?"

"At first he used to pretend he was all right when my mother would find him slumped in the armchair in the sitting room. He would bounce up when she'd catch him and joke about it, but his complexion was turning yellow and he just dragged himself around."

"When I went with Golda to visit him at Groote Schuur Hospital, we thought he'd never make it out."

"They just cut him up and sewed him back together. Couldn't do anything. And they sent him home to die."

"I didn't like you then, but I felt sorry for Golda and your mother and the little ones."

"And then we thought a miracle would happen when the two specialists arrived from London and said a new drug had been discovered: Penicillin. They gave it to him but he died that night."

Anya looked out over the mountain. "I think I'm beginning to understand why I hated you so much, Libka. You knew I hated you, didn't you?"

"I was never sure why, although I must admit I'm not always a friendly person."

"That wasn't the problem. Am I friendly?"

Both girls chuckled.

"I hated you, Libka, because I was jealous of you. Sometimes when I'd come over on a Saturday I'd see you sitting on the stoep with your father and you seemed to have such a special bond. I could never imagine loving anyone as you did your father and Maputo. I envied you because all I knew was hate and arguments.

"Maybe years ago my parents loved each other, but ever since I can remember there were only wars in our place. And if my mother hadn't been so timid and forgiving, it's possible both she and I would be dead. He used to get so violent — and over nothing! He'd come home drunk and play Russian records and sing at the top of his lungs. My mother and I would be sleeping, but if we'd ask him to be quieter he'd start beating us and yelling. I guess he was miserable because he was a failure.

"All these immigrants from Europe who peddled rags became so rich. And my dad, who had read every great book in Russian and Hebrew and could quote from them, he could never make a living. When he worked in the shoe store, he despised the owner, and he was no good at taking orders from anyone, especially people he had no respect for, those who were just interested in money."

"Maybe he shouldn't have come to South Africa," Libka mused. "Do you think he would have been better off in England?"

"For sure he would, but he's a difficult personality. If he admires someone, he would kill for them, but he can't tolerate many of these Jews who started out as peddlers and made their fortune in South Africa."

"Did your mother ever think of leaving him?"

"My brothers and sisters told her she had to leave him and they even offered to take her to Jo'burg or Durban, but I guess she couldn't or didn't want to."

Libka dissected the stem of a purple flower.

"Well, let's change the subject to something more cheerful," Anya suggested.

"Like what?"

They both burst into laughter.

"Like missing school... You must really pine for your Afrikaans class, Libka. Didn't you have a lot of fun there?"

"I sure did."

"You must miss all that history about the land that adopted you." Laughter lingered in Anya's tone. "Now, Libka Hoffman, don't you want to know when Jan van Riebeeck established the first Dutch settlement in the Cape Province? And what about the Great Trek of the Boers, and the Battle of Blood River? Do you know when diamonds were discovered in Kimberley? And what about the goldfields at Witwatersrand! Surely you can't expect to make a life for yourself without these vital facts!"

She imitated a teacher's glare at Libka, who now looked up and could not withhold a smile.

"You have to be sensible," Anya continued in the same tone. "There can be no life in this land if you do not memorize your dates. Answer quickly — you have two seconds: When did Bartholomew Dias discover the Cape of Good Hope?"

Now both girls broke into laughter.

"Gosh," said Anya, "how much they stuff into your mind! Just to leave no room for thought. Clutter the mind with hatred, with prejudice, with dangerous facts and statistics. Seriously, what did you ever learn in school?"

She looked at Libka but no reply came.

"I may not be ancient," said Anya, "but I will soon be fifteen ... perhaps 'a dangerously precocious specimen' ... ha ha, the words of Miss Bloemfontein. But I'm not going to become blinded to what's going on in this country. South Africa hasn't become bloody yet, but it will ... and it *deserves* to.

"I have a pen pal in London, this fellow who was in reform school. And my eyes are opening. Oh sure, there's hatred everywhere, but here it's like a time bomb, compressed, smouldering ... and when it bursts, I don't want to be around!"

Anya's eyes scanned the skyline. "It's a pity because this is such a beautiful country, with the Indian Ocean on one side, the Atlantic on the other and Table Mountain soaring over everything. Of course I don't have much to compare it with, never having been out of this country, but people could live in such peace here. Instead, we whites have become so corrupted. I guess it's hard not to be tempted, with all those diamonds and gold sprouting from the land and everything overflowing with riches ... crops bursting from the soil, flowers stealing through every crack and the sea overflowing with fish. For those Europeans for whom a soft-boiled egg was a big deal, who dragged water from the well to heat for a bath, it must have been paradise. But still, why did they get so greedy?"

Anya sighed, leaning back on her arms, casting her eyes upwards and catching the breeze.

"Well, who cares? There's too much to live for, Libka, much too much to tolerate this. You and I, I don't think we'll last here very long."

Libka's eyes had taken on a distant quality. "I have known for a long time," she said as though talking to herself, "that I just don't belong here. But where can I go? England? America? And how can I leave?"

"For me it's easier," said Anya. "What do I have to lose? I worry about my mother, but of what use can I be to her? But you're part of a family, and you care. It won't be so easy for you to pick up and leave like I will."

"Leave for where?"

"I have a base with this pen pal in London. I know he won't let me down."

"Will you really go to England?"

"I'll go, as surely as we're sitting on this mountain. I have to, Libka. Otherwise, well ... It's not that I'm afraid of going to jail, but what can you do from behind bars?"

"I met a boy from England," Libka confessed softly.

"You did! How?"

"He's a Malay boy."

"What are you saying, Libka Hoffman! You met a Malay boy?"

"Well, actually, I met his grandfather. He has the shop on Main Street near my house."

Anya's eyes were set on Libka.

"I used to see the boy in the store. He was always reading. And then one day I noticed him at Three Anchor Bay."

"And you talked to him?"

"Not really." Libka blushed. "But his grandfather told me he's from London."

Anya burst out laughing. "That's all you need, Libka Hoffman, to get chummy with a Malay boy! You'd be driven out of the country."

"I once saw him reading the Russian writer Dostoyevsky and his grandfather told me he wants to be a barrister."

"I can see why he's in London. In this country he'd be sitting in the back of buses and trams. Let's befriend him. I'll do it if you're chicken!"

Libka giggled.

The first ray of sunshine appeared over Table Mountain. Anya jumped up in exhilaration and held out her hand to Libka.

"Let's dance!"

Libka protested but Anya pulled her up and began twirling her around as she burst into song:

> If you were the only girl in the world
> And I were the only boy
> Nothing else would matter in the world today
> We could go on loving in the same old way.

Libka joined in the song, which Beryl was always singing. It seemed that every time she turned on the wireless it was broadcast from London.

> A garden of Eden just made for two
> With nothing to mar our joy.

The girls exploded into giggles.

"Come on, Libka, I'll race you down the mountain. The one who reaches that boulder first will be the first to get to London."

Like springboks they darted down, their gait light and swift, hair flying, and hit the mark on the same stroke, collapsing in a heap of laughter.

· fourteen ·

When the doorbell sounded a few mornings later, Libka was alone in the house so she didn't answer it. Her mother and the two younger children had gone to Adderley Street, Beryl and Golda were at school and Elsie had dressed in her Sunday best and taken the day off.

The ringing of the doorbell was persistent, and Libka became afraid that it might be urgent, so finally she went to answer.

"I'm Mr. Shmerl from Wynberg." The dapper man looked at her with lively eyes. "Remember me?"

Libka answered with hesitation. "I think so."

"I was at your father's funeral. Which one are you?"

"Libka."

"Ah, Libka. May I come in?" He removed his jaunty hat with the red feather.

"My mother isn't home but you can wait."

It had been a strange morning. Rarely alone in the house, Libka had taken the opportunity to search in her mother's drawers, and she found the dreaded garment. Removing her blouse, she stood before the mirror studying the pear-shaped forms on her body. But on this day they seemed less frightening. She strung the straps of the flimsy garment around her shoulders and let her body fill the cups. Growing in curiosity, she put on a red sweater that she had once considered too tight when her mother wore it, and pulled on a skirt with slits at both sides. By the time the doorbell rang, her feet were in her mother's high heels and a coating of red traced her lips in heart shape.

Now she was sitting opposite this man who looked at her in a way that was embarrassing.

"So you say your mother isn't home," he said, as though not minding at all. "And why you're not in school?"

"I didn't feel too well today."

"Ah, but you look good enough!" As he smiled she noticed the glint of his gold-capped teeth.

Libka smiled back shyly, and a strand of hair fell over one eye.

"I remember you from when you still lived in the rooms upstairs from your father's workshop. This was before I moved to Durban. I must say, you grew up to be a lovely girl." The man's eyes traced her from the high heels upwards. "Imagine, Yosef's daughter! Ah, he was a wonderful man, your father. We were neighbours, *landsmen,* in the old country, you know. Your father was an honest man. And what a hero! He swam the Black Sea and fought in the last war. Your mother still keeps his medals?"

Libka thought of the silver box in her father's bottom drawer.

"Yes, we still have them."

"And your brothers and sisters," Mr. Shmerl asked, "where are they?"

Without waiting for an answer, he bounced up from the settee and paced through the house, inspecting every corner.

Libka saw him pop his head into her bedroom. Pulling down her sweater nervously, she met him in the hallway. "Nice girl," he said, patting her on the shoulder. Then he led her back to the sitting room. "You don't mind if I wait?"

"It may be a long time. My mother went into town to check the lists to see if any of our relatives survived the war."

"Nobody survived," he said flatly. "Hitler took care of that."

As Libka sat down on the settee, he took the place beside her. She felt awkward, aware of his leg brushing against hers.

"So tell me about yourself. You go out already with boys? You got a beau?"

She blushed and looked down to allow her hair to curtain her face. And then she felt his hand on her back. Was it a father's hand or was it something else? And why did shivers run through her?

"You're a pretty lady." He spoke so faintly that she caught only the vibration of his words.

And now, when she felt herself being slid against him, she became frightened. She giggled like a child and brushed her hair aside.

"You don't like?" His face was aglow.

"I'll tell my mother you came," she said and sprang up from the settee.

Mr. Shmerl grew tense and his eyes darkened. Getting up slowly, he spoke in a harsh voice. "Your father and I, like brothers we were in Europe. We lived in the same *shtetl*. You know what that means?"

"The same little town?"

"And I know what it is when a father drops dead and a young woman is left alone with small children. Five you are?"

"Yes. Three girls and two boys."

"And you are already from the oldest?"

"I turned thirteen."

"Big deal, thirteen. So what you going to do, take in wash? Not in South Africa. That's why I came today, to work out a proposition with your mother. She knows me inside out. I don't have to show her my passport. And I'm considering that maybe we should go together into business."

Libka nodded cautiously.

"I can see that you don't feel comfortable with me. A little suspicious?"

"Oh no." She tried to sound innocent, but she remembered what those women at her father's funeral had said about him pinching a lady's behind.

"Don't give me no. I try to be like a father to you, and you get all ... oh, never mind."

"No, Mr. Shmerl," she said, becoming afraid. "I didn't mean to ..."

"Maybe you didn't. All right. Anyway, you tell your mother I got business to talk to her. You got a telephone in the house?"

"Not yet."

"Me, I got one. Well, I need it for business. Monkey business!" He chuckled as he popped on his hat. "Anyhow, you tell your mother I come back Friday — not tomorrow, not the next day, but Friday. Meanwhile, don't spend all your money."

With a flash of his golden teeth, he went on his way.

Was this the man who was going to manage her father's factory? Libka cringed at the thought and wondered why her mother seemed to trust him.

———

Golda came home from school that afternoon, flung off her satchel and disappeared. Sara, who was preoccupied with the other children, did not notice anything unusual, but when suppertime came and Golda had still not shown up, she sent Libka and Beryl to look for her.

Golda was sleeping in the lane by the rabbit hok, braced against the pomegranate tree.

Beryl shook her awake. "What's wrong, Golda?"

She startled and looked about in a daze.

"Supper's on the table," said Beryl. "Come on."

But Golda did not move; instead, she began to cry quietly.

Libka stooped before her. "Tell us, Golda, what's the matter?"

Golda tried to turn her face away but then jumped up and ran into the house. Not even Beryl could stop her as she fled straight into the bedroom and shut the door.

Sara and the children lingered outside, wondering what to do, but then decided perhaps Golda should be left alone.

When after a few hours she had still not appeared, Libka suggested they go in to see. "She's never like this."

They found her sitting on the floor, staring blankly. Her face was white.

"Goldinka!" Sara ran to her. "What happen to you?"

Beryl and Libka stooped down beside her.

"I c-can't go back to school," Golda cried. "I can't!"

"Where you can't go?" begged Sara.

Agony darkened Golda's face. "I'm finished with school," she said in a trembling voice.

They tried to get her to explain what happened but she could not speak.

"You've got to tell us," said Beryl. "How else will we know?"

"The whole school knows," she cried. "The whole school."

They waited in silence for her next words.

"They all asked me," she wailed, "whose turn is it ... whose turn is it to go in the b-bath last."

Sara cast her eyes on Libka and Beryl. "What is she saying?"

"Oh," said Beryl, "I get it."

"They know," squealed Golda, "the whole of Beachfront Junior High knows."

"It was bound to come out," exclaimed Beryl.

"What?" pleaded Sara. "Please tell already."

"The baths," said Libka, "didn't you hear? They know we all take baths in the same water."

"Aw," said Sara, "this is such a crime? What are we, diseased?"

"That's not the point," said Beryl. "It just isn't done."

"And your cousins Rochel and Berta, they starved in the war in Europe and a little sugar the *boba* didn't have to put in the tea."

"This isn't Europe," said Libka.

"Nonsense!" said Sara. "You have to cry so bad because of this! But I wonder how they find out."

"You don't have to wonder," said Libka. "Didn't Mrs. Peker barge in the other day when Golda and I just had our baths and you were bathing Shneyer and Dina?"

"Aw, aw! A criminal offence!"

"You can be sure she went home and told them all," said Libka. "And that Naomi Peker has as big a mouth as her sister Sally, so I'm sure she spread it through the whole of Beachfront Junior High."

"So they must know at Promenade High too." Beryl seemed in shock. "Our lives are being destroyed!"

"Worried about Joyce?" scoffed Libka.

"I sure am."

"Stop about Joyce!" Sara admonished. "And, Goldala, come up already from the floor. I am not ashamed. My children are all healthy and thank God they can bathe in the same water."

———————

Libka was waxing the passageway the next morning, evil thoughts of Mrs. Peker floating in her mind, and Shneyer was busy with one of his secret games when a convertible pulled up in front of the house.

Sara was hanging out the wash in the yard, and Elsie had not yet made an appearance. She had come home very late the previous night.

"Yoo hoo!"

It was Mrs. Peker. After yesterday's disturbance, the last thing Libka wanted was for the old busybody to attack her for doing "servants' work." She sprang up at the instant the front door opened, abandoning the rags, and fled to the dining room. She darted under the table to take shelter beneath the long tablecloth.

"Somebody home?" Mrs. Peker called as she entered. Spotting Dina on the slippery floor, she chimed, "Mama? Where's Mama?"

Dina gurgled, took a skid and crawled away.

As Mrs. Peker trotted past the entrance to the dining room, Libka saw the stumpy legs in the orange patent-leather sandals.

"Sara!" the visitor bellowed. "It's me! Rivka!"

She passed through the passageway to the rear, where she found Sara in the yard.

"So there you are!"

Sara turned apologetically and tried to tidy herself. "Aw, Rivka, I didn't hear."

"Look at you, Sara. What are the *shvartze* for? I'll wait in the dining room."

Libka tightened as the orange sandals entered and the chair at the head of the table was pulled out. She felt cramped and wondered how long she could stay in the same position.

"Yoo hoo!" the visitor called when Dina tottered in. She might have used the same tone for a squirrel or a chipmunk.

Libka was relieved when she heard her mother coming. Perhaps in the midst of conversation she might find the chance to change her position.

Sara's hair was pinned back, loose strands trickling out. Her black cotton dress was covered with an apron.

"Should I make tea?" she asked, trying to assume a cheerful manner.

"Not tea. I'll have a glass of ginger beer a little later. I have indigestion." Mrs. Peker burped loudly. "Who knows what the girl put in my omelette this morning."

"You feel all right?"

"Of course not, but let's get to the point. Sara, tell me plainly, what will be?"

Sara snuck into a chair. "Will be?"

"That's right," said Mrs. Peker. "First your Libka attacks a student in the school playground and gets expelled. Who ever heard of such a thing, a Jewish girl! And now there's a new rumour circulating in the school. And don't you be surprised if the health department comes to your doorstep!"

"Ugh! What is the crime? That the children wash up in the same water?"

"In Europe you could boil a *fendele* water and everybody washed up in the same basin. But here — no sir! Six people don't bathe in the same water."

"Uh! Uh! Rivka. And tell me, if it's such a disgrace, why you made such a big announcement?"

"Announcement? Me?"

"Who else?"

"Listen, I mention it to my children in a good way, like to teach them a lesson to be grateful. I say to them, 'Here's a family from good stock. Mrs. Hoffman was high class in Europe, and look how they are so ... conservative.' So even with the best of intentions, the story got muddled up in the playground. Listen, don't blame me."

"Golda come home crying and said she won't go back to school. Your Naomi had to spread it in the junior school also?"

"What do you mean also?"

"Well, we know that Sally can't wait to talk bad about everybody."

"Sara, how can you talk that way? My Sally is the most popular girl at Promenade High School."

"Our lives don't yet depend on Promenade High School," said Sara. "Really, I don't even see the wonderful things they learn. Libka read lately lots of books, the English classics *Jane Eyre* and *Pride and Prejudice* and the best philosophy and poetry. She even read the Russian classics. The other day she came back from the library with Dostoyevsky."

"Don't mix up my *kop*. Who's Dostoyevsky?"

"A important Russian writer. Yosef read him in Russian. I read him in Hebrew too — *Crime and Punishment*."

"I never heard from any of that. Anyway, so what are you saying, Sara, you want to take your children out of school?"

"I am not frightened from Miss Bloemfontein and her laws."

"So you want your children to grow up like the *shvartze*, with no education?"

"Don't tell me, Rivka. Please. Your father, what was he? A rag collector? And you should know what went on in my mother's house."

"That's why I'm talking," broke in Mrs. Peker. "I remember your bookshelves and the education books, and the music. You played the violin, no? And the poems you and your brothers wrote. And your brother Elka studying to be a doctor. Who knows what became of him. I remember, listen. You want me to deny it? That's why I'm talking to you. That's why I came today. Because I know how things used to be and I see what's becoming."

"What they learn in school here," Sara said, "is to be enemies. The only thing you can do is build castles in the sky and make with the servants and the chauffeurs in the limousines. I'm not impressed!"

"Well, that's the way it is," said Mrs. Peker. "You either go along with it or ..."

When Sara showed no sign of submitting, Mrs. Peker tried again. "Listen here, Sara, you got five children to think of. You want they should all be ruined? I'm very impressed what you tell me that Libka reads philosophy books and studies such serious things, but facts is facts. Many mental cases was smart people. Send her away to an institution in the Transvaal or maybe in the Orange Free State. Nobody has to know. For their information, she might be living with her uncle and aunt in America, in the United States."

Sara tried to protest but Mrs. Peker didn't give her a chance.

"And don't delay. It doesn't take long for a tragedy to strike."

"Everybody gives me lessons." Sara rose and smoothed her apron. "Rivka, I will bring you a glass of ginger beer."

"The girl can't bring it? You don't have a bell in your dining room? I keep a bell in every room."

"It's all right. Don't worry."

As Sara moved to the doorway, Dina scurried after her, thumping her hands as she chased her mother's feet.

Cramped beneath the table, Libka was disgusted with all the chatter she had overheard. She was tempted to leap out and give Mrs. Peker a heart attack.

In the silence she could imagine the woman eyeing the cobwebs above the cabinet display and the yellow food stain on the tablecloth.

When Sara hurried back with the glass of ginger beer, the baby's pace was frantic as she tried to keep up with her. When she caught sight of Libka crouched under the table, she shrieked in delight and headed straight to her.

"What's going on?" Mrs. Peker grabbed the glass and took a sip of the carbonated liquid, trying to belch.

Dina bounded out, gasped at Mrs. Peker and scampered back beneath the tablecloth. Now Mrs. Peker's curiosity was aroused and she brushed aside the cloth to look. She let it drop, then lifted it again, as though the first vision could not be real. "*Got in himel*, Sara! What am I seeing?"

———•———

"How much evidence do you need?" Beryl asked his mother.

"When one thing go wrong, everything follow," Sara said. "I can understand why she was under the table. She tell me herself. Mrs. Peker come into the house unexpected, and Libka didn't want to be caught with the old rags polishing the floor. You already saw what happened with your friend Joyce."

"Did you ask Mrs. Peker about the baths?"

"What is the difference?"

"Since she's responsible, she should know," protested Beryl. "Not only did that fat Naomi Peker spread it at Beachfront Junior High, but Sally made sure the whole of Promenade High knows."

"Uh, such a crime!"

"Well, they certainly did a lot of damage. I think this was the last straw for Joyce too. She acts like she doesn't know me. And all the excuses I make can't change the bare facts."

"Beryl, *mein kind,* don't feel so hurt about Joyce. There is other girls. Plenty."

"Keep out of my business," he said, but his pain was clear. He had waited for Joyce outside the Promenade High gate a day after the rumour had started. He had wanted to walk along Beach Road with her and try to explain, but the girl was icy.

"Sorry, Beryl," she said, "I can't go out with you anymore."

He had asked why, pleading for another chance.

She only tossed her blond ringlets and eyed him aloofly. "I'm seeing someone else."

Remembering this, Beryl pushed his plate of borscht and potatoes aside. Making his way out of the room, he ran straight into Libka.

"Watch out," he said.

She caught his tone and did not move.

"I said watch out."

"What's the matter, did Joyce ditch you again?"

The two glared at each other and a chase began. Libka fled, taking the steps two at a time, pursued head-on by her brother. She flung the gate open, dashing into the street, and continued her flight down the hill. Beryl could have caught her but he became aware of neighbours' eyes. Flexing his muscles, he retreated into the house.

Libka lurked around the corner. The safest place for her would be in the street where people passed or looked out of windows, for Beryl would never create a public scene. But after a while she became uneasy about her bare feet and cautiously went back towards the gate, keeping a watchful eye on the house.

On the stoep, Shneyer was playing with a rubber ball when the shuttered entrance to the rented rooms flew open and the soldier appeared.

"Stop pounding on the walls!" he shouted. "Do you want to wake my baby again?"

Unaware of Libka's presence, he advanced towards Shneyer.

"You knock that ball against the wall once more and I'll rip off your little hands."

Libka stepped up towards the stoep and said, "He's only playing."

Smit looked at her, his eyes glinting with evil. Then he said slowly, mouthing every word, "You have a beak like your mother!" He stamped across the stoep, kicked the black leather chair then headed back to his door. "Little Jew," he sneered, "you're asking for trouble."

His tone unnerved Libka. She took her brother's hand and entered the passageway, where she met Beryl. He had overheard the encounter, which overshadowed his anger about Joyce. Slowly they walked back to the kitchen, where Sara was kneading dough over a white tablecloth.

"He means business," Beryl said, and Libka noticed that the colour had drained from his face.

"What is that?" Sara stopped her work, wiped her flour-covered hands on her apron and peered into Beryl's face. "Something happen?"

"That soldier," said Beryl, "he was yelling at Shneyer again, and he insulted Libka. I didn't like the sound of it."

"Ugh!" Sara seemed undeterred. "Let him yell. Like I tell you, children, drum on the walls, drum on the piano, sing, dance, have fun. The more lively, the faster we will get him out. I'm afraid they will also burn down the house with their hotplate."

"I often smell something burning, but it's probably your cooking."

"So don't eat if you don't like. But who knows what is going on in their rooms? When he first came to apply I told him he could use the kitchen facilities. I thought one man alone, a soldier just back from the war, but it looks like they run a restaurant in the rooms."

"I'm not a coward," said Beryl, "but I would hesitate to start up with him."

"What is with you?" Sara reproached him. "We are not frightened of him."

"And Libka had to antagonize him." Beryl gave his sister a scornful look. "He's not a character one messes around with."

"How you mean antagonize?" Sara asked.

Shneyer pushed forward to defend himself. "I was only playing." Tears sprang into his eyes. "That's all I was doing, just playing." The rubber ball fell from his hands and he sank to the floor, crying his heart out.

"Shneyerel, don't cry." Sara stooped before him. "We will get that bad man out. You will see. We will get him out."

"Just try," said Beryl. "The way the law is, run by these Afrikaners, let's see how much luck we'll have. He's thick in with all those Boers. You wouldn't stand a chance."

"Beryl, please don't tell me," said Sara. "It is our house and we are not yet prisoners."

· *fifteen* ·

Mr. Shmerl from Wynberg returned the following Friday evening and this time the entire family was present. He joined them for the Sabbath meal and partook in the ceremony. Warm *challah* was heaped in the centre of the table and Elsie wheeled in the tea wagon with the first course of chopped liver, chicken noodle soup and *kreplach*. Sara had given her two yards of fine calico, and this appeased her for the evening. As the silver candlesticks from Europe gleamed on the starched white tablecloth, Mr. Shmerl held up his wine glass and gave thanks for the meal.

Shmerl had sent a message through Mrs. Peker announcing his visit and the family dressed formally for the occasion. Sara wore a jade-green suit with an emerald brooch. Libka and Golda were dressed in the identical yellow-and-white polka-dot organdie dresses their mother had made, with yellow silk bows in their hair. Beryl wore his white linen slacks and a blue-and-gold pullover Uncle Meyer had sent from America. Shneyer looked like an elf in the two-piece outfit the Shevahs from Claremont had brought for *Channukah*, and Dina was wrapped in pink ruffles.

"He is Daddy's old friend," Sara told the children in advance. "We worked together in the bank in Europe."

"What's he doing now?" Beryl wanted to know.

"Struggling ... They have a small variety store in Wynberg. But he's a capable engineer and worked for many years on the railroad in Durban. So we think he can make a success if he take over a ready-made business with all the valuable equipment and machinery. It is important to bring in somebody whose history we know."

Libka had not told her mother much about Mr. Shmerl's earlier visit when he found her home alone. She felt unsure of her feelings. But as her mother spoke, Libka's suspicions were not laid to rest. When she thought of the way he had touched her and the things those women had said at her father's funeral, it gave her a queasy feeling.

Yet when Motel Shmerl burst into the house that evening, she began to question her instincts. He shook hands with Beryl, kissed Golda and her on both cheeks, and soon Shneyer was propped on his knee. He told the children of the old times in Europe and how close he had been with their father.

After the Sabbath meal, the children dispersed and Sara and Mr. Shmerl moved to the sitting room.

"And your brother Meyer in America, he became a rich man?" he asked with a touch of envy, but Sara overlooked his tone.

"He didn't become a literature professor like he wanted, but he's a successful businessman. Whenever I get a letter from him I hope that from America maybe he will know more what became of the family."

Mr. Shmerl shook his head. "Uh, Sara, perhaps it is better not to know."

Sara unloaded her heart, recounting Meyer's efforts to bring the family to America. "But by the time Meyer's application was approved, it was too late. The borders were already closed. Only one other letter came after that, and then nothing."

"Sara, should we be sunk in the past? Let us rather look to our future."

"But, Motel, how can we forget?" said Sara. It relieved her to talk about it, though Motel Shmerl seemed restless.

"Yosef also tried to bring over the family, but he was so involved making a living that by the time we filed papers to become British subjects the trouble in Europe had started."

Mr. Shmerl patted Sara's hand. "Enough already, Sara."

"Uh!" she exclaimed tearfully. "To think that the old *shtetl* and everything is wiped out ... I wonder if we will ever know what became of the family. I run all the time to the Jewish Agency and the Red Cross but there is nothing on their list."

Mr. Shmerl shifted in his chair and reached for the *taiglach* on the tea wagon. "We must count our blessings, Sara. You got still your children, your health. We must do the best with what we got."

Sara and Motel Shmerl continued to talk in the sitting room until late into the night.

"Mr. Shmerl is interested," Sara announced the next morning. "He is a practical fellow and, after all, it is better to take in a manager that know your daddy from Europe than to bring in a stranger."

———•———

Golda returned from her music lesson that afternoon and went into her room. When she didn't come out after being called for supper a few times, Beryl went in to check.

"I don't want supper," she said.

"What's wrong?" he asked. "You look pale as a ghost."

Golda began to cry.

"Don't tell me they're giving you a difficult time at school again," he said. "What happened?"

Between sobs, Golda related that her music teacher had yelled at her. "She said I'm getting worse every time I come," wept Golda. "She said I m-might as well stop my lessons."

"It's no wonder," said Beryl. "How can you advance when you hardly ever practise?"

"But how can I with that man?"

"Golda, don't be a fool." Beryl moved to her bed and sat down beside her. "You mean you're afraid to practise because of that Smit character? Mom wants to get rid of him, anyway."

Golda's body trembled as she put her hands over her face.

Beryl pulled her up and led her into the sitting room. He pushed her onto the piano stool.

"Practise! If you're afraid, then I'll sit with you."

In the dining room the other members of the family were already seated around the table.

"Beryl ... Goldie ..." Sara called as she spooned the food into Dina's mouth.

"We're coming," shouted Beryl, but Golda sat on the stool like a stone.

Stuffing a dumpling into her mouth, Libka went into the sitting room. She knew that it took an extreme situation to make Golda behave in this way. No matter what she felt, Golda rarely showed it or complained.

"What happened?"

"Never mind," said Beryl. "Zip your lip."

"What's going on? Is it a secret?" asked Libka.

"If you can believe it," said Beryl, "Golda is now afraid to practise and her music teacher is fed up with her."

"You mean because of that tyrant?"

Golda broke into tears. "Stop, stop," she wept. "I shouldn't have told you."

"Of course you should have told us," said Libka. "Come and have your supper," she demanded, "and then you'll practise all evening."

They returned to the dinner table but Golda merely nibbled on her food. Sara watched with concern, and after they had eaten and she brought in the vanilla pudding for dessert, she asked, "Something bad happened, Goldie?"

"It's okay."

"It's not okay," said Libka. "Can you believe that Golda is terrified to practise her piano lessons because of that man? He's a Hitler."

"Mr. Smit, the boarder?"

"Who else?"

"All right, all right," Beryl interrupted as he gobbled down his pudding. "Libka, keep out of it or you'll create a scene as you do with everything."

"Really?" she said, offended.

"Yes, really. After dinner Golda will practise, and if she has any hesitation, I plan to be home this evening."

"Imagine," said Sara, "that we should be afraid to live normally in our own home."

Around seven o'clock that evening Beryl went into Golda's room and found her chewing her fingernails.

"What did we arrange?" he asked.

"All right, I'm coming."

Golda had scarcely settled into her practice, choosing a soft melody, when the door from the rented rooms flew open. Smit shot into the sitting room in his underwear, his hair standing up and eyes wild.

"Stop!" he yelled. "My baby's sleeping."

Golda's fingers froze on the keys.

"You start hammering on that piano again and I'll cave your head in!"

His thunderous voice reverberated through the house and in moments Beryl had emerged from his room and Libka from the stoep where she had been snuggling in her father's chair.

"My sister has to practise her music lessons," Libka told Smit. "Her teacher has been complaining."

Smit glared at her with mocking eyes. "You talk to me like that, you little mouse, and there'll be something coming to you."

"I don't think you have a right to act this way. It's still my mother's house."

"*Ja?* Your Jew mother?"

Sara had appeared in the passageway, the baby in her arms, a sleepy Shneyer trailing behind her.

"What is going on?" she asked as she looked at the hairy figure in his underwear.

"Mommy," Libka said, "he won't let Golda practise her music."

"Listen here, Mr. Smit." Sara looked up at the wild-eyed man. "If my daughter have to practise her music, you can't stop her. You can't make an invasion in my house."

"*Ja?*"

"*Ja,*" Libka repeated.

Beryl poked Libka stealthily in warning as the fury rose in Smit's face.

The man swirled around and it seemed as though he would strike Sara. "Jews," he hissed, "you're asking for trouble." He charged into his rooms, slamming the door violently.

Even Libka could not encourage her sister to continue. They all went back to their rooms.

———•———

Libka had a feeling that this was not the end of it. The anger boiling in Mr. Smit haunted her and she had a nightmare where he plunged a bread knife into her mother. Sometimes she was afraid to go to sleep because she felt she needed to keep watch and also feared the dreams where he emerged with a black mask over his face.

One night she had fallen asleep early and was in a deep slumber when something jolted her awake. She wasn't sure if it was real or in a dream. Light was coming from the kitchen so she knew her mother was still awake, probably sitting there with tears in her eyes as she read the old Yiddish books.

Suddenly, on some strange instinct, she shot out of bed and rushed from the dark room into the kitchen. Her eyes still misty in sleep she grabbed her mother's hand and tugged her from the chair, dragging the dazed Sara into her bedroom. She'd scarcely shut the door when they heard the lumbering boots in the passageway. Terrified, they listened to the intruder stumbling through the house, ramming at the walls, and then the shout rang out, "*Ek sal jou kry, Jood!* I will get you, Jew!"

Behind the closed door, Libka and Sara stood frozen as he prowled the house. His growls were loud and fierce, then became subdued, even more foreboding. Libka pinned herself against the door, but it bore no lock and she would have to rely on her strength. She thought of the children sleeping in the other rooms, of Shneyer and Dina and of her brother Beryl. But the drunken voice was now coming from the rear of the house. Libka thought of awakening Golda and sending her out through the window to seek help from neighbours, but then they heard him in the corridor again, and she braced herself against the door, preparing for the worst. His threats became muffled as he broke into Sara's bedroom where Dina slept in the cot. Libka heard his curses, thinking she should run to the infant's rescue, but she couldn't seem to move, only tightened her grip on the door. He swept out of that room, then Libka heard him staggering into the sitting room. "*Kom uit, Jood!*" he raged. "Come out." They heard furniture toppling over, and his voice began to crack as china cups and crystal goblets shattered on the tea wagon. "I'll kill you, *Jood!*"

The heavy footsteps hit the passageway again, and the bedroom door crashed open, sending Libka flying.

He stood, menacing, in the light from the passage, his curses bathed in the spit which oozed down the sides of his mouth. *"Goed!"* he exclaimed in satisfaction as he glimpsed Sara.

At that instant a dark shape hurled itself through the window behind them.

———•———

Just as Libka had awakened that night, so Maputo had sprung up from sleep in the alley by the shack. Something was amiss in his master's house and he wasted not a second in reaching it. He moved stealthily into the lane by the rabbit hok and listened.

He heard the soldier ransacking the house. He could not view the man from his position in the lane, but he could see into the bedroom of Libka and her sister. The room was dark, but he could make out the forms of Sara and Libka barricading the door, and he could hear drunken threats from the other side. Uncertain what to do, he crouched on the windowsill; but when the door flung open and revealed the man's violent face, Maputo leaped through the window and rammed the door closed. The impact sent the soldier reeling down the hall to shatter the stained glass doors.

Neighbours, hearing the commotion, called the police. By now Beryl, Golda, Shneyer and Dina were also awake. Even Elsie had emerged from her quarters in the courtyard.

By the time the two constables had pounded the gate open and made their way up the steps, Smit was on the stoep to greet them. He ushered them into the house.

"This bastard came to kill this lady," he informed the police in Afrikaans, pointing to Maputo who stood mutely backed against the wall. They took one glance and pulled his hands back, encircling them in chains.

Shaken, Sara tried to appeal. "No, Mr. Policeman, this is not the right man," she stammered to the arresting officer. "It is the other man." She pointed at Smit, who stood smirking.

"*Ja?*" said the Afrikaner constable, looking down in amusement at the dazed woman surrounded by her terrified children in their night clothes. "What is your name?"

"Sara Hoffman is my name."

"You live in this house?"

"Me and my five children."

"Of what nationality are you?"

"We are Jewish."

"And this man," he motioned to Maputo, "he attacked you?"

"No, no. The other man attack me."

The excitement had sobered Smit enough to play his part, and he winked at the two constables.

"The poor lady is confused," he said amiably in Afrikaans. "I saved her from the black bastard and now she accuses me. I'm a soldier, after all," he added, flaunting his uniform.

"*Jy is die vrou's man?*" the officer asked. "Are you her husband?"

Smit laughed, and pointed as his pregnant wife appeared, disturbed by the turmoil, and filled the passageway with her stomach. "*Nee, nee! Hier is my vrou. Marie!*" He put his arm around her and she nestled into him. "This Jewish lady," he continued in Afrikaans, pointing to Sara, "she's a widow so my wife and I rented some rooms to help her out."

Libka understood every word. Still in her nightgown, dazed and dishevelled, she stepped forward. "Policeman, don't listen to him. He's not telling the truth. He was going to kill my mother."

The two constables eyed each other in amusement as Smit and his wife looked on.

"*Ya, ya,* little girl," the constable said, "go back to sleep."

Libka turned to Beryl. "Say something to them!" she whispered. "You're a boy. Maybe they'll listen."

"What can I say?"

"Tell them the truth."

Beryl, half asleep and embarrassed to be caught in his pyjamas, approached one of the constables. "Sir ..." he began, but Smit stepped in front of him. Now in cordial Afrikaans conversation with the officers, he patted one on the back and accompanied them and the handcuffed Maputo onto the stoep. Libka heard them chat in Afrikaans, Smit joking, "I saved a Jew. Good soldier, eh?"

Chuckling, one of the constables whipped Maputo with a heavy leather *sjambok* as he stumbled down the stairs with his hands chained.

———•———

Several days after the attack, a lorry pulled up before the house; and the black men who a short while ago had lugged the clumsy furniture up the steps now sweated on the downward path. Smit had moved without paying the rent, and Sara felt so relieved that she did not even mention it.

Though the attack on the family and the jesting manner of the police preyed on Libka's mind, the coming of Maputo at this crucial time awakened a new belief in her. There was some communication, some power, that transmitted itself with an impact far beyond words, and it was this indefinable power that she had always sensed in Maputo. Why, she asked herself over and over again, had he appeared on this night?

She could see him now so clearly, his hands clasped in metal as the police led him away. Yet he held his head high and accepted the accusation without question.

Libka knew there could be no hope for Maputo's release, that the rest of his days would be passed in captivity. In this land where she lived, no black man could have a fair trial.

The stab of injustice pierced her, and at times her aching loneliness was so great that she felt she would die of it.

There was only one person with whom she could share her grief, and one afternoon she found herself going to Promenade High. She waited across the street as the droves of girls poured out of the gate, chatting and laughing happily. Finally, she spotted the lone figure of Anya Steinberg. She knew the girl would cross the street and take the solitary walk to the district in which she lived. Anya rarely took the tram and saved the change towards the purchase of a book or music.

When Anya saw Libka she sensed something unusual had occurred. What other reason would bring her to these grounds from which she had been expelled?

"Anya," Libka called, "can I tell you what happened?"

As they proceeded alongside the manicured lawns of Sea Point, strolling under the palm and silver leaf trees, Libka told Anya what had occurred the night of the attack.

"And Maputo submitted just like that?" Anya asked.

"When they put him in handcuffs he didn't make a sound. He acted as though he was guilty."

"The same as when that horrible servant of yours accused him of stealing?"

"He never defends himself. Even when the constable whipped him with that terrifying leather strap, he didn't make a sound."

"The police whipped him with a *sjambok?*"

"I guess that's what it is."

"You know the Voortrekkers used the *sjambok* with their oxen when they were migrating from the Cape in the Great Trek," explained Anya.

"It must have hurt Maputo so much, but he kept his dignity."

"Remember, Libka, as a black man he knows he doesn't stand a chance."

"I think it's even more than that with Maputo. He seems to feel there is some magical thing in the sky that leads us. Destiny, is that it?"

"I'm not going into that," said Anya. "He's a black man, and in South Africa they can do anything to a black man and he has no defence."

"It's so wrong, Anya. And you say in London it isn't like that?"

"Sometimes I think it's cowardly to escape to London," Anya said as they came to the area where the grass was unkempt and neared the neighbourhood in which she lived. "But if we fought back here, what would we accomplish? I'd be very happy to fight and even sacrifice my life, but would that change the situation?"

"The way the constables acted when they arrested Maputo, I don't think anyone would even listen. After all, I'm not a child, but when I tried to tell them what happened they told me to go back to sleep."

"I know they'd just laugh at your mother, but didn't Beryl try to reason with them?"

"Well, you know Beryl. He felt so embarrassed to be caught in his pyjamas, and anyway he was practically asleep. He did try to say something but the soldier just pushed him away."

"The Afrikaner police aren't much different from those Nazis in Europe. I'm sure they would be capable of operating concentration camps and gas chambers."

"But what did we Jews actually do to make everyone hate us so much?"

"If you'd read your history books, Libka, you'd see that this has been going on for centuries. Jews were always the scapegoats, blamed for all the misfortunes. In Germany many Jews were doctors, lawyers, rabbis and leaders of the country, and these were the people that were considered the greatest threat. The more successful the Jews were, the more they were hated. They were a threat."

Libka's mind was so clouded, filled as it was with the image of Maputo being led away.

"Do you think Maputo will be in prison for his whole life?"

"Who will come to rescue him?"

"Do you think if you and I got dressed up like grownups and went to see the guards, we could tell them what happened?"

"Libka, you have more faith than I do."

"And do you think they would let us see Maputo? All I'd want to tell him is that I miss him."

· sixteen ·

Feeling she would burst from frustration and confusion, Sara went to the house of Riva Peker. She did not expect to find consolation, yet she sought release from her gnawing thoughts.

She was pleased no one else was home. Mishka was busy with his deliveries, and Sheldon would probably not be home until nightfall with the three jobs he held down to provide for the household. The girls were at work — Bashka as a bookkeeper at an import/export firm, Hena a stenographer and Chana a salesgirl in a lingerie shop on Adderley Street.

Sara recounted the attack on her home, how Libka had sprung up from sleep, sensing danger, and she told Mrs. Peker of the strange appearance of Maputo.

"I told you what I think and what's the good to my telling you again?" Mrs. Peker spoke from her velvet divan in the parlour, her legs propped up on a matching stool. Servants in light blue cotton uniforms with ruffled aprons and caps scurried from room to room dragging buckets and mops.

Crystal chandeliers glowed overhead and the room was swathed in velvet drapes, oriental rugs and embroidered wall tapestries from the island of Las Palmas. Miniature china cups and silver goblets were arranged on the mahogany tea wagon.

"I warned you about taking in roomers. So what you want from me now?"

Mrs. Peker watched a servant shining the floor, and suddenly she pointed a finger. "You're missing spots!" she ordered. "There, there, there — to the left, more to the left, right there in the corner. There's a dull spot! I see it even from here!"

The frantic servant looked from her missus to the floor, seeking the spot that she had missed.

"These *shvartze*," Mrs. Peker cursed. "You need the patience of a god to deal with them." Now she turned back to Sara. "What's the use to come to talk to me, Sara, you listen?"

"But, Rivka," Sara pleaded, "try to consider my situation. After all ..."

"I would never be in your situation. I would never *allow* myself to be in your situation. You don't have to make a *shmate* of yourself because your husband is no longer living. He left you a good business. He left you a house. And you let everything go to the dogs."

Sara pressed her hands together as though for comfort, and she could not find the words to express the complex feelings that crowded her mind.

"And as far as what you tell me about Libka," Mrs. Peker continued, "it proves only what I told you. The girl is not normal. What else you want me to say?"

"But, after all," Sara said, "to spring up just at the same second, and *shlep* me to the room. And like I tell you, she was sleeping already for hours."

"You answer me," said Mrs. Peker, "that's normal behaviour?"

Sara looked at her beseechingly. "One thing I know in my heart: if I would still be sitting by the kitchen table, he would have finished me off. And he wouldn't be held responsible, especially if he was drunk. I already saw how the police act — Afrikaners, they all got friendly. To them it was a joke."

"So all right," said Mrs. Peker. "Why you put yourself in such a situation? Why you take into your house an anti-Semitic Afrikaner who openly spits in your face and calls you a dirty Jew? Why you do this to yourself, Sara? Answer me why you do this to yourself."

"How could I know, Rivka? He came in a soldier's uniform, official, and right away he pay me in advance for the first month. And he didn't tell about the babies, and to ask is against the regulations."

Mrs. Peker moved irritably and watched the fearful servant massaging the floor to a high gloss.

"Ugh, I'll have to let that girl go." She gritted her teeth. "Slow and clumsy, and eats worse than a pig!"

Mrs. Peker studied her puffy flesh oozing out of the orange sandal.

"And as for that Kaffir coming through the window out of the blue, it gives me goose bumps."

After the attack, Libka had told her mother that Maputo had not gone to the Transvaal and was living nearby, though she didn't give her the details.

"Well," Sara told Mrs. Peker, "he didn't go to the Transvaal. Libka said he sleeps somewhere not far."

"So Libka is still socializing with this Kaffir who stole your silverware?"

"I don't believe he stole."

"So who else?"

"Maybe I put it somewhere and forgot. It's hard to remember everything."

Mrs. Peker eyed her suspiciously. "I'll tell you for the last time and never again will I repeat myself. Send the problem away. That will clean up the atmosphere. So she and her Kaffir friend saved your life. Wonderful! But Libka will also kill you — you and every one of your children. And what you tell me about her springing up in the night, hearing things no normal person would dream of, this should make me change my views?... And now let's get down to business. You signed the papers already with Motel Shmerl?"

"Next week."

"Listen, it's a good break for him, and for you it's a golden opportunity. I told him so myself. A few days ago he came to my house and we had a frank talk. I have faith in that fellow. You can see it in his expression. Straight, no nonsense. With him you won't have problems like you did with those *ganef* brothers who cheated you out of the sawmill."

But Sara's mind returned to a conversation she had overheard when she went into the kitchen one evening. Libka and Golda were washing the supper dishes and Libka was saying, "I don't know why we shouldn't warn Mommy. After all, if that Mr. Shmerl turns out to be a crook ..."

The conversation changed when they saw her, but later that evening she asked Golda, "What did Libka say before about Mr. Shmerl? She don't like him?"

"Who said so?" Although Golda tried to appear innocent, Sara sensed her discomfort.

"Libka don't trust him, this Mr. Shmerl?" she asked again.

"How should I know? Of course we trust him. I mean, wasn't he Daddy's good friend?"

Sara had not wanted to broach the subject with Libka, but she was troubled by Golda's evasiveness.

"So there you go," Mrs. Peker went on. "Sometimes I think you don't know when you have gold in your lap. Sign the papers and finalize. You waiting for Motel to change his mind?"

That evening Sara asked Beryl, "And what is your opinion about Mr. Shmerl?" She was serving him an early supper as he was meeting some friends at the cinema.

"He's a nice enough man. Sure. Any more avocado salad?"

"I will chop up another egg and some onion. Too much avocado isn't left. And the good fruit and vegetable man, he didn't come on the wagon this week."

"Well, hurry up, I'm running late. How come you haven't made chicken lately?"

"I will make. In fact tomorrow, Friday, I will buy a nice chicken for *Shabbes* and I will also make soup with *kreplach*. You will maybe take the chicken to the *shochet?*"

"I wouldn't be caught dead running through the street with a live chicken."

"But, after all, to make it kosher."

"Anyway, I have a rugby game after school tomorrow." .

Sara chopped the egg and mixed it into the bowl with the avocado. "Tomorrow I must go to the lawyer," she said, "to look over the papers for the arrangement with Mr. Shmerl."

"So? Pass me the buns. Is that today's?"

"I bake fresh *bulkas* this morning. And tomorrow I will make *challah*." She passed Beryl the plate of buns. "I hope it will be a good thing with Mr. Shmerl, but who can tell?"

"Why shouldn't it work out?" Beryl reached for a bun and began buttering it. "Surely you're not getting cold feet now at the last minute."

"Who say cold feet? But, Beryl, you should realize it is a big step. We don't want the same thing to happen like it did with the sawmill."

"I wouldn't worry about it," he said. "Hurry up with the avocado. And I'll have a few of those Cadbury chocolate biscuits and a mango for dessert."

"Mrs. Peker also think it is a good thing. She tell me she think it is a *goldene zach*."

"Talk in English."

"She think it is a golden opportunity."

"So there you go. Any more chocolate syrup? And pass the milk while you're at it."

"Well, I hope so," said Sara. Tears were streaming down her face as she cut the onion. "Let's hope it will be the beginning of good luck for us."

———•———

Two days after Smit moved out, Elsie disappeared. It had not come as a surprise, for she had been threatening for some time. And after the attack on the Hoffman family, she had become unapproachable. She would slap the food on the table, and back in the kitchen they would hear her mumbling to herself.

"This is no place fit for a human to live," she told Libka one morning as she clanked the breakfast dishes in the sink. "It smells of death, and I don't even feel safe here no more. That swine Maputo! At last he's where he oughta have been long before. He coulda cracked my head open easy as he can a white man's."

In the other room Dina was raising a tantrum, and Sara hummed a monotonous tune to quiet her.

"And you, young missus, it's doin' you no good sitting around here day after day when everyone else's off to school. Gives you too much time to think up queer things. And it's rubbin' off on the others. I see it clear like daylight. You think the young master is the same? Flares up at me like I was just anybody's maid. Tells me to my own face how to fry my fish! Me, Elsie, who ran the household of the Dr. Reznik family. And there's no richer family in all of the Cape Province! But then, I asks meself, how's he to have respect for me? How's I to even have respect for meself when my own missus get down on her bare knees and scrub the floors? That's Kaffir work!"

There was a feeling of relief when Elsie was gone, but gradually they became aware of missing articles ... brightly coloured dresses that Sara had worn in happier times and children's clothing saved for special occasions. The antique clock from Europe was gone; and one day when Libka was sweeping under Elsie's cot in her old quarters, she discovered a silver bowl from the set that had disappeared.

She ran into the kitchen where Sara was making *kreplach* and chicken soup for supper.

"Look!"

Sara eyed the silver bowl in Libka's hand, then moved closer to study it. "From the silver set my mother gave me," she said in amazement. "So you find it, after all, Libkala?"

"Guess where?"

"Uh! Uh!" Sara exclaimed in joy.

"Shut up!"

Libka told her mother that she had found it under Elsie's cot. "And she set Maputo up as the thief by putting the goblet in his room."

Yosef's best suits had been removed from the closet. And one day when Libka stooped in the silent room and opened the bottom drawer, she noticed that the silver box had disappeared. She flung herself to the floor, unable to control the grief that poured from her. Now the secret reminders of her father were gone. She no longer cared if anyone heard her sobs. She wept for all that had happened since her father's death.

The creaking of the floor aroused her and she turned to see Golda clutching Dina in her arms. "What are you looking at?" Libka stormed, but Golda only bent down beside her and touched her hand. "Don't cry like that, Libka," she stammered as her own tears erupted.

With Smit gone, it was now possible for Libka to reclaim her own room, but Golda made no move to return to her former quarters. And Libka understood the reason. The children feared to go into the premises the soldier had occupied. Only Shneyer would sometimes venture in to call out "Boo!" and hear the word resound in the empty rooms.

Eager to escape the house that still exuded the stench of Smit, Libka decided to go to the surroundings of her old school. She would wear a new persona, for she hardly felt the person she was only months before. The white anklets and clumsy oxfords seemed childish to her, and she felt less timid about the new emotions within her and the awareness of her body.

She realized that she had no suitable clothes of her own, only the dresses her mother made for Golda and her. They ended above the knees and most were of organdie, with round collars, embroidery and tiny buttons. And then she would have to wear the patent-leather flats with the white anklets.

She searched in her mother's wardrobe for the dresses that Elsie had not bothered to take. Her mother was tiny like herself, and she knew she could wear the same size. She had already adjusted one of her mother's bras. With a few safety pins, it seemed to fit.

She found a floral silk peasant skirt with a wide ruffle at the ankles. The colours in the fabric dazzled her — shocking pink and gold and crimson, and the silk hissed as she moved. The skirt had a broad band at the waist, which she tightened and tied with a decorative cord. She put on a transparent pink blouse trimmed with lace, but hesitated about the bra strap that showed through in back. Perhaps if she stood very straight it would be less defined. She found a pair of red paradise sandals that revealed her toes, which seemed seductive. They flapped slightly when she walked, but she would get used to it. Her hair was freshly washed and a strand fell over one eye just like the actress Veronica Lake.

When Libka entered the kitchen, Sara was ironing. At first she simply continued pressing Beryl's sailor suit; but when she looked at Libka again, she put down the iron and a wondrous expression rose in her face. Her lips parted and her eyes shone as she fingered the lace on Libka's blouse. Libka had never seen her mother look this way. It was as though she had been transported to another world.

"I'm surprised Elsie didn't steal this outfit too," Libka said. "How do I look?"

Sara sniffed, her eyes moist. "*Oy!*" She began to cry.

"What's wrong, Mom?"

"*Her* they want to send away." Her face distorted in pain. "She is mad, crazy? Who would believe!" Drying her eyes, she found new strength. "Daddy should only have lived to see this."

"Oh, stop it, Mommy!" Libka herself had begun to cry.

"But wait, wait!" Sara persisted. "We will show them. We will show them all — Mrs. Peker and her daughters with the painted faces and the sailors. They should only look like this ... a little princess ..."

Libka and her mother struggled to regain their composure. Then Sara said, "I am proud. Believe me!"

When Libka went out onto the stoep, she found Dina tethered to a pillar, crawling around her prescribed area with her rubber bunny. With Elsie gone, Sara would secure the infant with a dog leash, freeing herself to do the housework. Dina had already tumbled down the stairs once, landing in the pot with the cactus plant; and Libka was blamed for this neglect.

"Hello, puppy," Libka chirped as she came onto the stoep, her shoes flapping.

Dina crawled towards the red shoes, licking them as she had seen the neighbourhood dogs do. Libka laughed as she released the infant from the leash and lifted her high into the air.

"Who's she?" Shneyer had emerged from the shuttered doorway, looking at Libka as though she were a birthday decoration.

"Who do you think?"

His eyes were entranced by the bright colours of the floral silk peasant skirt and he touched the fabric with awe. "Can I have it?"

As Libka put Dina down, she made an odd somersault, revealing her bare bottom. Then she lay with her legs kicking. Libka bent and tickled her belly.

Shneyer nestled around the silk fabric, hiding his face in it. "Will you be her new mommy?"

"I'm her sister," said Libka, "yours and Dina's."

The infant thrust her arms out joyfully, cackling as though she wanted the world to hear.

———•———

Libka set out for Promenade High that afternoon. Hovering under the silver leaf trees, the grey stone walls that shrouded the building seemed forbidding. She peeked through the gate, but there was not a sound in the playground. In an instant the clang of the bell reached her, and with it came voices. At first they were distant and muffled, but they grew louder and clearer as groups of girls in navy blue tunics advanced eagerly towards the exit.

The gate began to pound as girls in twos, threes and larger cliques poured out into the street. Some wore navy blue blazers over their tunics, with the blue-and-gold emblem sewn on the breast pocket. Most still wore the felt berets, but a few were wearing the summer uniform of white straw hats rimmed with the school band. All carried satchels on their backs and trod along in heavy brown oxfords.

Though Libka had not found the courage to look directly at the girls, she remained at the side of the gate where she was visible to them. As the babble intensified, she was seized with a feeling of foolishness, but as she turned to leave, the rustle of her skirt served as a magnet. In seconds she was surrounded by girls, some familiar, others strange.

"Look at that outfit!"

"Coming back to Promenade High?"

"She'd be stupid to come back. Look how much fun she's having."

"Is she the one who got into the fight? Wait till she hears about Anya Steinberg!"

Chatter fizzled around her and occasionally she grasped the words; but she saw in every face the look of awe.

More girls were joining the circle and, embarrassed by the attention, Libka sought to extricate herself. Waving to no one in particular, she turned and cut down a street that led to the sea. White mansions rose aloofly beyond the tall trim hedges, and gardeners plucked away every stray leaf. Fountains splashed over lush gardens. Chauffeurs waited in shiny cars, plump women in colourful outfits reclined on chaise lounges and servants set up trays under orange and yellow sunshades.

Libka strolled beneath the palm trees and savoured the salty breeze that intensified as she neared the ocean. She sauntered across the grass and removed her shoes as she reached the silky sands.

Laughter sounded and she turned to see the shapely form of Sally Peker wiggling along. She was no more than four foot nine, and despite her fifteen years, her body was developed like a full-grown woman. She had shed her school uniform and now wore clinging white shorts and a pink halter. She moved confidently in the high-heeled white sandals which revealed her painted red toes.

"Well, what are you doing here?" she exclaimed, tossing her golden locks. "For goodness sake, you're practically trespassing on Arthur's front lawn." She smirked at the shy boy beside her and took his hand.

"This is part of the Sea Point Pavilion," said Libka. "It's public property."

"But reserved for residents of the area, isn't it, Arthur?" Her baby-ish features looked stubborn.

When she saw Libka's determined look, she giggled nervously. "But that's all right. I mean, we're not exactly strangers, are we?"

"Unfortunately." Libka eyed her red toenails.

"Hey, come on," Sally said in her lilting voice. "That's a super outfit you're wearing, Libka. By the way, my mother found us this dressmaker, and you just wouldn't believe the things she can make. She's a coloured woman, but the work she does — you wouldn't believe your eyes!"

Seeing Libka grow restless, she tried to regain her attention. "By the way, did you hear the latest?"

Libka appeared disinterested. "The latest what?"

The boy seemed uneasy and motioned to Sally.

"I'll be over your house in a moment, Arthur," she told him. "There's something so very important I have to tell this girl."

As the boy walked off, she turned to Libka. "You didn't hear? My God, you should be the first to know. If anyone should be thrilled, you should." Her blue eyes gleamed with excitement. "It's about Anya Steinberg, the one who got you expelled."

"No one got me expelled."

"Very well," said Sally, "if you don't want to hear, I won't tell."

But when Libka began to rise, she could not bear it.

"Let's be friends. Come on, doll, can't we be friends?" she begged. "After all, we're practically related. Didn't your mother work in my mother's house in Europe?"

Libka scoffed. "I think you have the facts mixed up." She began putting on her shoes.

"Oh, I do? Anyway, let me tell you the story." Sally flopped down on the sand beside Libka and played with her hair. "You have such pretty hair, you know. It's naturally curly, you're so lucky. Anyway, poor Anya, she's really finished. If you think Miss Bloemfontein was mad at you, you should have heard!"

She twirled Libka's hair, piling it on top of her head, then fiddled with a wisp here or there.

Libka pulled away in irritation.

"It was awful, just awful," said Sally. "It started in Afrikaans class when Anya refused to speak the language. And my friend from the tennis club told me that during assembly Anya didn't sing the South African national anthem, but hummed 'God Save the King.'

"Do you know what Anya told the teacher? 'Somebody has to defend justice and you're all cowards!' So where do you think that got her? Right in Miss Bloemfontein's office!"

Sally lowered her voice and tried to sound mysterious. "And then the lunch bell rang, and where do you think this Sally disappeared to? Right under Miss Bloemfontein's window! So I heard the whole thing. Anya kept saying, 'You won't get me to speak Afrikaans.'

"Miss Bloemfontein explained that it was compulsory to also learn Afrikaans in school. 'I don't believe in segregation,' Anya said.

"Miss Bloemfontein called her a revolutionary and warned her where all this would lead. To jail, of course. 'You Boers treat the coloureds and blacks like dogs,' Anya said. 'Your police put my best friend's friend in prison because he's black.' Naturally, Miss Bloemfontein was horrified that Anya would have a friend who had a black friend."

"Why would she be horrified?" Libka cut in.

"Oh, come on, Libka, are you trying to be funny?"

"Listen here, little gossip," Libka said, jumping up and brushing the sand off her skirt. "I don't want to hear anything more from you."

"*You* call me a little gossip?" Sally put her hands on her hips. "How dare you! Don't you even have any bloody respect?"

"Not for you."

"But I haven't even told you the whole story." Sally could not stop herself. "When the headmistress asked her who her best friend was, guess what she said?"

"Shut your mouth."

"You, Libka. She said Libka Hoffman. Imagine, after she got you expelled."

Libka hurried off, but Sally pursued her.

"Then I heard Miss Bloemfontein say, 'Is this not the girl who we expelled from Promenade High?' Can you imagine!"

Libka turned and eyed Sally. "Do you want me to plug up your mouth with seaweed?"

"Listen," the other answered, "I guess it's true what everybody says about you. You stink. Are you the last one to bathe in that filthy water? You probably have lice in your hair!"

Libka did not stoop to answer and continued alongside the ocean, Sally sneering as she tossed her hair haughtily and walked off. Libka, her mind consumed by Anya, was oblivious of the girls and boys in colourful attire, chasing each other, laughing, bending to catch the ice cream leaking down their sugar cones. Back on Main Street she hopped onto a tram and got off when she saw the street vendors and derelicts in the gutter and recognized Anya's neighbourhood. When Libka tapped on Anya's door, it sprung open and her mother looked out fearfully.

"Come in," she said softly when she saw Libka. "I hope Anya will see you."

The house was dim and Libka was relieved that the fierce man did not appear in the doorway.

"I'll warn Anya." Mrs. Steinberg patted Libka on the shoulder. "How pretty you look in that outfit. Thank you for coming."

Mrs. Steinberg tiptoed towards a closed door. "Somebody to see you," she called.

She put an ear to the door, but no answer came. Smiling reassuringly at Libka, she tried again.

"What do you want?" came the toneless voice.

"A surprise."

"I don't want surprises!"

The words were like a slap, and Mrs. Steinberg looked apologetically at Libka. "I'm very sorry," she said. "You must know what happened to Anya today."

"That's why I came."

"You're a good girl. We'll try again."

Summoning courage, the thin woman in the shapeless housedress tapped gently once more.

"It's Libka," she called. "Golda's sister."

There was a long pause. The woman pressed her ear against the door; and when she heard a sound she darted a hopeful glance at Libka. "I think she's coming."

The door opened swiftly and Anya's eyes flashed first upon her mother, then on Libka.

"I'm in no mood for visitors," she said sternly to Libka, "but since you've bothered to come all this way, come on in. I was just listening to *Anastasia*."

There was a look of relief on the face of Anya's mother as she closed the door and left the two girls alone.

"So who made the big announcement?" Anya asked.

"Sally Peker."

Anya nodded. "What does that dummy know, anyway?" She fiddled with the gramophone. "News spreads like an epidemic, but I don't care. Why should I care?" She darted a hostile look at Libka. "Why did you come, and so togged up, to show your respects?"

Libka felt foolish in her outfit and shrugged.

"Well," said Anya, "you might as well sit down."

Libka knelt to the floor and wrapped her peasant skirt around her. Books and papers were scattered everywhere, and Libka's eye fell on *The State and Revolution* by Vladimir Lenin.

"What are you looking at?" asked Anya. "I don't suppose you've read Lenin or Karl Marx yet?"

"Not yet, but I plan to. When I was in the library I saw his book *The Communist Manifesto*." Libka had noticed this book in the piles in Anya's room. "Where do you buy all your books, Anya?"

"Jason's Rare Books on Adderley Street. That's the place to go. He's not out for the money. Just has a reverence for good stuff."

"Really? I'll go there when I have some money."

"So what did that big mouth Sally Peker tell you?" Anya asked. "And how would she know, anyway?"

"It turns out she was in the playground and hung around under Miss Bloemfontein's window."

"Snooping, as usual. I hope she at least gave you an accurate account."

"It's hard to know," said Libka. "But did you really tell Miss Bloemfontein about Maputo?"

"I told her the truth. I told her my best friend's friend was thrown in jail because he's black."

Libka felt embarrassed. "Am I supposed to be your best friend?"

Anya fiddled with the gramophone. "That's pretty pathetic, isn't it? I get my best friend thrown out of school. I guess I am crazy."

The girls laughed quietly, as though to themselves.

Anya wound the gramophone, which continued its scratched rendition of *Anastasia*. For a while the girls listened in silence.

"Well," Anya said finally, her voice low, "I've won my freedom." Then she imitated the headmistress's words.

"'We can't have anyone of your ilk among our pupils here. It is most unfortunate that we have you in our country.' This was my chance," said Anya. "'It's not even your country,' I told her. 'Maybe you forgot your history, Miss Bloemfontein. The British occupied the Cape in 1795 and controlled the sea route to the East. And you people fought them in the Anglo-Boer War of 1899 to 1902 but the territory remained under British domain. How's that for my history comprehension?' I asked Miss Bloemfontein."

"Did you really say all that?" Libka asked in awe.

"Every word of it, and this bought me my freedom. The great lady rose and pointed to the door. 'Get out!' she said. 'You are no longer a pupil at Promenade High School.' Isn't that terrific?" Anya shrieked with joy. "So, best friend, how shall we observe this memorable occasion?"

Libka smiled. "Maybe you should sing the British national anthem."

Anya stood up straight as a post and burst into song and Libka, giggling, joined in:

> God save our gracious King,
> Long live our noble King,
> God save the King:
> Send him victorious,
> Happy and glorious,
> Long to reign over us:
> God save the King.

It was late afternoon by the time Libka left Anya's house. "I'll walk you to the tram stop," Anya said.

The girls strolled down the gravel street, sidestepping the garbage and rags. Anya's mind was on the future. "There's change in the wind, Libka. Janny Smuts is a fair prime minister, but he's not going to be around forever. I mean, he's past three score and ten, and when he goes we'll really be in for it. There'll be a blood bath in South Africa. These Boers are afraid of any intrusion. They fought with the British, they fought with the Bantus and they're trying to strangle us Jews. No, I shall not submit to their language."

"Then what will you do, Anya? How can you fight against a country, a whole system of government?"

"A country is made up of people," declared Anya. "You and me. If we behave like cattle, then there's no problem ... at least not for a while. But we'll only lead the country to doomsday! This can't go on. How can we support this? Colour distinctions, class distinctions. Listen, I'm bitter. Maybe if I was rich and lived in a mansion by the Sea Point Pavilion, I'd feel differently, but I really hope I wouldn't. I really hope I couldn't be bribed so easily. There is nothing about it that tempts me, Libka. I despise it!"

As they stood on Main Street waiting for the tram, Libka asked, "Are you feeling like this because of what happened to Maputo?"

"I don't need a trigger, but when you told me how those Afrikaner police whipped Maputo with a *sjambok* and he didn't feel he even had a right to defend himself, that was the last straw for me."

———•———

Libka climbed the narrow, winding staircase to the upper storey of the tram and felt a flush of excitement as she looked down from the height. There was energy in the air and she was aware of things she hadn't seen before. She noticed more than ever the coloured children playing half naked in the gutter, infants guarding others still smaller than themselves. A little girl with frizzy pigtails wheeled a baby in a carriage of cardboard with bent wheels. Two children crouched in a lane, playing with rusty cans. A boy twirled a paper plane through the air. Everything seemed significant and meaningful.

She walked up York Road and peered into the alley where Maputo used to sleep and saw his tattered blanket and the pillow she had stolen from the closet lying in a heap against the wall. She rolled the blanket around the pillow. She would hide it beneath Maputo's old cot and keep it for him.

Nearing her house, she felt she had been away for a long time. It hardly seemed only that morning that she had selected the floral peasant skirt, the pink blouse and red shoes. The heady feeling gave way to exhaustion from everything that had happened — the unpleasant encounter with Sally Peker on the beach and Anya's euphoria over being thrown out of school. She couldn't wait to shed the gay attire from her body and feel normal again, to be back in her old clothes, alone with her thoughts.

Could she leave this country? Could she abandon her mother, sisters and brothers? Though her life seemed to have no clear path and she sensed that her destiny lay elsewhere, she was too perplexed to know in which direction to turn.

———•———

Restlessness invaded her body these days, and she often felt a fever to explore. Her time alone in the house dragged and she had taken to dwelling on the past, so when she found herself on a tram heading for Adderley Street, she decided on a whim to change for a bus to the industrial section. She hadn't been to her father's factory since his illness and had a yearning to see it again.

She got off at the corner of Nelson and Sir Lowry Road and strolled around. Factories dominated the area, with sooty black windows that gaped and metal doors that creaked when opened and shut. As she passed the leather tannery, she inhaled the once-familiar stench and almost welcomed the hammering of machines that pervaded the area. The streets were a confusing mess with screeching cars, lorries and buses. Nelson Street ran off the main thoroughfare, a narrow unpaved street where punctured cans and bedraggled clothing littered the gutters and coloured children played. Black workers passing in the street called lustily to one another.

It was here in this district that Libka was born. She remembered sitting on the high chair in the rooms above their workshop while Mrs. Shevah would fuss over her. "A *sheine popkele*," she would exclaim while she twirled Libka's hair into banana curls. She would pinch her fat creased legs and say, "A beauty she will grow up to be."

She strolled past the confectionery factory and looked up at the bleak windows. The building resembled a prison, yet she remembered coming here often with her father. It was owned by another immigrant from the old country. She recalled the heaps of chocolates they would come away with, bags brimming with sweets in coloured tinsel. And she used to insist on opening every one, biting into the cream fillings, tasting and searching. And her mother would shout when she found chocolates with fillings stuck to floors and furniture.

As Libka entered the doorway of her father's factory she heard familiar voices. She pulled open the inner glass door and then caught the words: "She needs to know only what we tell her, *farshteyst?* Nothing more, nothing less —"

Mr. Shmerl's words were cut short by Libka's entry. His face was sweating and his shirt sleeves were rolled up to the elbows. Next to Mr. Shmerl, looking timid, sat her father's accountant, Mr. Adelson, a man whom Libka had always liked.

But there was nothing else in this office that she could recognize. The old oak desk of her father was gone. And where was the armchair on which she used to swivel? Harsh fluorescent lights had replaced the bulb on the string, and the green walls were now a glossy white.

"You know who this is?" Motel Shmerl's face flushed as he moved around the desk and came close to Libka.

"I should not know already?" Mr. Adelson rose and offered his hand. "My favourite girl." He had always kissed her, but now he seemed tentative. He shook and pressed her hand. "My, so grown up. I would hardly recognize her." He stepped back and viewed Libka approvingly as she stood in her ruffled peasant skirt and sweater, her toes showing through the red paradise sandals.

"So you decide to join the business?" chirped Mr. Shmerl. "Where you want to operate from, the factory or showroom?"

"Such a pretty girl you would hide behind the machines?" Mr. Adelson smiled.

"We're building a showroom," Mr. Shmerl said briskly. "Your mother tell you?"

"Where?" asked Libka, looking about.

"Upstairs. Upstairs in the back."

Mr. Adelson caught Libka's forlorn look and said tenderly, "You must have so many remembrances. The rooms upstairs, that's where you lived when you were a little girl. I remember well."

"Ah, the old fool is getting sentimental again," cut in Mr. Shmerl. "We're putting the space to good use. Want to see? Come with me."

Libka followed the brisk little man. As he led her past the pounding machines, she looked for a familiar face. Where was Fortune, the loyal foreman; and Bongani, who had replaced Maputo when he went to work in their house in Green Point? Where were Kwanele and Njabulu and Mhambi, whom her father had valued so much? Every face at the machines was strange to her. Where had her father's old workers gone?

Mr. Shmerl stepped aside and prodded her up the steps where she used to totter as an infant. Though it was dim, she was conscious of her bare legs and tried to restrain the motion of her hips as she went upwards.

She found herself in a large open area with walls in the process of being plastered. She looked around for the tiny rooms where the cribs used to stand, the pantry, the kitchenette, the vestibule where she played with her rubber dolls. But the rooms had been demolished.

As she lingered, she became aware of a strange look in Mr. Shmerl's eyes, the same gleam when he had caught her alone at home. Here in her childhood surroundings the expression was even more bewildering.

"Thank you for showing me the showroom, Mr. Shmerl," she said, trying to appear casual. "It's very nice."

"But you didn't hardly look. Come, let me show you."

What should she do? She remembered how angry he had become at her house that day, and she was afraid to upset him.

"Come," he said, "I'll show you around."

He took her by the hand and led her into a cubicle. "You remember this? Maybe here you used to sleep in your crib?"

An image flashed before her: the golden-haired Miss Ingrid sitting on the edge of her cot, reading an English fairytale.

A stained mattress with cigarette burns now dominated the area, a plaid blanket heaped at the foot.

"This is where I live, see?" said Mr. Shmerl. "Here I eat, here I sleep, here I live. My wife she has no use for me, so now I'm all alone." He looked at Libka. "You feel sorry for me, huh?" He came close and she felt hardness as he pulled her against him. "A little bit you feel sorry for me?"

"No," she said, twisting her head to avoid his breath.

"Just a little bit maybe? An old man all alone. You want to make me happy a little?"

"No," she said, then, "I mean ..."

"Come. Let's talk a little. You know that your father and I, we were like brothers?"

He was easing her onto the mattress.

"Sit down. You're a big girl."

She felt herself stiffen, but tried not to show him she was afraid.

"You're a pretty girl, you know. I bet your father was proud of you. Yes?"

"I don't know ..."

"Ah, just a little shy, yes?"

He put his hands around her face and drew it towards his mouth. She tasted the sourness of a sticky tongue and pulled away in revulsion.

"Thank you very much," she said loudly. "The showroom's very ..."

"What's wrong?"

As she stumbled towards the stairway, she could feel his eyes glaring menacingly out of his flushed face. She had meant to act grownup and confident but now she could not find her voice.

She clattered down the stairs and almost bumped into Mr. Adelson. His face filled with concern, but she blundered past him and out into the street, afraid that if she stopped she would burst out crying.

Motel Shmerl panicked. Who knows what she might tell her mother? Sara Hoffman had acquired a telephone shortly after he took over the factory, so he decided to ring her before she got Libka's side of the story. Right in the presence of Mr. Adelson he lifted the receiver and dialled.

"My dear Sara," he said with unusual gentleness when he heard her voice, "more problems you don't need, but tell me, please, what's with your Libka?"

"Why, something happened?" Before she could gather her words he went on. "Mr. Adelson and me, we were sitting here going over the ledgers when suddenly she come in. Tell me, she still isn't in school?"

"Well ..." Sara was confused.

"But that's not my business, though of course as a *landsman* I consider it my business. Anyhow, Mr. Adelson and me, we gave her a fine welcome. Then I took her up to see the showroom we're building ... Listen, Sara, maybe I was wrong to call you, but to neglect would be even worse."

"So tell me already, Motel," said Sara, fearing the words that may come.

"I don't want to make a *skandal* in front of Aaron Adelson, such a strong devotion he also feels for Yosef's family. But when she flew out from the factory, we wanted to stop her, to calm her down. But faster than a rabbit she was gone."

"*Oy!*"

"Sara, it takes the life from me to call you with such a *maise*. I didn't believe what Rivka Peker was filling my head with, but ..."

"Libka didn't tell me she was going to the factory. I wonder why ..."

"Why!" Mr. Shmerl mocked. "I should know what goes on in the girl's head. Why did they expel her from the school? You tell me!"

"But something must have happened."

"Maybe she didn't like that we tore down the rooms. Who can know what's in another's head? Listen, Sara, if there's anything I can do ..."

For the rest of the afternoon Sara waited anxiously for Libka's return. She paced the floors, and each time she heard a sound, she rushed to the stoep.

But when Libka returned, she crept into the house, listening, then stole into her bedroom. Her mother was cooking in the kitchen and did not see her. Libka removed her tight sweater, gaudy skirt and paradise shoes, and changed into a pair of black pedal pushers. When Sara found her, she was sitting on her bed, staring at the pages of *Wuthering Heights*.

"I make this afternoon *taiglach*," her mother said. "You would like some with a glass of milk?"

Libka recognized the patronizing tone. "No," she said curtly.

"But I know you like always ... warm just out from the honey."

"I don't want!"

"All right! All right!" Cautiously Sara left the room.

But later she came in again.

"It is after six. Beryl and Golda and everybody eat already. There is borscht and potatoes on the table."

"Go choke on your hot potatoes!"

"*Oy vey!* What you want from my life?"

"I'm leaving! I'm going to that boarding school."

Sara stepped back, her expression tragic.

"Get out!" Libka shouted.

When Sara began to cry, Libka jumped up. "I said stop that!" And when still her mother did not show strength, terror seized Libka. She tore the glasses off her mother's face and flung them to the floor.

"*Oy mein Got!*" Sara wept, dazed without her spectacles. "My glasses she break!"

Libka saw her horror-stricken mother stoop down to search for her glasses, and as she continued to wail, Libka fled onto the stoep.

When she returned to the bedroom an hour later, she was relieved that Golda was not there. She was aware of faint conversation in the kitchen, but she could not bother to listen. As the evening progressed, no one came to her door; and then the house sank into darkness.

They are afraid of me, she thought, and this terrified her. She prayed she had not broken her mother's glasses, for her mother was lost without them. To take away her glasses was to take away her eyes. But what frightened her most was the awareness that she might not have stopped at that.

If she had tried to tell her mother what had happened at the factory, everyone would think she had invited it, wearing the sweater that was so tight on her. She remembered the gossip about a girl at school who accused the caretaker of making passes at her. Sally Peker claimed she saw the girl at the Sea Point Pavilion flirting with a man old enough to be her father, and word travelled around that she was a free woman. The headmistress held her responsible for provoking the caretaker and she was ridiculed. Libka feared this might happen to her.

She paced the room, finding no peace. She had not eaten since that morning, but a sick feeling throbbed in her stomach. Maybe there was something in her that invited the strange behaviour of Mr. Shmerl. She tried to think of other girls, fun-loving girls like Sally Peker and Joyce, and she was sure that scary old men didn't do such things to them.

Why had she gone to the factory at all, looking so grown up? Was there something that drew her to this horrible man?

It could never happen to Golda. It could never happen to all those laughing girls who flowed out onto the school playground. It took the devil to invite it, and the devil must lie within her.

—————

For two days she spoke to no one, slipping into the kitchen only when she could avoid everyone. She filled her mouth before the open refrigerator, then sneaked back into her room. But on the afternoon of the third day she encountered her mother in the passageway.

"Come out already," Sara pleaded. "What are you doing to yourself, *mein kind?*"

Why was it that her mother's gentleness made the tears come? It might have been easier if her mother had reprimanded her and slapped her. Then she could fight back and feel justified.

She was relieved that her mother wore her glasses and they seemed intact. She had had a nightmare — eyeless, her mother was wailing in the house.

"D'you have any food?" Libka asked, though not feeling hungry.

"Come, my child, a crumb you didn't put in the mouth for days."

Libka went into the kitchen. She tried fiercely to fight her tears, but her mother noticed.

"*Sha* already! So I will send you to the boarding school. Whatever you want."

Ah, so her mother now agreed that she was mad and was at last submitting!

"How come you're so agreeable all of a sudden?" Libka asked.

"What you mean, agreeable?"

"Why are you so eager for me to go to boarding school?"

Sara mashed an avocado pear and sprinkled salt and pepper into it. Then as she began cutting the onion, tears pierced her eyes. "Who can tell? Who know what is right?"

"I'm sick of avocado pear," Libka shouted. "I thought you had some decent food for a change."

"What you want from me? I bought today the good avocado pear from the Malay man on the wagon."

"*Muzeltov!*"

"You want *lokshen* pudding?"

"No!"

Sara peeled and chopped a hard-boiled egg and added it to the avocado pear. Libka could see that her mind was weighted with thought. She served the food in silence, sitting opposite Libka and seeking reassurance.

"Maybe you can tell me what happen in the factory," she said at last.

Libka looked straight at her mother. "The factory? Who told you I was there?"

"Mr. Shmerl telephoned."

"And you didn't tell me this! Why did you keep it from me?"

"You give me a chance to tell? How can we talk like human beings when you act so wild?"

"You start up again," said Libka, "and I'm leaving this minute!"

"*Sha, sha,*" her mother begged, "but I got a right to know."

"To know what?" Libka was afraid if she looked at her mother she would see too much.

"He show you the showroom and you run away. He tell me you act wild."

"I act the way I want to act!" She eyed her mother. "And I don't like dirty-Jew crooks!"

"*Sha!* To talk like this about our own people ..."

"He's worse than the bloody Smit! He's worse than those Voortrekkers who stoned our house! He's the slimiest, dirtiest, crookedest ..."

"*Sha!*" begged Sara. "*Sha* even for the deaf neighbours. What did he do to you that you talk so bad?"

How could Libka tell her mother that he had stuck his slimy tongue into her mouth like a poisonous snake and that he touched her under her sweater?

"I've had enough of the Jews!" she fumed. "I'm dropping out of *cheder*."

Sara clasped her hands. "*Cheder* also you will stop? After all, a person needs a Hebrew education."

"You get your Hebrew education! You think I want to become a rabbi!"

Libka sensed her mother knew she was evading the issue and she was relieved that Sara didn't press for more details because she had no way of explaining what had happened.

· *seventeen* ·

Libka longed to be alone and to free her thoughts. She was terrified of being sent away to a place for troublesome girls, yet she worried what she might do at home. Though Elsie was gone and Beryl was out of the house most of the time, she could not clear her mind with Dina tottering around and Shneyer emerging from hidden corners. Golda was quiet and cautious when she came home from school, even stopping her piano practice when Libka passed by.

Sara was involved with the housework, preparing meals or doing the washing in the yard. She looked worn and defeated and mumbled to herself.

On a bright Tuesday afternoon Libka decided to go down to Three Anchor Bay, even though she couldn't swim at this time of the month. Tucking a wad of toilet paper inside her bloomers, she put on her navy blue pedal pushers, a white blouse and leather sandals. Then she snuck into the pantry and stood on the ladder to reach the jar of confectionery that her mother hid on a high shelf. She grabbed a handful of butterscotch toffees to curb her sudden craving for sweets.

As she strolled down the cobblestone street, she passed the small white dwellings, where she heard people speak in Afrikaans. Once on Main Street she lingered around the Malay shop where heaps of pomegranates, loquats, mangos and avocado pears were displayed in front. Pretending to look at the fruit, she peered through the entrance but could not see the Malay boy.

She cut across the Commons and walked through the fields of dry grass until the rocks became visible and she could hear the pounding of the waves.

The area was deserted, not even a fisherman to be seen on the rocks. She was removing her sandals when she noticed a form in khaki shorts and shirt a slight distance away, and when he turned his head in her direction she recognized the Malay boy.

She could not understand the longing she felt to make contact with him. Was it the loneliness she sensed in him, the isolation, his eyes searching the ocean, or the fact that she had seen him read the same book as her father?

She sat down on the sand and watched the waves explode on the shore, hoping he might come her way; but when she again glanced in his direction, he was lying on the sand.

She would soon be going off to boarding school and no longer be able to come to Three Anchor Bay. The thought of never seeing the boy again filled her with sadness.

The afternoon was passing and she must soon head home. The boy was now reading. She remembered Anya's words about befriending him and not being afraid to talk to a Malay boy.

A sense of defiance drew her in his direction, and when she came close to him, he lowered his book and looked up at her.

"Are you lost?" he inquired gently.

"No. This is my favourite swimming place."

"I've seen you here before," he admitted.

She lingered awkwardly as he lifted his book.

"I go to your grandfather's store sometimes," she said.

"I know."

"I once saw you reading a book called *Crime and Punishment* that my father used to read in Russian."

"Dostoyevsky is a fine writer."

Since the boy made no attempt to continue the conversation, Libka stooped down beside him. "Can I look at your books?"

"By all means."

The boy opened his satchel and removed a number of books, piling them on the sand. Among them was a volume of speeches by Sir Winston Churchill. Libka recognized the name. He had taken over as prime minister of England when the war started. The book blew open to a page with a heading "We Shall Fight on the Beaches."

There was also a book by someone called Gandhi, and another of the poetry of Robert Browning. The volume he held in his hands was in an unfamiliar language.

"I'm not sure if any of these will be meaningful to you," he said in a voice like those who announced the symphonies on the BBC.

Libka glanced at the book in his hands. "What language is that?"

"It's called Gujarati, which my grandfather taught me. He's an admirer of a spiritual leader of India: Mohandas Karamchand Gandhi. And I wanted to read him in the original language."

"What kind of book is it?" Libka studied the lettering in fascination.

"It's called *The Story of My Experiments with Truth*. To summarize, it deals with achieving change in a non-violent way. Gandhi spent some time in South Africa and had discouraging experiences."

"Like what?"

"He was thrown off a train at Pietermaritzburg after refusing to move from the first-class coach, even though he had a first-class ticket. And when travelling by stagecoach he was beaten by the driver when he didn't relinquish his seat to a European passenger. He had all kinds of humiliating experiences, so he dreamt of a better world."

"Is that how you feel?" Libka was surprised at the intimate way she was able to talk to the boy.

"My grandfather believes we're in this world to make a difference."

"I spoke to him one day and he told me you live in London."

"Yes."

"And you come to visit him?"

The boy nodded. "I'm very close to my grandparents. They raised me because my parents were working." He caught Libka's passionate eyes and leaned closer. "My grandfather ..." he began, then stopped himself and returned to his book.

Feeling she had been too aggressive, Libka rose, and now the boy closed the book and looked up at her.

"I don't mean to be distant," he said, "but I suspect it isn't wise for you to talk to me."

"Why?"

"I would expect a girl like you to be in Sea Point, not wandering around here in Three Anchor Bay."

"Sea Point doesn't interest me."

She looked directly at him and this time he didn't turn away.

"I don't belong there," she went on. "If you'd like to know, I want to go to England."

"But Cape Town is so magnificent — the splendour of Table Mountain, the serenity of the veld, the ocean ..." He seemed embarrassed, but she could not remove her eyes from him. He sounded like a poet.

"May I ask why you'd like to leave South Africa?"

As she looked out to sea, the words came unbidden. "I don't think things are fair in this country. We had a Bantu man in our household who was like a member of our family, and now he's in jail. A Boer attacked my mother and when the Afrikaner police came and saw Maputo, they handcuffed him and threw him in jail."

The Malay boy looked up at Libka in confusion. "Wait a minute, slow down! First of all, why did the Boer attack your mother?"

"We're Jewish and I think he hated that. He was a boarder in our house and used to see my mother reading Hebrew books from Europe."

"And how does the Bantu man fit in?"

"He was just there, that's all. His crime was that he's black."

"So they didn't determine what really happened but imprisoned him because of his race?"

Libka nodded.

"But you know such things are not unusual in South Africa."

"And when I was a child living in Newlands the Voortrekkers threw rocks at our windows and drove us away."

"I know Newlands," he said. "There are many Boers living there. Before my parents relocated to London, we lived in the Malay Quarters at the foot of Lion's Head."

"I liked Newlands better than where we live now."

"But don't you feel welcome in Sea Point?"

Libka shook her head. "The people there are so different from my family."

"How do your parents find living here?" he asked.

"My father's dead. He's buried in Pinelands Jewish Cemetery."

A silence fell between them and Libka suddenly felt awkward confiding in this strange boy. "Well, I better go." She turned to leave.

"Wait!" He gathered his books. "I'd like to walk with you. Do you think I can?"

"I live in Green Point, not far from your grandfather's store."

They slithered their bare feet through the sands in the sultry afternoon, avoiding the seaweed that the waves had hurled onto the shore, and then paused to put on their sandals as they reached the prickly grass. Approaching the Commons, the boy removed the book of Robert Browning's poems from his satchel and handed it to Libka.

"I'd like you to have this. Maybe we'll meet in England someday," he said, then with a shy smile he hurried off towards his grandfather's store.

Libka watched him cross the Commons, then opened the small, leatherbound volume. There was an inscription on the flyleaf. In the same calligraphy she had been taught at school were the words "Sayyed bin Noor," with a London address beneath.

What an unusual name, she thought. Maybe he is a poet, the way he spoke about the splendour of Table Mountain and the serenity of the veld. And his eyes have such a dreamy look. As she strolled up the street towards her house, she felt that things would never be the same.

She was jolted out of her magical state when her mother met her on the stoep. "Libkala, *mein kind,*" she said, "I have news for you."

Sara had enrolled Libka at Kirstenhof Girls' Academy, a boarding school near Simon's Town. She had hoped to send her to a school in The Gardens neighbourhood, a place primarily for Jewish girls, but the expense was too great. The fact that it was away from an affluent district appealed to Libka. She had no interest in mingling with snobbish Jewish girls, though she pretended her mother was responsible.

"We are not abandoning you, *mein kind.*"

"Anything to get out of this house," she told her mother.

"Things will be better, my child. After the summer you will start a new life."

—·—

Since her expulsion from school, Libka often went to the library on Adderley Street near the Botanical Gardens. Her mother accompanied her the first time when she registered to take out books. After several visits, Libka had come to know the librarian, Miss Higgins, who spoke with a precise British accent. At first Libka had been worried that Miss Higgins would ask why she's not at school, but the lady never questioned her. When Libka would approach, she would remove her spectacles and smile. "Hello, Libka," she'd say to show she remembered her name, "what are you looking for today? Something in our Eastern European collection?"

After seeing Libka take out countless books by Tolstoy, Dostoyevsky, Chekhov and other Russian writers and poets, she commented, "Shall I presume your parents are from Eastern Europe?"

"Yes, they're from Lithuania."

"And they must have instilled this love of literature in you."

"Maybe. My parents brought very little over when they came to Cape Town, just a few feather pillows and silverware my grandmother gave them for a wedding gift. My father told me that most of their luggage contained books."

"I admire that," Miss Higgins said with a big smile. "The Jewish people from Lithuania have contributed vastly to our country. They place so much value on culture and learning, and of course the *Talmud*," she said reverently.

"Well, my father was always reading books in Russian and Hebrew, and sometimes I wish I could read them in the original language."

"Maybe someday you will. You're a most astute young lady," Miss Higgins said as she checked out the pile of books Libka had selected. "You have more items here than we normally permit a member to take out at one time." She winked at Libka. "But don't tell anyone, I'll make an exception."

Libka sought out this librarian when she planned a visit to Maputo's prison. It was two months since he had been put in jail and Libka was intent on seeing him. She spent long hours at the library, checking maps and guidebooks to determine the location of the prison.

"Someone important to me was put in jail," Libka told Miss Higgins. "Could you help me find out where the prison is and how to get there?"

Whatever Miss Higgins may have thought, she handled Libka's request with the same dignity as her search for other literature.

"Of course, my dear," she said gently. "Let's see what we can find."

When Libka told Anya she was taking a train to visit Maputo, her friend said, "Count me in. I've never seen the inside of a prison and it's time I did."

The platform was crowded with black women in colourful attire, baskets balanced on their heads, babies tied to their bosoms. As the train chugged into the station in Cape Town, they flocked into their designated section. Libka and Anya were almost the only passengers in the European compartment.

The train whistled as it pulled out of the station and swept through areas Libka had never before seen. The lush landscape gave way to barren lands. Smoke rose from fires in Kaffir huts. Industrial sites and tin-roofed shanties swept by.

As the train moved on, past and present blended into a kaleidoscope of her life. She was glad Anya left her to her thoughts. What would the boarding school be like? Perhaps at Kirstenhof Girls' Academy she would find a teacher like the librarian Miss Higgins. She thought of the Malay boy, who was studying fascinating things. She had read the book of poems by Robert Browning that he gave her, memorizing some of the verses, and had even read about the poet's life, especially intrigued by his secret marriage to Elizabeth Barrett. She tried to identify with Elizabeth Barrett, who had showers of dark curls falling over her face and large exotic eyes. She would look in the mirror and imagine herself in that image.

She hoped there would be a library at the new school where she could explore the British poets Percy Shelley and John Keats. She hadn't even read William Shakespeare, though she had heard of his plays *Julius Caesar* and *A Midsummer Night's Dream.* Her mother knew many of Shakespeare's verses by heart and could recite them in Hebrew and Russian.

After two hours the train chugged into an area from which only a grey structure with barred windows was visible.

"We're here!" Anya poked Libka. "Don't forget the pillow."

Libka grabbed the feather pillow, which she had retrieved from its hiding place beneath Maputo's old cot, and the bag with the biltong she had stolen from the pantry.

The grounds of the prison were enclosed in barbed wire. As Libka and Anya approached, a burly figure lumbered up, a rifle at his side.

Libka told him they had come to see a friend.

"Name of inmate?"

"Maputo. He used to live in my house."

"Offence?"

"He killed my father," Anya blurted out, a mischievous gleam in her eye.

"Anya, stop it!"

The warden dismissed the girls and marched away.

"Please, mister," Libka called through the barbed wire, "all I want is to see him. We came from so far. I just want to give him this." She held out the pillow and the paper bag.

"What do you have in there?"

Libka displayed the strip of biltong.

The guard smirked. Then, catching the despair in Libka's eyes, he released the gate and the girls scuttled through. As they followed the man into the grey structure, Anya whispered, "I'll wait here. You go alone to see Maputo."

He was lying on the cement ground of his dark cell, his eyes on the ceiling. When he heard a stirring and caught sight of Libka through the bars, he leaped up. "My little missus," he murmured, "my little Libka."

She pressed her forehead to the bars. "Maputo," she breathed, and was sure she could feel her heart pound. "Maputo, my friend," she repeated, this time so he could hear.

A rush of tears poured down his face, and as Libka stood there, her own tears began to flow. There was so much she wanted to tell him, so much to share, but she remained speechless. When the guard led her away, she realized she was still clutching the pillow and the bag of biltong.

· *eighteen* ·

When December came the family did not go to Muizenberg as they had in previous summers. How Libka had longed to be in that beach house by the sea that they had rented each summer. She used to awaken with the light, climb the white mounds of sand to the topmost peak, then abandon herself to the downward flight.

She craved the trickle of the sands through her toes, to balance on the peak of the cliff and look down on the landscape of the cactus and the glorious flowering proteas, to hear the explosions of the waves. Into these waters she would race, avoiding the sting of the blue bottles and defying the waves that towered above her. She would watch them grow taller and fiercer, and in that moment before they'd burst she'd hear the lifeguard's whistle from the shore and know she must turn back.

Then she would feast on the sun, letting it soothe away the chill of the waters, and always there was the tropical breeze when the sun became too intense. With her brothers and sister she'd run to the ice

cream parlour for the special treat. Which flavour would she choose:
The guava? Mango or pawpaw?

Libka especially remembered the summer when her family and
the Garfinkels had rented beach houses near each other. Mr. and Mrs.
Garfinkel had come from Lithuania on the same boat as her parents
and they seemed so similar. Next to Mr. Oberg, the tall Danish man
who had studied in Leningrad with her father, she knew her father liked
Mr. Garfinkel best. Though he was wealthy and lived in a mansion in
Camps Bay, he was humble and had none of the airs of some of the Sea
Pointers. And his wife Hena was like a sister to her mother. They were
distant cousins, but no sisters could have been closer. Hena was also
uncomfortable with the Sea Point women and kept to herself. Libka
liked being around their children. They were several years older than
her. Annette was already married, and Simon was studying engineering
at the University of Cape Town. Although the youngest son, Andrew,
was about four years older than Libka, she felt at ease talking to him.
He had dark, passionate eyes and black curls falling over his forehead,
and always seemed far away.

Libka knew that Andrew had also loved Muizenberg, but it had
ended for him the year his mother died and his father withdrew in his
grief.

"Mommy," Libka begged, "can't we go to Muizenberg even for one
week?"

"We have to be careful with the money. We don't have a daddy
anymore."

"We still have the factory."

"You know already that we are losing our best contracts."

"Because of Mr. Shmerl?"

"Customers that Daddy had for many years are cancelling their
contracts."

"Then shouldn't you get rid of him?"

"It's easy to talk."

Libka had still not told her mother what had happened the day
she went to the factory. She couldn't dispel the fear that she may have
invited it. Why had she gone up that dark staircase with him and dressed
like those seductive actresses in the bioscope? She had already suspected

he was slimy from the way he acted when he found her alone in the house. And even if she wasn't guilty, they would think she had exaggerated or invented the story.

She dismissed the thought and turned her attention to Shneyer and Dina. If they couldn't go to Muizenberg, at least they could swim closer to home. With Beryl away at Habonim camp with a group of Jewish youth, the other children fell into a summer routine. Every day Libka would gather Shneyer and Dina, and she and Golda would take them to the Sea Point Pavilion. Here there was a pool for small children, where Dina enjoyed being dipped in to her chin. She gasped and splattered and shrieked as Libka submerged her, then lifted her high up. She'd kick her chubby legs and babble for more; and finally when she'd be taken out, she would cry and tear at a strand of Libka's hair.

It was also a struggle to get Shneyer out of the water. He would run back to the deck chairs, shivering, and Libka or Golda would wrap him in a towel. Then Libka would bound up the ladder to the high diving board, do a somersault in the air and glide into the deep end of the pool.

———·———

That summer Libka spent more time at the library, and whenever Miss Higgins saw her standing on the stool to browse on the upper shelves or lying on the floor to study the books on the lower levels, she came over and asked, "Are you finding what you're looking for today, dear?"

One afternoon she found Libka exploring the section on immigration and was surprised to see her there. When she hovered around, Libka turned to her. "Miss Higgins, is this where I can find information about Jewish immigration to Cape Town?"

"You're close enough," Miss Higgins said. "What exactly are you seeking, Libka?"

"Well, my father once told me that the ship on which my parents came from Lithuania was the last one of immigrants allowed in this country."

"I see." Miss Higgins pondered. "So that restriction would have been due to the Quota Act. When did your parents arrive here, dear?"

"They left Lithuania in December 1929 and arrived here in January 1930."

"It's fortunate your parents escaped Europe in time, but there must be sadness in their hearts."

Libka felt she was being untrue by not revealing that her father was dead, but she was afraid the lady's reaction would be so gentle that it would only make her cry. If there was anyone with whom she dreamed of sharing the many things her father had told her, it was Miss Higgins. She imagined being tucked away in a secret corner of the library and telling her the story of her father and his brother Dov-Ber when they were studying in Leningrad before the First World War, and how they had to go into a village in the hills at night because Jews were not allowed on the streets after sundown. And she wanted to talk about her Aunt Liba, for whom she was named, her father's favourite sister who played the violin before she could even read, and who died of polio when she was twenty-two.

Libka turned to Miss Higgins, but a few people were now standing behind her, so she hesitated. Miss Higgins reached for a black volume on the shelf. "This book will give you more background on the immigration issue, Libka. You may also check it out if you wish. It covers much of the history of the times and also the Aliens Act that was passed in 1937, further curtailing immigration."

Libka retreated to a corner in the library and leafed through the volume. She had many questions. Was this restriction only for the Jews and was it because of the National Party and the Afrikaners' hatred of them? Was it due to the war? She opened a section that dealt with the influx of the Jews, and the Afrikaners' vision of them as conniving and stealthy. She read what she had already learned at school, that the Boers believed the country was theirs since they were the first Europeans to settle in South Africa when the Dutch seafarer Jan van Riebeeck arrived in Table Bay in 1652. At that time the local inhabitants were the Hottentots and Bushmen, who thousands of years earlier had adopted a pastoral lifestyle herding sheep and cattle.

Libka was riveted when she came upon the section on Eastern European immigration and the passing of the Quota Act and later the Aliens Act.

"The Aliens Act was aimed at curtailing Jewish immigration to South Africa as it was increasing due to growing anti-Semitism in Germany," she read. It went on to say that an Immigrants Selection Board screened every immigrant from outside the British Empire or Ireland. One of the qualifications was "assimilability." Since the Jews were criticized for failing to assimilate, it was used as a pretext for excluding them.

Libka had become so engrossed in the book that someone had to tap her on the shoulder to remind her that the library was closing.

It was dusk by the time she hopped onto the tram at Adderley Street and realized her mother would be worried. She was astonished to see the Malay boy sitting in back with the coloured and black people. His eyes were on the floor but she sensed he may have noticed her.

She slipped into a seat near the front and pretended to be reading the immigration book, but her thoughts were on the boy. She remembered what he had told her that day on the beach: about the spiritual leader of India who was thrown off a train at Pietermaritzburg when he refused to sit in the third-class coach.

She wondered if the boy felt embarrassed sitting in that special section. After all, he lived in London and she believed that there he could sit wherever he pleased. But much as she wished to speak with him, she wouldn't dare go back to sit with him.

She considered getting off earlier to avoid him, but finally decided on her regular stop near his grandfather's store.

She lingered, not daring to look back but listening for someone behind her. When she cast a furtive glance over her shoulder, she saw him a distance away. She slowed down, hoping he would catch up, but the distance between them seemed to grow. Why was he avoiding her? Had she acted childishly that day on the beach? But then he had given her the book of Robert Browning's poems. Would he have done that if he didn't care? She had spent many hours reading the book and had so much to ask him. Should she turn up York Road and head home or continue on Main Street to his grandfather's store, pretending she wanted to buy something?

She dropped her book, giving her another chance to look back. He was leaning against a post, an open book in his hand. Driven by the same courage she had found when she approached him on the beach, she went straight towards him.

"I thought you might have gone back to England by now," she said.

He looked up at her gravely. "Next week," he replied.

"I'm going away too." Other than to Anya, he was the first person to whom she made this confession. "My mother is sending me away to boarding school."

Sayyed shifted his position and looked around apprehensively.

"Are you going to your grandfather's store?" she asked.

"I'm not sure."

When Libka lingered, he seemed concerned. "Shouldn't you be going home? It's dark already."

Ignoring his question, Libka rambled on. "I've been reading the book you gave me. I like Robert Browning's poems."

"I thought you might."

"Are you a poet?" she asked, remembering his words on the beach.

"Why would you think that?"

"Oh, just the way you talk, the way you described the mountain and the veld when I saw you on the beach. Remember?"

The boy shrugged and acted as though he wanted to escape.

"I may never see you again. Don't you want to talk to me?" She could not believe her words but felt an urgent need to hold onto this moment.

"Of course I want to talk to you," he said, "but we can't do it here."

She recalled how, when he gave her the book of Browning's poems, he had said, "Maybe we'll meet in England someday." Perhaps this was his way of telling her that he really wanted to talk to her but was afraid it would get her into trouble.

"Maybe we'll meet in England someday," she said, "and then we could talk and not be afraid."

"That would be nice. Anything is possible."

As she turned up York Road and headed home, she clung to his words.

· nineteen ·

When summer ended, Libka went off to Kirstenhof Girls' Academy. It reminded her of the prison grounds where Maputo was held. The grass was dead, the branches of the trees like spikes. She was put in a cubicle with swinging doors that left an exposed area at the top and bottom. Her iron bed was hard, and she could not settle into her private world for she never knew at what instant the harsh matron would plunge her face above the swinging doors.

"Welcome to the club," a tall girl from the Transvaal announced upon Libka's arrival. "I'm Cornelia Vanderberg. You English or Afrikaans?"

"English."

"*Jou naam?*"

"Libka Hoffman."

"And what did you do to deserve this?"

Libka shrugged.

The girl was lanky and fair and she looked at Libka with cold blue eyes. "You didn't come here for fun, by any chance?" She spoke with a Dutch accent. "Or maybe you like to have your knuckles chopped with a metal ruler and eat lumpy porridge every morning. And don't forget," she said as she turned away, "talking after lights out is verboten."

Libka became aware of an anger smouldering within most of the girls. Even the fragile blondes had a hard look, and they viewed their surroundings with suspicion. Often at night there were fights. Girls would be wrestling, and long hair was the favourite target. But the moment a matron was heard, the girls would disperse and silence would fall on the floor. Here at Kirstenhof Girls' Academy no one's history was solid enough to withstand another scar.

Strange bonds were formed at the boarding school. Two girls would seclude themselves from all the others, holding clandestine meetings, hotly guarding each other; but sometimes these same girls would fight each other violently.

Despite the dismal atmosphere, Libka felt content in her cubicle. The angry eruptions around her seemed to calm her own tensions.

As she lay on her bed in the evenings, she thought of her mother and brothers and sisters and felt they were better off without her. She had only stirred up trouble. Beryl and Golda never interfered, though things were no different for them. Maybe the girls at this boarding school were like her, trying to change things and only creating problems. She did not dislike Cornelia Vanderberg and the other girls, though they were often petulant and scornful, and she felt it was pointless for them to behave in this way.

She began to review all that had happened since her father's death. She had not meant to create arguments and battles. She had wanted to protect her family but it had come out all wrong.

The worst day of the week for Libka was Sunday. Buzzers would ring all day and girls dashed down to meet a visitor.

Sara wrote that she hoped to see Libka but burdens of the house and business prevented her. Libka feared there were growing problems in the factory, though her mother's notes were short and restrained.

———•———

One Sunday when visitors' time was almost over, the buzzer announced a caller for Libka. She slipped into a capped-sleeve green dress and ran down the stairs. She could not imagine who it might be.

As she reached the last staircase she saw the form of Anya in the lobby. The girl might have heard Libka's footsteps or felt her presence, yet she remained with her back to Libka, like the day in Anya's room with the cracked *Anastasia* record.

"You came to visit me?" Libka asked, coming up gently.

"No. I came to see how the privileged live."

"It's almost as far as the jail. How did you get here?"

"Horse and carriage. My footman is parked by the white pillars."

They went out onto the bleak grounds. Libka longed to venture beyond the towering stone walls, but knew it was forbidden. In the two months since coming to Kirstenhof Girls' Academy she had not seen the world outside the gate. A special permit was required, and this could only be obtained through the intervention of a parent or guardian. A visitor coming to the premises had to ring a bell, which sounded in the caretaker's office.

As Libka and Anya strolled through the dead grass, the trees bare and the sun harsh, Anya commented, "Remind you of Maputo's quarters?"

"I don't think my mother realized how it was."

"Mrs. Peker's influence," said Anya. "She and her daughter Sally, the whole lot of them! Does that parasite still sneak flour and sugar from your mother?"

"I don't think so."

"Remember how she'd use up all her rations, then sponge on your mother when there wasn't enough to go around for you children! Why does your mom associate with that shrew?"

"She's lonely, I guess, since my father died. I wonder if it's better for her without me around."

"According to Golda, it isn't. Things are even worse. Beryl is never home and there's no one to look after Shneyer and the baby. Golda may have to drop her music lessons."

"Do you know what's going on in the factory?"

"Only that creepy Mr. Shmerl is there now."

"So you think he's creepy?"

"He's slimy. I think he's a lecher."

"What's that?"

"Someone who molests women."

This was Libka's chance to tell Anya what had happened. Though she knew her friend would believe her, she was still not able to bring it up.

"Why doesn't your mother dump him?"

"I asked her the same question. I guess it's not so easy."

Two tall blond girls passed by, casting vindictive glances at Libka and Anya.

"Friendly here, huh?" whispered Anya, eyeing them back.

"There are so many fights on the floor. Sometimes I think the girls are killing each other." She glanced at Anya, grateful for her friend's presence. "How come you decided to visit me?"

"I had nothing better to do. You know, Libka, it made me sick sitting on a soft seat in the European compartment of the train that was practically empty, while the others are cramped into the smelly cars."

"I was thinking the other day," said Libka, "if I ever rode on a train with that Malay boy, we would have to sit in separate compartments."

"Aha! You still think about him?"

"When I met him on the beach, he was reading a book in some strange language by a spiritual leader in India. He has a name that ends in Gandhi."

"Mahatma Gandhi," said Anya. "He believes we can improve the world without violence. I'd like to believe that, but I have my doubts. So what about this boy?"

"He gave me a book of Robert Browning's poems and on the front page it had his name and address in London. He has the most unusual name — Sayyed bin Noor."

"That's a Malay name. Don't tell me, Libka, that you have a crush on this boy!"

"Maybe it's because of the book, but I think of him sometimes. I saw him once just before I came to this place, but he was afraid to be caught talking to me. I mean afraid for me, not for himself."

"What a disgrace!"

Anya looked across at the cold-eyed girls sitting on the stone benches. "Cheerful atmosphere. And here I thought you'd be part of a cosy clique." Then she grew serious. "I think it's horrible that they sent you away. Your mother has been influenced by ignorant people, and they're the most dangerous ones. I love not being in school. Did it help me to understand my father? Did it help me to face the situation I was in? Just one thing it taught me: there's no understanding when you need it most."

She tore off a wilted blade of grass. "My father left us, you know. Guess he left for our good as much as his. Would you believe I miss him?" Her eyes flashed in the sunlight. "Anyhow, I'm going away. Goodbye, good old South Africa. Thanks for giving me the chance but I can't live here."

Libka was filled with wonder. "You're going to England?"

"Where else? And what about you, Libka? What'll happen to you?" There was concern in Anya's eyes. "You're not going to grow up in this country and, heaven help you, get stuck with some stiff South African and have a staff of servants?"

Now it was Libka who reached for the blade of grass and avoided the other's eyes.

"I know you tried to help your family, Libka, but where did it get you? Into reform school! And I don't have to remind you that you're about as suitable for this country as I am."

Libka saw the truth in Anya's words, yet she could not imagine a place where she would really belong.

"There's no easy answer," said Anya. "We live in a world saturated with wrongs. Is it right for your father to be dead? Is it right for Maputo to be in jail? And, I must admit, it isn't even right that you should be confined in this place. In your own crazy way, you were just trying to take responsibility for your family."

The visit from Anya lingered in Libka's mind. As she lay on the iron bed in her cubicle far into the night, she thought of Anya's words: "You're about as suitable for this country as I am." But where could she go? Her mother had thoughts of America, but Libka didn't imagine she'd have more of a chance there than she did in South Africa. Beryl, of course, was tempted by the things he had read about the glamorous lifestyle there and the films he had seen with the Hollywood stars, but it seemed alien to Libka.

Her thoughts kept returning to the Malay boy. His dreamy eyes haunted her and his book of Browning's poems lay at her bedside. Often she would look at the inscription on the first page. He would now be in London.

One night she took a sheet of lined yellow paper from her notebook and began to write.

> *Dear Sayyed bin Noor,*
> *You will probably not remember me but I am the girl you once spoke to on the beach at Three Anchor Bay and then I saw you another time on the street but we couldn't talk. I know where you are because you gave me a book of poems by Robert Browning and it had your name and address on the front page.*

*I look at it a lot here in my little room at Kirstenhof Girls'
Academy, which is near the naval base in Simon's Town. My
mother sent me away to boarding school, but I think this place
is really a reform school because the girls seem rather wild. I
guess my family considered me wild too.*

*I have to admit I get lonely, but most of all I don't feel I
belong in this country. I think I even told you that on the beach
that day.*

*I have one friend. Her name is Anya Steinberg and she is
also Jewish like me. She has a horrible father who beats her and
her mother, but she is a girl who isn't afraid to speak up. She
and I used to fight but we really care about each other. Anyway,
she was expelled from Promenade High (I was too!) and now
she's planning to move to London. I suppose that's my dream
also, though it seems scary. I'm really not sure what I'll do with
my life.*

*I wonder why I'm telling you all this. I was even surprised
at what I told you on the beach that day, about the Bantu man,
Maputo, how he was thrown in jail so unjustly. My friend and
I actually visited him in prison just before I came to this place.
There are a lot of Boer girls here, and even listening to them
reminds me of when the Voortrekkers threw rocks at my house
in Newlands.*

The page was full but Libka could not stop her thoughts. She had
only two sheets of paper left on her pad and needed them to write an
essay about the Afrikaners, but she did not care. Dipping her fountain
pen into the inkwell, she started a new sheet, writing about how she
hated Promenade High and how the girls had ostracized her because
she didn't behave like them. *Not that I ever wanted their approval,* she
wrote, *but it still hurt me. I blamed my mother. I was always attacking
my mother for everything that happened to me, but secretly I admire
her for the way she is. I would have hated it if she acted snobbish like
the other Jewish mothers.*

Libka then went on to pour her heart out. *I think my father's death
was the last straw for me. I loved him so much, and he never criticized
me no matter how bad I was. And I was a bad child. My sister Golda
was so agreeable and she always did what was right, and my older
brother Beryl was only interested in dressing up and flirting with girls.*

But I always felt out of place with everything. It was easy to blame it on my mother's European ways or the aloof Sea Point crowd, but I really despise this country. I guess what made it unbearable to me was when Maputo was thrown in jail.

She wrote how much her father loved Maputo and how the two of them understood each other without the need for words. *I know when my father died, Maputo's heart was as broken as mine, but still he kept comforting me.*

As her pen raced along, filling the lines, she panicked that she would run out of paper. There was so much that flowed from her heart.

She remembered when she hopped onto the bus after the library and found Sayyed sitting in the rear section. She was not sure which one of them felt more ashamed. And afterwards he avoided her. Why was she writing these personal things to a boy whom she hardly knew, a boy from a world forbidden to her?

Finally she pulled herself together and squeezed in a few more lines:

You probably don't remember me and may not even receive this letter, but I'm writing it because I trust you.

> *Faithfully yours,*
> *Libka Hoffman*

As Libka crawled into bed after midnight she felt at peace despite what she had written; but it took several days before she found the courage to mail the letter.

· twenty ·

Libka often lay awake at night, her thoughts drifting over her life. Sometimes she still cringed at the recollection of Mr. Shmerl.

Unknown to her, her father's accountant, Mr. Adelson, was also plagued by the scene he witnessed at the United Engineering Works and troubled by the manner in which Libka had fled after being led upstairs by Mr. Shmerl. Holding a deep fondness for Sara and her family, he hesitated to alarm them and hoped that perhaps he had overreacted. But on his weekly visits to review the ledgers, he continued to observe Motel Shmerl, once even encountering him behaving improperly towards a new secretary, and he felt it was his duty to share his concerns with Sara.

Mr. Adelson lived in Woodstock; but one evening after a session with his client Abe Garfinkel in Camps Bay, he was passing through Green Point and decided to drop in and see Sara.

It was after eight o'clock by the time he arrived. The younger children were already in bed and Golda was in her room, reviewing her Hebrew lessons and studying for exams. Beryl had gone out with his new girlfriend. Eleanor, who had come from England with her parents, was cheerful and not at all critical. Beryl felt that even if she knew what went on in his house she would not condemn him for it, as Joyce had done. In fact, he had been to Eleanor's house and noticed that her mother did her own cooking and dusting, and he didn't feel the presence of a staff of servants. When they served tea, Eleanor had carried in the crumpets from the kitchen, and then she had helped her mother clear the dishes off the table. Yet she was as pretty as Joyce, with a willowy figure, long golden hair and blue eyes.

Sara, who had been sitting in the kitchen reading Tolstoy's stories in Russian, was startled when she heard the doorbell. Since Yosef's death very few visitors came to the house. During the last weeks of Yosef's life, Rochel and Reuven Shevah had been constant companions, taking turns to sit beside his bed through the night so that Sara could get some sleep. Their eldest son Yankel, a medical student at the University of Cape Town, would often forfeit his weekend dates to perform this task. And it was Rochel who fed Yosef his final spoonful of water as he uttered "*Genug,* Rochel" and closed his eyes and died. They had made an effort to remain supportive to Sara in the first few months of widowhood, but gradually life intervened and a trip from Claremont to Green Point was a major undertaking.

The Scandinavian couple, Ingrid and Oberg, who were also regular visitors during Yosef's illness, now rarely came since the bond had mostly been between Oberg and Yosef, who would relive their student days in Leningrad. Mrs. Peker still barged in, but this usually occurred during the daytime when Mishka was making deliveries and the son and daughters were at work.

When the bell rang again, Sara moved tentatively to the door and was startled to see Aaron Adelson, looking pale and apologetic.

"Sara, my dear, I should have telephoned before coming, but I was passing through Green Point and hoped you wouldn't mind a short visit."

"Aaron!" Sara reached over to embrace him. "Please come inside. What a nice surprise."

She led him into the sitting room and served tea and *taiglach*, which she had made earlier that evening. For a while they spoke of the old times in Lithuania. Adelson was from a neighbouring *shtetl*. He and his wife Hinda had arrived in South Africa in 1928, a few years before Sara and Yosef. He was a humble man who never acquired the material success of many of the Jews in the new country. He was a meticulous accountant who tended to undercharge his clients and he worked long hours for a modest fee.

"How is it in the factory with Mr. Shmerl?" Sara finally asked.

"I wish I could give you a good report, Sara," Adelson said. "Though it is always a pleasure to see you, my visit tonight is not a happy one."

He proceeded to tell Sara that he was concerned with the manner in which Shmerl ran the firm and that several of Yosef's long-time clients had recently withdrawn their contracts. His inventory records also indicated that steel, bronze, brass and other valuable metals and tools that were so scarce during these war years were missing. One of the lathes had also disappeared. When he inquired about this, Shmerl had dismissed it abruptly, claiming Adelson's records were outdated. Also, he had fired Fortune, the devoted foreman, and several other loyal employees.

"Maybe I am wrong," Mr. Adelson said, "and I hope I am, but how could he discharge Yosef's best workers now in wartime when skilled labour is so hard to find? After all, Yosef trained them for over twelve years, and they were more than skilled workers, they were loyal friends. They wouldn't touch a sliver of steel unless Yosef gave it to them. I tell you, Sara, Mr. Shmerl's actions trouble me and I felt we should talk it over."

"What do you suggest?" Sara asked. "You think I should go over to the factory and try to inspect?"

"It's hard for you," Mr. Adelson said, "all alone in this country and with five young children. And I understand you don't have any help in the house now. How are you managing, my dear Sara?"

"I manage," she said quietly. "I do what I can."

"And the tragedy of our people in Europe. Is there any news of your family or Yosef's?"

Sara nodded grimly. She looked at Adelson as he sat with his head lowered. "And you, Aaron? You also had eight brothers and two sisters and the parents and your *boba*. You or Hinda hear of any survivors?"

"Nothing."

They sipped tea in silence, then Aaron Adelson said, "I understand that Libka is now away at a boarding school."

Sara nodded.

"How fast she grew up. I hardly recognized her when she came to the factory."

"Yes, the time passes. Aaron, maybe you know why she ran out so fast, like Mr. Shmerl tell me?"

"Motel Shmerl is not like the rest of us, Sara. It is hard to know what is in the man's mind. I myself couldn't understand why she ran out after he took her upstairs there to his showroom."

"What kind of a showroom is he building?"

"*Ver vais*. Libka never explained what happened when he took her up there?"

"I tried to ask but she didn't want to talk about it. She is a moody girl and sometimes she exaggerate, but I could tell that this time something bad happen."

"She ran through the plant like a storm, and I didn't like the look on Shmerl's face."

"Maybe sometime she will tell me," said Sara, "but if I try to press, she can get wild."

"I would not trust a daughter of mine with him. He's a funny fellow. I think you need to keep an eye on him, Sara. I know it isn't easy for you to get away, but maybe you and Beryl should go into the factory and have a look."

· twenty-one ·

Late one afternoon Libka was summoned to the headmistress's office at Kirstenhof Girls' Academy. The stern woman, Mevrou Vandermerve, reminded her of Miss Bloemfontein at Promenade High. She waved a blue airmail letter.

"You're Libka Hoffman, *ja?*"

Libka nodded.

"I regret to have to summon you here on a most unsavoury matter." She held the letter out to Libka. "Do you recognize the name on the return address?"

In amazement Libka read the name "Sayyed bin Noor" and the London address inscribed in the Browning book.

"Yes," she said.

"Though it is unthinkable to ever censor the mail belonging to another individual, an exception had to occur in this case. Who is Sayyed bin Noor?"

"Someone I once met."

"This is not a British and nor is it a Dutch name. In our opinion it is of Malay origin. Is that correct?"

"Yes. His grandfather has a store near my house in Green Point."

"And you know this boy, no doubt?"

"Yes."

"How do you know him?"

"I used to swim at Three Anchor Bay near my house and he was sometimes there."

"So you associated with a strange Malay boy?"

"I often bought sweets and toys for my little brother at his grand-father's store."

The headmistress eyed Libka gravely. "With a letter bearing a name Sayyed bin Noor coming to one of our pupils you will realize why we had no recourse but to inspect the contents." She surrendered the letter to Libka. "I will step out for a moment while you read it. You will then understand the seriousness of this investigation."

Mevrou Vandermerve rose and made her way out, footsteps heavy in her brown laced shoes. When the door clicked shut, Libka began to read.

Dear Libka,

I did not know your name but of course I remember you. What European girl would speak to one of my kind, a Malay, on a beach in South Africa? And, yes, I do remember all you told me about the servant you loved who is now in jail, and how your family was driven out of your home by the Dutch in Newlands. I had never spoken to a European girl in Cape Town before, so all this was a revelation to me.

Now that I'm back in London, things are different, and here at Oxford I have the good fortune to be considered a peer among my colleagues. I hold a fondness for Cape Town as my birthplace and I still have my beloved grandparents there; but my parents, both being physicians, could not make a life in South Africa, which is why we left for London many years ago.

I was deeply moved to receive your letter and to know that you remember me. I gave you that book on Browning because those poems are special to me and I wanted to share them with you.

I'm sorry that you, a Jewish girl, find life in Cape Town so difficult, but the Dutch are threatened by newcomers, particularly the Jews who have made such a material success of their lives and contributed immensely to the country.

If you should ever decide to relocate to London, please know that I will help you in any way. From this vantage point I will have a right to interact with you and perhaps we can even sit together on a tram or train. That would be an adventure!

Truly faithfully yours,
Sayyed bin Noor

———•———

When Mevrou Vandermerve returned to her office she was accompanied by Libka's Afrikaans teacher, Mevrou du Plessis. Both women seated themselves opposite Libka.

"You read the letter from this individual?"

Libka nodded.

Mevrou Vandermerve reached over and retrieved the letter from Libka's hands. "So you understand, *ja?*"

"Understand what?"

The headmistress and Mevrou du Plessis looked at each other, indignation in their expression.

"It appears that you and this ..." she checked the letter, "Sayyed bin Noor are engaged in a conspiracy against the original settlers of this country, the Afrikaans people."

"I don't think they were the original settlers," Libka said quietly.

"*Ja?* So who were the original settlers?"

"According to my history books, the Hottentots and Bushmen lived here two thousand years ago. They herded sheep and cattle and had peaceful lives. They weren't slaves to the white people."

Mevrou Vandermerve cleared her throat. "Since you claim to know your history, have you ever heard of the name Jan van Riebeeck?"

"I think I have."

"You *think* you have?" Mevrou du Plessis intervened. "Have you not memorized your facts and dates?"

"I don't believe in memorizing things."

"Perhaps we should jog this girl's memory," suggested Mevrou Vandermerve. "In your elementary class surely you learned that the first European to settle in South Africa was the Dutch seafarer Jan van Riebeeck. When do you suppose that occurred?"

Though Libka knew that the Dutch East India Company set up a station on Table Bay in 1652, she feigned ignorance.

The women eyed each other. "Is her grasp of Afrikaans any better than her knowledge of our history?" Mevrou Vandermerve asked her colleague.

"I have reported to you," the answer came. "She fails to hand in her compositions and seldom appears in Afrikaans class."

"Why is that?" the headmistress addressed Libka.

Libka slouched in her chair and mumbled, "I prefer to do other things."

"Your diction is atrocious! And do you mind sitting up straight!"

Libka did not change her position.

"So you prefer to do other things, *ja?*" Mevrou Vandermerve tapped a metal-edged ruler on her desk. "Other things such as entering into threatening communication with a man of another class, a Malay? I understand you are a Jewess?"

"My parents came from Lithuania."

"And your people invaded our country in droves and took what they could, while our people, the original settlers, struggled to survive with gruelling labour on the farms. The Jews descended on us, usurping our land of its valuable resources, and now you, a young Jewess, enter into a conspiracy against our country with another intruder, a Malay. Can you not understand our outrage?"

"I think the Jews helped to build up the country." Libka mumbled on purpose to annoy the women. "And, anyway, I understand the doors are now closed to immigration from Eastern Europe."

"Thank goodness for the National Party. We don't have enough of these peddlers with their black beards and ragged attire who went knocking from door to door, not knowing a word of our language! They grabbed, they stole, and now they consider themselves the kings of our land, *Suid-Afrika*. Surely you, a Jewess, should show appreciation for what this country has given to your people. A little different from Adolf Hitler in your ancestral land, *ja?*"

Libka began to get up and reached for the letter Mevrou Vandermerve clutched in her hand. "Can I have my letter back?"

"No. You cannot have it back."

"It's from my friend."

The two women eyed each other in dismay.

"Before you leave this office," Mevrou Vandermerve stated, tapping the ruler, "you will take this letter and rip it to shreds. *Ja?*"

"I won't do that."

"If you refuse my request, the repercussions will be immense." She flipped the pages of a document before her. "Our records indicate that you have already been expelled from Promenade High School in Sea Point. There is now a question as to whether we will permit you to remain at Kirstenhof Girls' Academy."

Libka remained steadfast in her refusal. Even though the headmistress confiscated the letter, the incident only deepened her loyalty to Sayyed.

Sara received a letter from Mevrou Vandermerve a few days after the visit from Aaron Adelson. She was still pondering all he had implied about Mr. Shmerl's activities at the factory but had not discussed the matter with anyone. She would have liked to talk it over with Rochel and Reuven Shevah, but she could not travel to Claremont. Since the departure of Elsie and Maputo, the household tasks fell to her; and with Libka away at school, there was no one to tend the younger children. Though Golda tried to help, she was a serious student and Sara did not want to distract her from her studies and music practice. Beryl was involved with social life and was usually present only for meals. Several times Sara thought of talking with him, but he was always hurried and she could never find the right moment. Mrs. Peker was ever-present, but Sara did not feel she could share such thoughts with her.

When the letter from Mevrou Vandermerve arrived, Sara could no longer withhold her concern. After she had served supper and the children had gone off to play and Golda was washing the dishes, she placed the letter before Beryl on the dining-room table.

"What's this," he asked, "from Kirstenhof Girls' Academy?"

"Read," Sara said, "and then we will talk."

> *Dear Mrs. Hoffman:*
>
> *I am writing you in reference to your daughter Libka, a student at our institution.*
>
> *I regret to inform you that an event has occurred which we must direct to your attention. We cannot reveal the details in this letter, but it is essential that you make arrangements to visit this office at your earliest convenience. We can then have a full discussion of this unfortunate event and determine the necessary action.*
>
> *Looking forward to hearing from you at your first opportunity.*
>
> > *Cordially yours,*
> > *Mevrou Vandermerve,*
> > *Headmistress*
> > *Kirstenhof Girls' Academy*

"What is this all about?" Beryl asked. "The headmistress refers to an unfortunate event, but doesn't give any details."

"I hope Libka is all right," said Sara. "You think we should telephone her?"

"How would I know? And since she didn't mention anything in her recent note, she may not even know about this letter."

"How can I make such a trip? And where do I leave the *kinderlach*?"

"Couldn't you leave them with Mrs. Peker?"

"I don't like to ask favours from her. She will only find more things to criticize, like the clothes they wear and how they eat."

"That's true." Beryl reached for a Marie biscuit, then said, "You know something, Mom, I'm not that excited about my studies. I don't have to tell you that. Why don't you telephone the headmistress tomorrow and set up an appointment and I'll take the day off from school and keep an eye on Shneyer and Dina."

Sara was impressed with Beryl's offer. "You mean I can depend on you to stay with them? I would have to leave early in the morning, and who knows with the connections when I can come home."

"Leave it to me, Mom."

Sara looked at her son in gratitude. "One more thing, Beryl, since you are such a good boy, maybe you can call the headmistress and make the arrangement for me. With my accent she won't even understand, specially over a telephone."

"Sure. Leave it to me."

Since Beryl was so compliant, Sara took the opportunity to bring up Mr. Shmerl and the factory.

"I will tell you, Beryl," she said. "You have a minute to talk?"

"They're not broadcasting the rugby matches from Newlands tonight, so I'm in no hurry."

Sara sat down opposite her son.

"Mr. Adelson, the accountant, was here the other night," she began.

"Oh yes? Where was I?"

"I don't know. Maybe in Sea Point with the girl."

"So go on."

Sara relayed the conversation of that evening as Beryl listened without interruption. "So you have continual doubts about this Mr. Shmerl, do you?"

"I can only go by what I hear. I myself am not in the factory, as you know."

"You think we should keep a closer eye? You said he was a capable engineer."

"It is his character we are not sure of. But Mrs. Peker compliments him to the sky."

"Well, Mrs. Peker! It's time we stopped listening to her."

"Mr. Adelson, a honest and devoted man, is not a fool. Maybe he is quiet and not pushy, but I think he has good judgement. And I know he would not come here to talk like this if he didn't have reason."

"Yes, he's a good man, refined. I know Dad had a high opinion of him."

"So what do you recommend, Beryl?"

"Maybe if we had kept closer watch on the sawmill, those partners couldn't have cheated us. We have to avoid that in the future."

"But how can I keep a closer eye? Would it be possible for you to go with me to see what is going on?"

"Well, who else? Isn't it my duty? After all, Mom, I'm sixteen already, and Dad isn't around anymore to do those things."

Sara eyed her son in awe. "Beryl, *mein kind,* would you like a nice chocolate bar for dessert? I have with caramel filling."

"Don't bribe me. And I'll tell you something else. I'm going to the factory alone to check things out. I'm not appearing with my mother. I'm quite capable of doing this myself. But first let's get on the phone tomorrow and see what's going on with Libka."

Sara climbed the ladder in the pantry and removed a chocolate bar from an upper shelf, placing it at her son's side.

The next morning she watched as Beryl, dressed in his sailor suit, lifted the telephone and made the call. She was proud of his precise English diction as he made arrangements with the headmistress. "She sounds cordial enough," he commented when he hung up, "but one never knows. And now guess where I'm headed?"

Sara looked at him, handsome and vibrant in white attire and golden skin, and said, "You won't go to school in your sailor suit."

"Anyway, classes started an hour ago. I'm off to Dad's factory."

Sara, who was feeding Dina her porridge, looked up at Beryl with shining eyes. "So you will go?"

Shneyer ran in, thrilled to see his brother still home. "Can I go with you?"

"No, *mein kind*," Sara said, "you stay home with Mama and Dina."

"But I want to go with Beryl!" He clung to his brother. "Please, can I go with you?"

"Another time. I promise."

After Beryl had gobbled down his cereal and mango, he reached for a chocolate bar in a platter Sara had displayed in the centre of the table. "Last night and now again? How come chocolates for breakfast?"

"Once in a while for a special occasion." Sara smiled.

"Can I have chocolate too?" begged Shneyer.

"Not so early. Later maybe."

Beryl marched out of the house, his head high. He hoped the adults on the street would notice him in a sailor suit when other children were in school. When he reached Main Street, he took the tram to Adderley, where he changed for a bus to Sir Lowry Road.

Getting off at the corner of Nelson, memories flooded back to him and he wondered why he had not visited the factory since his father's death. He reproached himself for being so involved in athletic activities and the struggle to impress Joyce. It seemed that no matter how much he tried, she had always been aloof. And why was she this way, he asked himself. Just because her family had a fancy house in Sea Point? Her father was a salesman in a clothing store, yet her mother behaved like a queen, always being chauffeured to the beauty parlour and returning with prickly red hair and nails the colour of blood. It now dawned on him how superficial Joyce was and how much better off he was with Eleanor.

As Beryl passed the factories on Sir Lowry Road, he remembered when his father would take him to visit the *landsleit* who were beginning their lives in the new land. They all spoke in Yiddish, and this was the only language Beryl knew until Miss Ingrid taught them English in their rooms above the workshop. She was such a pretty lady, even more glamorous than the starlets in the American films. He was sad she and Mr. Oberg rarely came to visit since his father's death. He remembered how Miss Ingrid used to sit at his father's bedside during the last weeks of his life. She took time off from her nursing job at Groote Schuur Hospital to be at Yosef's bed, fluffing his pillow, massaging his legs with eau de cologne and feeding him apple sauce.

The memories that rushed back were warm and he choked away a tear. It was a pity his father had died so young. It would have been fun to take him to rugby and cricket matches. Hadn't his dad been a hero in the First World War?

He had never really known his father. It was Libka who used to sit with him on the stoep in the evenings as he told her about the stars and planets. Beryl always thought that when he grew older he would get closer to his father, but that time never came.

As he turned onto Nelson Street and saw the black and coloured children playing in the gutters infested with rags and broken bottles, he remembered how he had played here as a child. It brought back to him the face of Maputo who was always there to watch over the family. He recalled that when they bought the house in Newlands and his parents had invited Maputo to live with them, he was determined to remain in the factory where he could watch day and night. If only he was still there, thought Beryl, what a comfort it would be. And he was struck by a sense of injustice that Maputo, who had saved his mother when the soldier came to attack her, should now be in prison. No one had defended Maputo when the constables handcuffed him, whipping him with the *sjambok* and dragging him away. His mother didn't stand a chance with the Afrikaner police, who only mocked her Yiddish accent. He, an English-speaking South African, could have made a better impression, but he had done nothing. It was time to review his attitude. He had become too heavily influenced by the Sea Point crowd.

Maybe Libka had a point to her rebellion. And perhaps she was really not so shy and withdrawn but it was her way of avoiding contact with that group. He had seen her dressed up and she was capable of looking no different from other girls; but she seemed to want to be an outsider. Maybe there was more to her than he had thought. She was smart, he knew that, much smarter than he could ever be. She didn't have to study long hours to get good grades. But she was so opposed to the political system and couldn't accept the superior attitude of the whites. Of course she had gone overboard with Maputo, but that was her tendency.

Whatever her problems, it didn't seem fair she had ended up at reform school, no matter what polite name they gave it. She couldn't even go outside the grounds of that place without special permission. And now he wondered what that letter from the headmistress signified. He would rather not think how his mother's session would go, as she struggled to express herself in English.

As Beryl stepped onto the threshold of the factory, he heard pounding in the office. "Hello?" he called. A buxom redhead bounced into the entry.

"Yes?" Her manner was hostile as she scrutinized him. "Who do you want?"

"Is Mr. Shmerl available?"

"He's busy in the factory. Can I help you?"

Beryl followed the woman into the office where she sat down at her desk and continued pounding on the typewriter.

"I just stopped by," Beryl explained. "This is my father's factory."

"Your father's factory?" She eyed him suspiciously. "Well, you can wait."

Beryl ignored her and entered the plant. Everything was different. There were about a dozen workers, all unfamiliar, who stood fearfully at the machines that vibrated and set off sparks. His mother had told him that Mr. Shmerl had fired Fortune, his father's long-time foreman; and he could see no sign of Bongani, Njabulu, Mhambi and Kwanele. He had remembered the place as tranquil. Though the machines rumbled, especially when the war contracts poured in, there was never a sense of fear. The workers his father had employed were cheerful and relaxed, and there was always Maputo to light up the place with his glowing smile.

"Beryl!" came a voice from behind him. He turned to see Mr. Shmerl in a white shirt with armbands and an orange tie, his face imperious. "I didn't think you even still remembered where the place was."

"Oh, I remember. As a matter of fact, I have the day off from school, so I thought I'd drop in. It's about time."

"The day off from school? Why?"

"Why not!" Beryl looked around. "The place looks so different."

"Of course it's different," Shmerl said with pride. "I had to make major changes to make the United Engineering Works a going operation."

"And why is that?" inquired Beryl. "My father certainly knew how to run an engineering factory."

"Things can go downhill very fast," said Shmerl. "After he died, everybody took advantage. Take take take, that's all people are interested in. And let me tell you ..." he pointed his finger, "these *shvartze* and coloureds have to be watched like hawks. They're natural thieves."

"Really?" said Beryl. "Not in my experience. I don't know if you remember my father's long-time employee, Maputo, who later worked in our house. I would trust him with my life."

"Beryl, my son," said Shmerl, tapping him on the shoulder, "you have a lot to learn. And this man you would trust with your life is now in prison, I understand."

"It was a complete misunderstanding," Beryl said. "The only pity is that there was no one to defend him. And I blame myself as much for that as anyone."

"Don't blame yourself so fast. You stick up for a Kaffir and you'll end up in jail too. Keep your hands clean, my son."

Beryl felt offended by Shmerl's intimate tone and he moved away.

"I'm just going to look around," he said, walking off into the plant.

"Help yourself," Shmerl called cheerfully as he retreated towards the office.

Beryl moved around, nodding cordially to the workers who eyed him fearfully. He didn't quite know what to look for to support Mr. Adelson's suspicions. He noticed the small room that had always been under lock and key was now open. Once he had wanted a piece of metal for his submarine model but his dad had said in these war years it was too scarce to use for toys. He had guarded fragments of metal, steel cutters and knives as though they were diamonds. Now Beryl peered into the room where the precious items had been stored and saw empty cartons toppled over each other. But how could he know what was missing when he hadn't been here for so long? And certainly Mr. Adelson knew more about Shmerl's accounting practices than he would ever know. He wondered of what value his visit would be. It only seemed to evoke so many memories.

Beryl stayed a short while, thanking Mr. Shmerl and the secretary as he set off.

"Come anytime," Shmerl called. "We burn the midnight oil here." He winked at his secretary. "Right, Marie?"

"We sure as the devil do," she exclaimed in an Afrikaans accent.

Beryl sidestepped the empty liquor bottles on the sidewalk and caught a whiff of dagga coming from a figure crouched against a wall. He knew that was the drug many coloured men smoked and remembered the night when Libka, in an unusually talkative mood, had told him about the man under the bridge in Newlands who tried to tempt her with a sixpence. He remembered when she described the crazed look in his bloodshot eyes and the smell of dagga coming from his mouth. How frightened she must have been, he realized now.

As Beryl turned onto Sir Lowry Road, crossing the busy thoroughfare to catch the bus, he heard someone calling his name. He swirled around to see Mr. Garfinkel, whose shoe manufacturing factory was nearby. Beryl had last seen him during the week they were sitting *shivah* for his father. He remembered how close the Garfinkels had been with his parents and the summer when both families had beach houses in Muizenberg.

"Beryl!" Mr. Garfinkel shook hands vigorously. "You're visiting your father's factory?"

"Yes, I decided to come down."

"And how is it going?"

"I'm not sure," said Beryl. "You know that Mr. Shmerl is now managing the place."

"I know very well."

There was a tone in Mr. Garfinkel's voice that prompted Beryl to ask, "Do you think he's doing a decent job?"

Mr. Garfinkel took Beryl by his arm. "You're in a hurry?"

"Not especially. I was just heading home."

"Then come in and have a glass of ginger beer with me. There are a few things I feel your mother and you should know."

Abe Garfinkel was a discreet man who found it hard to be critical of anyone. He sat down with Beryl in the office of his factory and closed the door, informing his secretary he wished no interruption.

"I admired your father deeply," he said. "I remember well when he returned from Leningrad after his engineering studies. Although he was an outstanding engineer, there were no opportunities in the *shtetl*, so Yosef had the foresight to establish the Jewish People's Bank. He travelled from *shtetl* to *shtetl* setting up branches, and he did the same in my village, Rumshishok, and installed me as manager. And when you work with a man, you get to know his character.

"We came together to South Africa on the same boat in early 1930. In fact, our vessel was the last one of Eastern European immigrants who were permitted to enter due to the Quota Act. I remember when the ship anchored on the island of Las Palmas and the *landsleit* wanted to buy whatever their eyes saw, but we were without a penny in our pockets. Your father was more established and gave generously, and so in Cape Town he had to start from scratch like all of us. Why am I telling you all this, Beryl?"

"Please continue," said Beryl, "there's a lot I didn't know about my father."

"Well, you're a young man. What are you, sixteen or seventeen?"

"I'll be seventeen next year."

"And your mother, how is she managing?"

"She's doing her best, Mr. Garfinkel, but it would be untrue of me to say it's easy."

"Of course. Your mother is a fine woman. She and my wife Hena, may she rest in peace, were very close in the old country. In fact, Hena was a distant cousin of your mother. Of course, that wasn't unusual in

Lithuania. Many cousins even married each other. Our *shtetlach* were like one big family."

Beryl remembered Mr. Garfinkel's wife, who had died a few years ago. It was during his father's illness, but his parents had gone to the service at the Sea Point *shul* and then to the burial at Pinelands Jewish Cemetery, where his father now lay.

"Anyway, Beryl, you're a young man and busy with your own life, but I'm not sorry I ran into you. I know that Motel Shmerl is now managing your factory, and I have certain reservations. Perhaps it is best if I talk more privately with your mother. Sadly, I haven't seen her since Yosef's death. It reminds us that life cannot be taken for granted and we must show interest in those we care about."

When Beryl returned from the factory, Sara heard the gate and ran out onto the stoep.

"*Nu*, Beryl?"

"*Nu*, shut up! Don't attack me the minute I get in."

"No, of course not. You want some refreshments?"

"No."

Later on Beryl approached Sara when she was in the kitchen making supper. "So do you want to hear or not?"

"Aw, you ready?"

"You attack me before I walk in the door, and now I can't even get your attention."

"Then let us sit down. You want to talk in the sitting room?"

Beryl had changed into his khaki shorts and blue knitted shirt.

"Stay where you are, but give me a chance."

Sara listened keenly as Beryl told her of his visit to the factory. "For some unknown reason," he concluded, "even though I have no evidence, I don't like the looks of that man. I know one shouldn't judge from external appearances, but his manner seems uncouth to me. Also, there's this gross woman in the office. Dad would never have hired someone like that. It doesn't matter that she isn't Jewish, but it almost looks like they have some conspiracy going on, the way they laugh and signal to each other. And the workers look terrified. There's no one left from Dad's day. It was never that way when he was around. It reminds me of what Mrs. Peker does to her servants. I don't know, Mom, but I sure didn't like the atmosphere."

"But what did you see? What did you notice? After all, Mr. Adelson is not a dramatist. If he came to report, he must feel something."

"Will you give me a chance to talk?"

Sara lowered the heat on the stove and slipped into a chair. "I'm listening."

"It's impossible to talk to you," complained Beryl. "I don't know why I even bother."

"What do you want from my life? So don't talk!"

He leaned against the stove. "The best thing I got out of this trip is that I ran into Mr. Garfinkel."

"Garfinkel!" Sara's eyes lit up. "Abe Garfinkel? Where did you run into him?"

"As a matter of fact, I was leaving the factory and had just crossed Sir Lowry Road to catch the bus when I heard him calling."

"Ugh, it is also a shame that we are losing contact with the few nice *landsleit* we have. Next to Oberg, Abe Garfinkel was Daddy's closest friend."

"And he said you're related to his late wife."

"Hena. Also a tragedy. Still a young woman when she died."

"Anyway, let's not stray," said Beryl. "Here I've wasted my whole day. Mr. Garfinkel wants to talk to you. He doesn't seem happy about Mr. Shmerl, though he gave me no details. He asked if he can come by and have a talk with you."

Sara jumped up in a little dance. She was amazed at the transformation in her son. "Beryl, *mein kind,* you are a good boy. Please arrange for him to come as soon as possible."

When Mr. Garfinkel arrived that Sunday afternoon no one else was home. Golda had taken Shneyer and Dina to the Sea Point Pavilion, and Beryl was out with Eleanor. It had been planned that way because Sara knew they would be talking about confidential matters and she felt it best that the children not be exposed to it.

Sara was consoled by Abe Garfinkel's presence. She had often felt so alone in the country since Yosef's death and was now reminded that she should reach out more often. Of course the children consumed all her time and energy, but there were occasions in the evening when she could unload her heart to someone.

Abe Garfinkel evoked these feelings in her. She had known him for many years. Naturally, the Jewish women of Sea Point tried to match him up after the death of his wife, but Mr. Garfinkel showed no interest. He lived quietly and modestly, despite his magnificent home. Mr. Garfinkel's house stood on a high cliff in Camps Bay, affording a spectacular view of the ocean. He loved the sea and his yacht was moored nearby. He lived alone except for his maid, an old woman who would have had difficulty finding employment among the demanding ladies in the area. This woman had been with the family for over fifteen years and Mr. Garfinkel felt protective towards her. She had helped raise his three children and mourned the death of his wife as deeply as all the family.

Sara found herself opening up, even shedding a tear when they spoke of those they had left behind. Nothing had been heard from their families since 1940, and from the rumours that circulated, they had little hope that Hitler had spared any of them. Words like "ghetto" and "concentration camp" floated among the Jewish people as their hope slowly faded.

Sara and Abe Garfinkel moved naturally into Yiddish. She appreciated the fact that he was a cultured man who knew the *Talmud* intimately. He was a scholar by temperament, though in the new land he had proved to be an astute businessman. And he seemed so much like Yosef in his approach. She remembered how Hena would sometimes say he's too kind to his workers, treating them as equals, and she was afraid they would exploit him. But his kindness elicited a deep loyalty from his workers, much like Maputo and the other employees expressed towards Yosef and his family.

With utmost gentleness Abe Garfinkel recounted what he had witnessed earlier that week when he was driving home. As he veered onto Nelson Street close to nine o'clock, he spotted a dim light coming from the United Engineering Works. The door was open and Shmerl was directing two workers as they manoeuvred equipment through the entrance towards a lorry parked in front. A red-haired woman stood on the sidewalk, surveying the street like a guard. Garfinkel moved his car a distance away, turned off the engine and observed through the rearview mirror. Time and again the workers dragged out piece after piece of bulky equipment and loaded it onto the lorry.

"It was unusual for this to be happening so late at night," Mr. Garfinkel said, "and with the woman standing there watching. I would have contacted you anyway to ask if you knew about this, so it was providential that I ran into Beryl. He indicated there was concern about Mr. Shmerl, so I knew it was time to act."

"It looks then like my judgement was not the best. Mr. Shmerl kept saying how devoted he felt to the family, so maybe I wanted to believe."

Abe Garfinkel volunteered to keep watch on the factory. Shmerl would have recognized Abe himself, so Garfinkel appointed one of his trusted workers to the task. The man blended in with the shabby atmosphere of Nelson Street. Disguised in rags and torn shoes, he crouched on the sidewalk among the debris, a bottle in hand. The stealthy movements in the darkness confirmed the suspicions about Motel Shmerl.

———•———

Unaware of what had been uncovered, Shmerl burst into Sara's kitchen, rattled and impatient.

"I've had enough of that Aaron Adelson," he told Sara. "I had to get rid of him."

Sara was alarmed. "Aaron Adelson?"

"The man is getting soft in the head. I've tried to be patient, but he'll drive the business to ruin."

Sara led him out into the passageway. She didn't offer tea, even though it was the middle of the afternoon. Beryl and Golda were still not home, Beryl at rugby practice and Golda at her music lesson. Shneyer was wandering around in the house or garden, and Dina was playing with her wetting doll in the bedroom.

"But Aaron Adelson was with Yosef from the beginning. What you mean soft in the head?" Sara demanded.

"Just like I said, soft in the head. He's messing up the books, he's messing up everything. How many more customers do you want to lose because of him, Sara?"

Sara ignored him and did not allow him into the sitting room.

"When you have your back turned, anything can happen," Shmerl rambled on. "I also was shocked. I thought he still had his marbles. His ledgers are all screwed up, he doesn't keep track of the inventory, his records are outdated, and he bills clients for jobs we didn't do. There's no end. Yesterday I had a call from Aba Rabinowitz. He's cancelling his contract."

"Aba Rabinowitz!"

"And after that I had to take action. I called Adelson in and told him plain and simple, 'We can't keep you anymore. We're not running a charity house.' Finish!"

Sara did not pursue the matter with Shmerl. She had already decided she must terminate the arrangement, and he was making it easier. For Shmerl to accuse Aaron Adelson was like jumping from the frying pan into the fire.

When Beryl came home she told him what had happened.

"I'm not a mind reader," he said, "but I can tell you that Mr. Shmerl's account is fabricated. Don't we know by now that he's stealing our valuable materials?"

"The equipment is so scarce you can't get it for money. It is more valuable than diamonds in these times of shortages."

"And he's trying to lay the blame on Mr. Adelson," said Beryl. "I would have no trouble discharging that Shmerl myself."

Sara was eager to discuss the matter with Mr. Garfinkel. They had been in regular contact since his visit, and a personal feeling had developed between them that surprised Sara. This made it difficult for her to initiate a call to him, as she felt it was proper for him to take the first step. But tonight she lifted the telephone without hesitation.

When Mr. Garfinkel heard Sara's voice, he was joyful. "Sara, my dear, what a pleasant surprise."

"I will tell you, Abe, I should telephone you in happier circumstances." Sara briefly related what had happened that afternoon.

Realizing that she was deeply troubled, Mr. Garfinkel arrived at her home the next morning even before Beryl and Golda had gone off to school. He cancelled all appointments at his plant and spent the rest of the day with her.

"I'll handle it," he told her. "Don't worry yourself, my dear." He reached for her hand and she let him hold it for a while as they sat silently together.

———•———

As Abe Garfinkel appeared at the factory the next day, the secretary eyed him coldly. "Mr. Shmerl is busy. What's your name?"

Her suspicion had been aroused by a telephone call a few days earlier. Someone who would not identify himself requested to talk to Mr. Shmerl. When he got on the line, the caller said, "If you won't treat Mrs. Hoffman right, you will pay with your life." Shmerl had slammed the receiver down but he repeated the words to his secretary.

Although Sara did not know about this call, when Rochel Shevah had phoned soon after the visit from Aaron Adelson, Sara confided in her; and when Mrs. Shevah passed this information along to her son Yankel, he was outraged and decided to make the call. He had once been to Motel Shmerl's variety store in Wynberg and the man had tried to cheat him, so the accusation did not come as a surprise.

Mr. Garfinkel ignored the secretary's probing eyes and went straight into the plant. He found Shmerl ordering the workers around.

"Listen here," he said in a tone uncharacteristic of him, "come upstairs to your showroom."

Shmerl was stunned. What was this distinguished shoe manufacturer doing here? He knew nothing of his relationship with Sara, nor could he have surmised that Garfinkel's worker had been monitoring his activities.

Shmerl tried to prevent Mr. Garfinkel from going upstairs, but the latter led the way confidently and Shmerl stumbled after him. It was hardly a showroom that Mr. Garfinkel found. On the soiled mattress lay a woman's bra and red lace panties. Empty liquor bottles leaked on the floor.

"Pack up your things and clear out," Mr. Garfinkel ordered. "Your term as manager is over."

When Shmerl tried to protest, Mr. Garfinkel spoke in plain words. "You're a thief and a liar. You should be ashamed of yourself to take advantage of Yosef Hoffman's widow. Have you no conscience? You're a disgrace to our people. Clear out this minute or I'll summon the police."

"What are you talking about?" Shmerl countered. "Here I take over a dying business and try to make something of it. Besides, who are you to —"

"And you'll return all the stolen merchandise, you hear me! You'll bring back the bronze and brass and tools and everything else. We know exactly what's missing."

"What right do you have to accuse me of such things?" shouted Shmerl. "I'll sue you!"

"And when you go out that door," Mr. Garfinkel continued, "that secretary of yours goes with you!"

"You think you can get away with this!" Shmerl faltered, sweat breaking out on his forehead as Garfinkel led him downstairs. "I'll straighten this out with Sara. What right do you have to interfere?"

In the office Mr. Garfinkel lifted the telephone and dialled Sara's number. "I'm putting a friend of yours on the telephone," he said gently when he heard her voice.

Shmerl was stunned by Mr. Garfinkel's familiar tone but he grabbed the receiver. "Sara," he said like a dying man, "what is going on? Here I'm struggling to keep the company afloat, and this shoe manufacturer accuses me of unheard-of things. I will not put up with this. I'll sue him and I'll sue you if you take sides with him."

"Mr. Shmerl," Sara responded calmly, "you shouldn't expect to take advantage. I have five small children to bring up. After all, you are not the beneficiary of my husband's estate."

When Shmerl got furious and tried to protest, Sara simply added, "I trust Mr. Garfinkel to deal with you."

Shmerl hung up the receiver, the colour drained from his face. Mr. Garfinkel stood with folded arms and watched him gather his personal items. "Come on, Marie," Shmerl said to his ruffled secretary, "don't waste your time here anymore."

As the two made their way out, Mr. Garfinkel added, "Tonight I'll be waiting here for your lorry to unload the stolen goods. How about nine-thirty? By then it will be good and dark."

———•———

The day after Shmerl returned the stolen equipment, Mrs. Peker barged into Sara's kitchen. She found her dressed in a primrose pink paisley, singing "Reyzele" as she stirred raisins and prunes into the carrot *tsimis.*

"No more black dress, huh?"

Sara swirled around, feeling a touch of annoyance at the sight of the woman. She had been up very late with Mr. Garfinkel and was now reliving their evening. He had come to her house immediately after Shmerl returned the merchandise. Long after the children were asleep, she sat on the settee with him and they drank schnapps that he had brought to celebrate the occasion.

Now Sara hardly acknowledged Mrs. Peker, who hovered behind her.

"No more black?" she repeated. "Well, it's time. How long can you go on mourning?"

Sara continued stirring the *tsimis,* adding a tablespoon of honey into the pot.

"I don't have much time," Mrs. Peker said. "I'm running a cake sale at the *shul.* So you want to sit down and listen?"

"I'm busy."

"Motel Shmerl came over last night," she said accusingly, "and I've never seen him so upset. What is this with Abraham Garfinkel, the manufacturer who lives in Camps Bay?"

Sara ignored her.

"Did you tell him to throw Motel out? What's going on, Sara Hoffman?"

"I don't have to give you a report, Riva."

"You're acting very strange, Sara. But how can you accuse a *landsman* when the *shvartze* workers stole from the factory! Motel was so involved trying to save the sinking ship, with Aaron Adelson messing up the records — I understand he's gone soft in the head — so how could Motel see everything? But when Mr. Garfinkel accused him, he looked around and saw what happened. And when the *shvartze ganovim* returned the goods because Motel warned them he would report them to the police, what does this Garfinkel do: he made Motel unload the heavy machinery that the *shvartze* had stolen."

Mrs. Peker's words were lost to Sara, who continued blithely in the kitchen.

"Are you listening, Sara, or am I talking to myself?"

"It is better that you talk to yourself," Sara answered sharply.

"Oh my! What is going on! I haven't seen you with such a temper, Sara, but I guess you got plenty of problems. I'm starting to think what you accused the sawmill partners was also only in your *kop*."

Sara ignored her and went into the bedroom where Dina was dragging things out of the drawer. "Come, my baby," she said, "I will make you a warm bath and put on a nice little pink outfit."

As Sara ran water into the tub, feeling the lukewarm temperature, Mrs. Peker watched. "A bath just for the baby? That's an improvement," she said sarcastically.

"I would appreciate it," Sara said, now giving Mrs. Peker a stern look, "if you would not interfere."

"Interfere? If not for me, who do you have to give you advice, your daughter Libka? By the way, how is she doing in that reform school? Are they straightening her out?"

"You straighten out your own children," said Sara.

Huffing and puffing, Mrs. Peker went to the telephone in the sitting room and dialled. "Mishka," she said, "you finished with the morning deliveries? Jump into the yellow automobile and come get me. I'm at Sara Hoffman's house and she is *nisht fraindlech*, not friendly at all!"

· twenty-two ·

Sara hired Aaron Adelson as interim manager of the United Engineering Works. Beryl and Mr. Garfinkel also rehired Fortune as foreman and as many as they could find of the other long-time workers that Shmerl had thrown out. Not only did they get their old jobs back, but they received an increase in their wages.

Beryl would now go into the factory after school on many days. He placed this even before his cricket and rugby games. He felt he had a purpose, and being in the factory revived good memories of his boyhood.

The workers liked Beryl and he did not permit them to call him Young *Baas*. "Call me Beryl," he said, but they were not able to take that step. They merely bowed and smiled when he entered.

Mr. Garfinkel's son Simon came to the plant whenever he could get away from his studies at university. He had a good understanding of how the machinery operated, having apprenticed with Yosef for a few summers. In less than a year he would be earning his engineering degree from the University of Cape Town.

Unlike his brother Andrew, who was determined to make his life in England, Simon planned to remain in Cape Town. He and his fiancée intended to marry as soon as Simon graduated and they would buy a place in The Gardens neighbourhood.

One Sunday Mr. Garfinkel invited Sara and the children to spend the day at his home in Camps Bay. Simon was there for the weekend and he served as guide. Beryl was honoured to be in the company of someone so much older; and now that he was helping in the factory, he no longer felt like a schoolboy and had a sense of accomplishment.

Simon took Beryl out fishing and they sailed to Seal Island on the yacht. Beryl had joined the Sea Scouts and was adept at operating the boat. Golda built sand castles on the shore with Dina, and Shneyer flew a kite.

Abe Garfinkel and Sara sat on the veranda overlooking the palms. The scent of the tropical flowers and honeysuckles filled the air and the birds trilled. They could hear the pounding of the ocean down below. For the first time since Yosef's death, Sara felt a joy in life.

The old maid steered in a wagon with tea and biscuits. Mr. Garfinkel jumped up and helped her unload the cups from her trembling hands.

"My life has been different lately," he told Sara when they were alone again. "I am grateful to you."

"I should be grateful to you, Abe."

"For what?"

"Not everybody would take such a interest and make big sacrifices. After all, what am I to you?"

Garfinkel sensed that Sara was seeking reassurance. "You are everything to me, my dear Sara," he said, taking her hand. "Though I would never impose myself, it is a gift to spend time with you."

Sometimes Sara wished that he would be more assertive, but she appreciated his gentle manner. She knew she brightened his life as much as he did hers.

———•———

Rumours about Abe Garfinkel and Sara Hoffman began circulating among the Sea Point Jewish women. He was considered a great catch, and since the death of his wife numerous attempts had been made to match him up with a young widow. There was even an old maid, Rebecca Finkelstein, whom they considered. She was born in Siauliai, northern Lithuania, and had arrived in South Africa with her parents and siblings in 1926. At thirty-two she still lived with her parents and worked as a bookkeeper at Ackerman's on Adderley Street. Although she was cross-eyed and walked with a limp, she was warm and had a friendly disposition.

But Mr. Garfinkel never agreed to meet any of the candidates. Though the women hounded him with telephone calls at home and even at his office, he always politely declined. "It is still too soon," he would say.

But now he was seen on occasion with Sara. They had been spotted during High Holy Day services at the synagogue in Sea Point and one evening at a candlelit table in a romantic seaside restaurant. A Mrs. Kuperschmidt had witnessed it and word spread like lightning.

Mrs. Peker got wind of it, and though Sara had not been receptive that morning when she came to complain about Motel Shmerl, she was too curious to nurse a grudge.

One Sunday afternoon she appeared at Sara's house as though nothing had happened. Sally, in tennis outfit, delivered her in the convertible.

"Thank you, doll," Mrs. Peker called as they pulled up beside the Hoffman house and the servants jumped out, unloaded a wheelchair from the trunk and manoeuvred the corseted and decorated woman into it. A cast covered her right leg, and she primped and complained as the servants dragged her up the steps.

Mrs. Peker had broken the leg when she skidded on her slippery floor a few weeks earlier. In her restrained position her bearing was even more imperious. To deflect attention from the plastered leg, she adorned her chest with a blinding array of jewels; and her hat could have been plucked from the Kirstenbosch Gardens.

Sara didn't comment on her plastered leg. Mishka Peker had reported the event when he delivered the milk one morning, accusing a servant of foul play; but Sara couldn't pretend to be sorry. In her heart she felt that perhaps it was justified.

"I still can't believe that Motel Shmerl is a *ganef*," Riva Peker told Sara after the servants had eased her into the armchair in the sitting room and placed her damaged leg on the footstool. "After all, from the same *shtetl*. And here I thought I knew the fellow. In Europe he didn't know such tricks. And you can't climb into a person's head. But you listen to me, Sara, and learn already a lesson from all your mistakes."

As Mrs. Peker spoke, Sara's mind drifted, as it did so often these days. She almost felt guilty that her thoughts were so consumed by Abe Garfinkel. After their times together, she would relive every moment. She should be thinking about her children and the future, but her thoughts always lodged on Garfinkel. She was indebted to him for the way he had taken control, sparing her the ordeal of disposing of Shmerl and helping Aaron Adelson settle in. She felt secure knowing Aaron was there to oversee the operation. He treated the workers with respect, as Yosef always had, and in return they gave their loyalty. When Mr. Adelson took over, he called the clients, and soon the long-time relationships with Yosef were re-established. Adelson was also interested in involving Beryl in the firm. "Even if he won't become an engineer," he told Sara, "it would be good for him to have this responsibility. You are tied down with the younger children. Someone in the family should oversee your business."

Beryl was proud to accept this role; and the more he helped the family, the more devoted he became. His dates with Eleanor were now limited to weekends, and he tended to study in the evening. "I might as well improve my marks," he told Sara. "There's no reason for me to be a dunce. And it would seem appropriate for me to attend university. Wasn't that what Dad had in mind for me?"

"Of course," said Sara.

"So listen," Mrs. Peker cut into her thoughts. "Is it true what I hear, that you're keeping company with Abraham Garfinkel?"

Sara resented her question. She did not want to hear his name on Mrs. Peker's lips.

"You don't have to tell me the details," Mrs. Peker said petulantly, "but it's not bad to be in such company. The Sea Point women have a new respect for you."

"I don't need their respect."

"No matter how you look at it," Mrs. Peker continued, "Abraham Garfinkel is a catch. One in a million." She made coughing sounds. "You have some tea, Sara? My throat is dry. And I wouldn't mind a few *taiglach*."

Sara made no move to accommodate her.

"By the way, Sally was driving me along Beach Road in the convertible the other day and we saw Beryl. A handsome boy! And he speaks such a good English. The King's English. I heard recently he was selected King during Habonim camp. I imagine the girls must kill for him. He's still seeing the blondie Joyce?"

"I don't know."

"I'll tell you the truth, if he was a little older I would make a match with one of my own daughters. Sally is already spoken for, but maybe Betty or Helen."

As Dina tottered in, Sara reached out to her. "Come, my baby. I will make you some warm milk."

Mrs. Peker looked around, annoyed at the interruption. "Maybe now that you're in such company, you should make some improvements in the house. Get rid of stuff. What you need the memories? This will remind you of that ... that will remind you of this ... And, besides, it's junk!" She kicked the armchair with her good leg. "So tell me, he has serious intentions, this Abraham Garfinkel?"

The doors between the sitting and dining room slid open and Shneyer wandered in. "Mommy, I'm hungry." He leaned on his mother as Dina began to tug at his hair.

"Of course, my child," said Sara. "I will make something to eat."

With the children clinging to her, Sara made her way out of the sitting room, ignoring her visitor.

"The *chutzpah!*" Mrs. Peker mumbled loud enough for Sara to hear. "To treat *landsleit* like that!" She opened her jewelled clutch bag and removed her bell, ringing it urgently. Her servants, who had stood in waiting in the passageway, rushed in with the wheelchair.

"Lift the telephone and ring my number," she ordered.

As one servant wheeled her over to the telephone, the other one dialled and put the receiver in Mrs. Peker's hand. After a delay, she heard Mishka's voice and said accusingly, "What took you so long to answer? Don't tell me you're sleeping again! Enough sleep in the day! Sally went off with the convertible, so get yourself into the old car and come for me. I'm at Sara Hoffman's not even half an hour and I'm ready to leave. Didn't ask about my broken leg, didn't offer a sip of tea. I've reached my limit!"

· twenty-three ·

In the midst of the events in the factory Sara travelled to Kirstenhof Girls' Academy for a meeting with the headmistress, Mevrou Vandermerve. Riding in the train she recalled the session with Miss Bloemfontein a year earlier when Libka was withdrawn from Promenade High. She wondered now, as she had many times, whether she should have taken the headmistress's advice so seriously. The Afrikaners were anti-Semitic and when they encountered a vulnerable Jewish girl they took the chance to pounce on her. If it had involved a girl of their own nationality they would have been more lenient. In any case, what crime had Libka committed? Anya may well have provoked the fight in the school playground. Libka rarely gave details. She was defensive and withdrawn and it was hard to talk to her in a reasonable way. Despite the difficulties she created, her absence in the household was felt. Shneyer and sometimes Dina hovered around her bed and a few times Shneyer was found sleeping in it.

"Why are you not in your own bed?" Sara had asked.

"When will Libka come back? Is she gone like Daddy?"

Who knows what's going on at the new school, Sara mused. She was nervous about the appointment with Mevrou Vandermerve and feared she would not find the proper English words. The children were right to insist she speak English at home, but she found herself drifting into her mother tongue.

When she arrived at the school grounds, worried and tired after half a day of travelling, it seemed so much bleaker than when she had come here with Libka for registration.

Yosef would not have permitted this. He was a reasonable man who resolved family problems calmly and he would have been undeterred by Miss Bloemfontein's words. He would have supported Libka, for he felt she was special. Though she never made an issue of her studies, she rated top grades at school; but all this was ignored when she was expelled.

Sara pressed the bell on the gate and the caretaker permitted her to enter. The grounds of the boarding school seemed ominous as she trod along the path to the entry. It was unusual in this country to see land so barren, here where trees and flowers sprouted from the rich soil. The benches were hard and cold and the structure was grey and solemn. There was no colour, no life. The branches of the trees were spiky and leafless, and even the chorus of the birds was missing.

When Sara appeared before Mevrou Vandermerve, the large square woman looked down on the frightened immigrant who seemed to lose her tongue.

"So you are Mrs. Hoffman, the mother of Libka, *ja?*"

"She is my daughter."

"You're new in the country?"

"In Lithuania I was born. I am here in South Africa now since 1930."

"1930. You're lucky you got in. It's a good country, *ja?*"

"For some people it is good."

"Not for you?"

Sara balanced on the edge of the chair, finding no words.

"It's not a good country for you?" Mevrou Vandermerve persisted.

"Sometimes it is good."

"Would it be better in Europe?"

"No. There it would not be better."

"If immigrants don't like it here, maybe they should go back where they came from. *Ja?*"

Sara shrugged, looking fearfully at the headmistress, who began shuffling papers.

"Clearly your daughter Libka has been a problem to you, and in the short time that she is here at Kirstenhof Girls' Academy unfortunate events have occurred. Most unfortunate!"

"What is it?"

"What is it? Could you speak up, please? I'm having difficulty understanding you, or maybe it's your accent. You're finding English hard to learn?"

"I am trying."

"And what about Afrikaans? You realize in this country it's compulsory to master both Afrikaans and English. Have you made an effort?"

"I am trying."

"After all," Mevrou Vandermerve continued, "you say you arrived in *Suid-Afrika* in 1930. You're here in our country sixteen years. Isn't that long enough to master the languages of the country that adopted you?"

"It is hard with a big family. And my husband, he died recently."

"Excuses! Excuses! Now when you were in Lithuania, what language did you speak?"

"In the home we spoke Yiddish or Hebrew."

"That has no value. What value does that have in *Suid-Afrika?* And here in this country, what language do you speak at home?"

"With the children, English."

Mevrou Vandermerve eyed her sceptically, then returned to her papers.

"Perhaps the problem with Libka originates in the home. After all, parents need to guide their offspring. Of course the essential learning takes place in the classroom, but there are certain ethical standards that should exist in the home. Are you aware, Mrs. Hoffman, that your daughter has been in cahoots with a Malay boy?"

"Cahoots with a Malay boy?"

"Do you understand me? I sense you have difficulty following me."

"Maybe you will explain."

Mevrou Vandermerve produced the blue letter and flapped it before Sara. "There's no point showing you this because you don't read English, *ja?* So I'll summarize for you. A letter arrived here at Kirstenhof Girls' Academy addressed to your daughter. Libka Hoffman, *ja?*"

"My daughter."

"And our mission here is to protect our students against negative influences. We therefore make a preliminary check of incoming mail. So when we saw the name Sayyed bin Noor on the letter to your daughter, it signalled trouble. Does that name mean anything to you?"

Sara indicated not.

"On investigation it appears that your daughter randomly picked up a Malay boy on a beach."

"That cannot be," said Sara.

"*Ja?* You know of Three Anchor Bay?"

"It is a beach near where we live in Green Point."

"And this is where the incident took place. She interacted with a Malay boy on the beach."

"She never told me."

"Of course she wouldn't tell you. These strange girls have deep dark secrets. But not only did she consort with him on the beach, but it appears they are now in correspondence, blackening the name of our country *Suid-Afrika*. This Malay boy who has escaped to England is in conspiracy with your daughter to attack the very premise of this country. The Malays, the Jews, the blacks! Where would they be if not for this rich land from which they have profited? As I speak to you now, Mrs. Hoffman, it becomes clear that your daughter is a threatening influence, and we fear what thoughts she may inflict on her fellow students."

Sara's mind could not absorb all these facts and the swift, severe manner in which they were delivered. She remained speechless, her eyes bright.

"Have you understood me? Am I making myself clear?"

When Sara finally found her voice, she asked, "Is it possible for me to see my daughter?"

"Regretfully, not now. She's in detention until we determine what course of action to follow."

As Sara sat in the train going home, she did not feel defeated. Though she had difficulty grasping the headmistress's words, she understood the essence. This was not a country where her family was welcome. Although Beryl and Golda seemed to blend in, it was a great struggle for Libka. She was, of course, influenced by Anya, who was over a year older and read books by Marx and Lenin. Her parents were believed to be Communists. Sara had noticed that Libka had taken such books out of the library and read them at night.

Sara had not told Libka that she would be meeting with Mevrou Vandermerve. Since Libka had not mentioned any trouble in her last letter, Sara and Beryl decided it was best to keep it to themselves.

Sara would have liked to know the contents of the letter but wondered what was so criminal about corresponding with a Malay boy. She remembered Libka mentioning a Malay boy at his grandfather's store where she often went with Shneyer. Maybe it was the same boy. Libka always spoke so fondly of the storekeeper, saying how generous he was when she and Shneyer wandered in to buy toys or sweets.

Libka seemed comfortable with the servants and people who were considered of the lower class. How she had loved Maputo. It had crushed her spirit when he was imprisoned. After all, it was Smit who should have been jailed, not Maputo, who had come to her rescue. She knew Libka had never recovered from this injustice.

As the train fled by shanties and the open veld, Sara's mind took on an unusual clarity. She did not remember a time when she was so alone with her thoughts, and the motion of the train seemed to propel her mind to new levels.

Maybe she should consider the advice of her brother in America. After Yosef's death, Meyer urged her to emigrate. He did not have faith in South Africa. He wrote that with the passing of the Quota Act and then the Aliens Act in 1937, the writing was on the wall for the Jews. It was not only the threat of the Afrikaners, he insisted; many were also afraid that there'd be such an upheaval in South Africa that the large black population would drive the whites into the sea. Meyer Marcus had been an aspiring poet in his youth, so he tended to get dramatic, though Sara knew he had wisdom and foresight. His dream had been to study literature and philosophy in America; and after a delay of five years in Havana, he managed to enter the country in 1927 but ultimately abandoned his goal and became a businessman. Sara had been close with Meyer in their youth, and she kept every letter he wrote during the years he was stranded in Cuba. Sometimes at night she would read these letters and wish they could be closer.

From Meyer's letters, Sara believed that for someone with ideas like Libka, America would be far more accepting.

And for Beryl it would be better too. If Yosef was alive, he would have encouraged him to study and made a man of him. Beryl had improved since he assumed more responsibility in the home and factory, and Sara felt that an uncle could guide him in the right direction.

What do we have left in South Africa? Sara mused. In America I would have my brother and a sister-in-law, and my children would have cousins.

———•———

It was already dark when Sara returned home from the visit with Mevrou Vandermerve. As she quietly pushed the gate open, she was surprised to see Beryl appear out of the doorway, followed by Golda and the two younger children. Beryl ran down the steps and took the package she held in her hand. She had awakened very early that morning and baked *taiglach* for Libka and packed them in an ornate Black Magic Chocolates tin.

"How come you brought this back?" Beryl asked in amazement. "Didn't Libka want the *taiglach?*"

"I will explain," Sara said cordially. "*Sha,* Beryl."

She embraced her children as though she had been away for a year. Despite the fatigue of the long trip and the session with the headmistress, she felt animated.

"Why everybody is still up so late?" she asked, pleased by the welcome.

"Golda tried to get them to sleep," Beryl explained, "but they wouldn't hear of it."

"I went to sleep," Shneyer said.

"Sure you did." Beryl tossed his hair.

"But Golda put together a decent supper of fish and chips," Beryl said. "And for once they weren't burnt."

Golda was pleased with the compliment. "I'll try to put them to bed now," she said. "Mommy, shouldn't you rest?"

"All right, *mein* Goldala. It is nice to know I have such good *kinderlach.*"

When the children had gone to sleep and Golda was studying in her room, Sara went to make herself a glass of tea. Beryl was weight-lifting in his room, but when he heard his mother he joined her in the kitchen.

"So what's going on with Libka?"

"You want to listen, Beryl, so late?"

"Then forget it if that's how you feel."

When Sara had told Beryl about her session with Mevrou Vandermerve, he was angry.

"These Boers are all the same. Jew-haters. I guess Hitler didn't help, but the Afrikaners have always resented the Jews. It appears it's because our people made such a success of their lives in South Africa. Resentment."

"It is not a good environment for Libka, even if they let her stay in that school."

"You keep saying school, Mom. The fact is that it sounds like a reformatory to me."

"They called it a school for girls with problems, but Mrs. Peker claimed it would straighten Libka out."

"Well, Mrs. Peker! Stop listening to her."

"You are right, Beryl, but who else do we have?"

"Too bad the Shevahs aren't around much and live so far away. They're sensible people. I was really impressed with the service Mr. Shevah conducted at Dad's gravesite."

"You know he was a cantor in Lithuania, and he was very devoted to Daddy. The Shevahs are older than Daddy and me, so they were almost like parents to us."

"I wish they'd be around more. There was no nonsense about them."

"That's what happens. Everybody is busy making a living."

"And Mr. Oberg and Miss Ingrid don't come anymore. They were always around during Dad's illness. Just like the Shevahs. I still can't get over that Yankel Shevah gave up his Saturday night dates to sit at Dad's bedside."

"They are wonderful people, but that is how it was in Europe. People helped each other."

"Remember that Saturday when our doorbell rang at midnight and there stood Yankel in a tuxedo just coming from a dance. 'Go get some rest, Mrs. Hoffman,' he told you, and he sat beside Dad's bed all night."

"Yes. I was ready to hire a night nurse, but Rochel insisted the *landsleit* take turns to sit with Daddy."

"The way Mrs. Shevah used to scold us! 'You can buy everything in stores for money,' she'd say, 'ice cream, sweets, toys. But tell me, in what store can you buy a mother?' That's how she'd carry on," Beryl said with a chuckle.

"I wish we lived nearer. It is hard for them to come from Claremont and not easy for me to travel."

"But you don't go out of your way either, Mom. Like that Mr. Garfinkel. Frankly, I was impressed with him. Seems like a decent man, and I recall Dad was keen on him too."

"Daddy would trust Garfinkel with his life. You know he made him manager of the bank in Rumshishok?"

"Yes, I know. But what's going on with Libka? How come you didn't give her the *taiglach?*"

"The headmistress wouldn't let me see her. Tell me, Beryl, what means detention?"

"To hell with it," said Beryl, "whatever it means. Though Libka has given us sufficient problems, I don't think she deserves that kind of treatment."

"Yes," said Sara, "Daddy would not approve."

"Dad would not approve of many things that have taken place in this house, and I think it's up to us to do something about it."

When Beryl went back to his room, Sara took out a sheet of paper and began a letter to Libka.

· twenty-four ·

As Libka remained in isolation she was not unhappy. It was almost a gift from Mevrou Vandermerve to permit her to escape the classes.

Alone in her cubicle her thoughts soared. Everything seemed attainable. She was convinced Anya would follow her dream and move to England. And since hearing from Sayyed, she felt she too had an anchor there. In her mind she had already responded to him.

She wondered why she had been sent to this place, with an atmosphere reminiscent of Newlands. Her mother seemed to have become confused. Miss Bloemfontein had unnerved her, and Mrs. Peker's advice had not helped. But her mother had always been clear minded. In fact, she was more practical than her father who was the adventurer, eager to seek new horizons. If it had not been for him, her parents would not have settled in this country. After Sara's engagement to Yosef, she had encouraged him to consider Palestine, but he believed South Africa held more promise. Jewish immigrants, many from Germany, had been settling there since the pogroms of the 1880s, finding safety and the means to build good lives. Still, if her parents had not left Lithuania, they might have vanished with all the other Jews and she would never have been born. Perhaps, she reflected bitterly, that would not have been such a bad thing.

One morning her cubicle doors rattled and the prefect who brought her porridge also left a letter. It was from her mother. Though Libka was ravenous, she tore it open before attacking her porridge.

> *My darling daughter Libkala,*
> *Everything at home is fine, but I think there will be good changes for all of us. South Africa has not been so good for us, especially for you, mein kind, and my brother Meyer write that we should consider America. Maybe it would be better. What do you think?*
> *It is hard for me to write too much in English and it would be better if we can talk, but in the meantime please don't worry about anything. Better things will happen for our family.*
>
> *Your loving mother, brothers and sisters*

When Sara showed Beryl the letter before mailing it, he remarked, "But this doesn't say anything. What's the point of it?"

"It is hard for me to explain everything in English. How can I write about the Malay boy and the headmistress? The time will come when we will talk in person. After all, Libka is not condemned forever. But I think we should take her out of that school and bring her home. What do you think, Beryl?"

"Suddenly you're asking me. If you hadn't listened to that headmistress at Promenade High and the stupid Mrs. Peker, the whole thing would never have happened."

When Libka received her mother's letter, she suspected she was withholding something, but was relieved just the same. She knew it was the policy of the school to notify a parent or guardian of any problems, and Mevrou Vandermerve had indicated there would be repercussions.

Yet how could she blame her mother for being evasive when she herself had never disclosed what had happened? Perhaps if she had a chance to see her mother, she could explain, but she knew Sara couldn't make the trip and had no one with whom to leave the children. She would not keep Beryl and Golda out of school; and on weekends Beryl was involved with social life and Golda studying and practising her music.

But Libka still had a hope her punishment would be confined to detention and her family would never know about this incident. It wasn't that she was ashamed. In fact, she felt proud that this boy had remembered her, though she was uncertain of her family's reaction. Her mother might not condemn it, but she would not consider it appropriate to mingle with a Malay boy. And Beryl might be shocked, not only because she had spoken with a Malay boy but associated with a boy at all.

In her solitude she often thought of Maputo and the love she felt for him. Though the image of him crouched in his cell lingered, she could not dispel from her mind the dignity with which he bore the whip of the Afrikaner police, or the sight of him, handcuffed, as they led him away. Perhaps if she had been more alert, she could have explained what had happened; but the police had only mocked her as she stood there in her nightgown. And her mother's attempts in broken English had only amused the constables.

Beryl should have helped, being a boy, but what did he care that Maputo had been unjustly accused. He was a typical South African, she thought, just like the other Sea Point boys. She had seen girls prancing with them along the pavilion. They seemed interested only in fun, and Beryl was eager to blend in. He wanted to be popular with the girls, and she had seen what had happened when Joyce discovered things about the family. She wondered if Beryl had come to his senses and realized how false she was.

If they moved to America, her mother would not be as lonely and maybe she would be cheerful again. Libka remembered how Sara seemed to become spirited when she read the old letters. "Libkala," she once said, "maybe one day you will meet your uncle in America. When he was a boy he also dreamed of being a writer."

——•——

Though Libka missed her family, she feared the prospect of seeing them. Would they detect her nights of loneliness and the strange thoughts that now dwelt in her mind?

Her period of detention passed and she was permitted to return to her former schedule. The girls at school had paid no attention to her confinement, and when she reappeared in the cafeteria and classroom it was as though she had never been away. Not that anyone showed friendliness towards her, but there were no probing eyes. Her teachers also acted as though nothing had occurred. It seemed that a period of detention at Kirstenhof Girls' Academy was a routine occurrence.

She concluded it was best that she had not told her mother of this event and assumed there had been no communication from Mevrou Vandermerve.

When Sara wrote that she and the children would be coming to visit, Libka feared that her two worlds would collide. But her mother never came, and in her place Golda and Shneyer arrived. They were dressed in outfits Libka had never seen before; and Shneyer looked proud in his new blue shorts and sparkling white shoes.

"Mommy couldn't come," Golda explained. "Dina's got a rash and she was up all night."

"Why you live in this funny place?" Shneyer wanted to know. "Don't you like us anymore?"

Libka hugged her brother and asked, "What's wrong with the baby?"

"Mommy thinks she's got chickenpox," said Golda.

"But she's bad," complained Shneyer. "See!" He held out his hand. "She bites me."

"I don't see anything," said Libka, "but just the same, I'll kiss it better."

Shneyer held out his other hand. "You can kiss this one better too."

Libka strolled around the grounds with her sister and brother. Shneyer burst with questions. His curls had grown longer and his cheeks were radiant.

"Is Mom still thinking of America?" Libka asked her sister. "Does our uncle still write that we should come?"

Golda gestured uncertainly.

"Well, doesn't he want us to come?"

"I think he does."

"Then why aren't you excited?"

When Golda seemed evasive, Libka sensed trouble. "Well, what's wrong? Aren't Beryl and Mommy excited?"

"Beryl is," Golda mumbled.

"Mom isn't?"

"I'm not sure."

Libka eyed her sister suspiciously and changed the subject.

"What's going on in the factory with Mr. Shmerl?"

"Maybe when you see Mommy she'll tell you."

"You live in that house and you don't know anything. Why did you even bother to come here?"

"Something's different," Golda blurted out.

"What?"

Golda felt trapped. She looked towards Shneyer, who was digging for worms in the gravel. Suddenly he came dashing up to Libka. "Take off my shoes," he yelled as he fell on the damp ground.

"What beautiful shoes," she said.

"*He* gave it to me," Shneyer shouted. "You like Golda's shoes?" He pointed to the new black patent leathers. "*He* gave that also."

"Who?" Libka looked at her sister as she tugged the new shoes off her brother's feet.

"He did! Mr. Poo Poo!" Feeling free, Shneyer sprang away. "Mr. Poo Poo," he shouted as he ran off.

"What's he talking about?"

Golda's eyes were guarded. "Somebody just gave them to us."

"Somebody?"

"Look," she said, "stop questioning me!"

"Can't I know?"

Golda did not answer.

"Is there a mystery about it?" Libka insisted.

Golda sat motionless on the hard ground. Then suddenly she jumped up as though to flee. "Mommy has a man friend and he gave us the shoes," she said, darting a fearful look at her sister.

Ice sped through Libka's body. How could all these things be happening?

"I think he likes Mommy," said Golda.

Libka sprung up. For a moment she stood frozen, then she lifted Shneyer's shoes and sent them flying.

Shneyer was delighted at this game, racing after them like a puppy.

"How can she!" Libka fumed. "Daddy's dead not even two years!" She turned on her sister. "Go home! Is this the news you came to bring me?"

Libka's world turned black. She ran away to hide the tears, and when she regained control and went back to find her sister and brother, there was no longer any trace of them.

The ensuing days were shrouded in fog. Mechanically Libka got up in the morning, dressed in her ugly green tunic, laced her shoes and went to class. She sat at her wooden desk but did not hear a word. At mealtimes she sat at the long tables and sensed girls revolving around her and plates banging, but she didn't taste her food. Sometimes she caught sight of the headmistress or one of the prefects, but nothing penetrated the mist.

On the fourth day she awoke and ran for a pencil:

> Dear Mom,
> Please let me come home for a visit. I miss the house and I want to see Dina. I'm here for over three months now. Please write to the headmistress, Mevrou Vandermerve, and ask her to give me a weekend permit. Mama, you will make me so happy if you do this. Libka

It was risky to have her mother contact the headmistress, but Libka believed that if she could come home she could set everything right. The man couldn't be that important. It was probably because her mother was lonely. Though Libka was not tempted by America, it would be an escape from this horrible place and it would get her mother away. They would go to America where she would be with her brother and forget about this man.

When a letter finally arrived from home she ripped it open even before entering her cubicle.

> Darling daughter,
> Golda and Shneyer brought a nice report. Golda say you look good and improve. She say you are more patient and calm, and they had a very nice time. I am so proud and happy to hear this. I would write the headmistress for a permit to come home but meantime we are arranging to come out the weekend after this. Somebody will bring us with a car.
>
> Your loving mother, sisters and brothers

· twenty-five ·

Abe Garfinkel's mind was preoccupied with Sara. When he had first observed the way in which Motel Shmerl had exploited her, he was surprised at the outrage he felt. He generally took life in stride and had even accepted the loss of his beloved Hena, grateful she had given him three devoted children.

When he would leave Sara after an evening during which they would discuss the old times in the *shtetl*, wistfully remembering beloved family members and friends, he would feel emptiness as he drove back to Camps Bay. For a long time he had grieved over Hena and had never envisioned that anyone could fill her place.

He had always admired Sara, ever since the time in the *shtetl*. Though she had been capable at home and helped her mother run the family inn, she was passionate about the books at the local library where she worked. She was also a gifted performer. He remembered her portrayal of Irena in Chekhov's *The Three Sisters,* and her role in

The Dybbuk. And she sang and danced, looking ravishing in the costumes she herself designed. She was spirited and adventurous, yet solid and sensible. He remembered her lengthy engagement to the prosperous Sholom, who had bought land in Palestine and pleaded that she build a life with him. Everyone had encouraged this union, considering it a triumph that the fatherless girl would find such a match. Furthermore, he requested no dowry, an uncommon arrangement. After he left for Palestine to develop his land, Sholom's parents visited Sara's mother, asking that she encourage her daughter to join their son. They emphasized that he had many prospects but Sara was his chosen one.

Since Garfinkel's young wife Hena was a cousin of Sara and they were also close friends, Sara would pour her heart out to her. She knew it would have brought *naches* and relief to her mother, for at twenty-six she was in danger of becoming an old maid, yet she found herself unable to make the commitment. Then, miraculously, Yosef arrived in her *shtetl* to set up the Jewish People's Bank. Handsome and brilliant, just returned from his engineering studies in Leningrad, Yosef took up residence in her family inn. Here he had a chance to observe Sara and he soon felt himself falling in love. Now in his late twenties, he had been engaged to a girl from his home *shtetl* for over seven years and it was assumed they would marry soon after his return from Leningrad. But his beloved had an elder sister who could not find a suitor, despite the matchmaker's efforts, and it was unthinkable for them to marry until a candidate appeared for the elder one.

Both Sara and Yosef found themselves in a perplexing situation. Sara had never known the feeling of love, except through the books she read and the plays in which she performed. And though Yosef had been deeply in love with Nechama, Sara awakened him to new feelings. She wasn't as ravishing as his beloved, but Yosef was drawn to the passion and depth in her. After setting up the bank in the *shtetl* of Butrimantz, Yosef hired Sara to work as a teller. She had been hesitant to accept the offer because she felt committed to her job at the library, but he convinced her that the books would still be available for her to read. Thus, as they worked closely together, their feelings for each other grew.

Abe and Hena Garfinkel had witnessed the relationship from the beginning. Yosef had recently set up a branch of the bank in nearby

Rumshishok, where they lived. And when Sara broke her engagement to Sholom, they were the first to know. Sara found it painful to sever this relationship, as Yosef did with his long-time fiancée, and they would both share these feelings with Abe and Hena.

These memories returned to Garfinkel as he drove back to his home one evening. He felt that Sara shared many things with him and she was as alone as he was. But did she feel that anyone could ever replace Yosef? This was something he longed to know.

During the past months he had become a regular visitor. By now Shneycr would seat himself on Mr. Garfinkel's lap and Dina would fight for the opportunity. The problems in the factory had brought him closer to Sara. He felt protective towards her and found himself increasingly drawn to her.

The children would see him in the evenings and he would remain with Sara long after they had gone to sleep.

Garfinkel was often present in Sara's thoughts. Though she still read at night, she did not feel lonely, for she knew he would soon come to see her. She had even confided in him about her visit to Mevrou Vandermerve.

"Do you think it is such a crime that Libka would write to this boy in England?"

"Sara, though South Africa has been good to many of our people, it is not a perfect country. In my opinion, a girl should be allowed to correspond with a boy in England. My son Andrew, who is now study-ing politics at Oxford, does not even want to come home when he's on holiday. He has very bad feelings about this country."

"And yet, Abe, you made out so well."

"It isn't hard to make a success in this country. I make a good living. I made money in the shoe factory, and I have a fine home. Listen, Sara, I'm not a politician, but I'm not comfortable with the situation here."

"I notice you and Hena never mingled much with the Jewish peo-ple in Sea Point."

"Hena was even more uneasy with them. As you know, she never socialized much. We went to synagogue in Sea Point on the High Holy Days, but not much more."

"Yosef also didn't want to live in Sea Point. Before we bought this house, we saw a few places there, but he didn't like."

"If you want to know the truth," he said, "I'm disappointed in how many of our *landsleit* behaved in this country. Of course it's no reason for anti-Semitism, but it seems some of them have gone overboard with luxuries."

Listening to Abe Garfinkel, Sara realized how similar his feelings were to those she and Yosef had shared. She knew Hena felt that way, but she had never spoken about such things with Abe.

"Libka also isn't at home in this country," she told him. "Since Yosef die my brother has been encouraging me to settle in America. Of course we want to be closer, but Meyer also believes it will be a better place for the children to grow up and be educated."

Garfinkel was pensive for a while and sadness crept into his face. "He may be right, Sara. As long as Jan Smuts is still our prime minister, we Jews feel relatively safe here, but he's getting along in years and the National Party is strong. America may be more secure, but how would you feel transplanting the family? It's not easy with five young children. Also, I understand that visas to America are not readily available."

"Naturally, it is easier to talk," Sara said. "Who can tell what the future will bring."

Garfinkel often joined the family for dinner, and now Sara prepared dishes such as she used to make for Yosef. He also relished the fatty brisket, roast potatoes, *lokshen* pudding and carrot *tsimis* that Yosef used to enjoy, and for dessert Sara served compote, *taiglach* or *imberlach* with a glass of tea and raspberry jam. She resumed her wine-making in the barrel, and she and Abe would sometimes have a glass of red wine with their meal. Beryl felt proud when he was allowed to join them.

"I have come to know your children and I like them very much," Garfinkel told Sara one night. "I haven't seen Libka since Yosef passed away. I would be happy to drive you to visit her and we can take along the family."

———————

For the first time since his father's death Beryl felt he was part of a family. Sometimes Mr. Garfinkel would bring Simon with him. Beryl was honoured to associate with this young man who was almost five years his senior. He once invited Simon along on a Saturday to watch him play cricket, and after that they played together a few times. Simon was involved in his studies, for he was in his last year at university; and when Beryl observed his dedication, he took his own studies more seriously.

Beryl was also impressed by Simon's girlfriend, who was pretty and lively. When she accompanied them to a cricket match one afternoon, Beryl decided to introduce his girlfriend, Eleanor, even though she wasn't Jewish. He was relieved when no one seemed to know the difference and was proud to be seen with her as they drove in Simon's red sports car with the roof down.

Beryl was always happy to find Mr. Garfinkel at home when he returned from a date with Eleanor. Sara and Abe would usually be in the sitting room, talking of the old times. Beryl was pleased that his mother no longer wore the dreary black dress and now appeared in colourful outfits he had never seen before. On a few occasions she had gone to Adderley Street and returned with parcels. When he asked her what she had bought, she said, "Nothing important," but he would later see her in a new garment or with a glittering ornament in her hair.

"This is the way you should always look," he told her. "It makes a world of difference. You don't seem like an old lady."

"What you mean, Beryl," she chuckled, "I am not young anymore."

"What are you, forty?"

"I am already a few years older."

"And how old is Mr. Garfinkel?"

"He would be around the same age as Daddy. In the later forties. Why do you ask this, Beryl?"

"For no reason in particular, but I think he's a decent man."

Beryl also noticed that Sara no longer talked to herself. Though it had never bothered him as much as it did Libka, it sometimes made him uneasy. And one day after rugby practice when he went into the kitchen, he caught her laughing to herself as she punched the dough for bagels.

"What's so funny?"

She turned around in embarrassment. "Aw, Beryl, I didn't see you was back."

"Something tickling you?"

"Tickling? No." She waved a dish towel playfully at him.

She also bathed more frequently and groomed her hair, sometimes piling it on top of her head in a carefree fashion.

"What's that?" Beryl asked one day. "You look like you're going to a dance."

"Why not?" she said and blushed.

· twenty-six ·

When Libka saw Mr. Garfinkel with her mother on the school grounds, her sisters and brothers following, she was not sure how she felt. She could still picture him and her father playing chess at night while Mrs. Garfinkel and her mother sat in the sitting room talking about the old times in Europe. She knew that Mrs. Garfinkel was a cousin of her mother and they had been close. Mr. and Mrs. Garfinkel always seemed so happy together and she would be surprised to see grownups holding hands, as they sometimes did at Muizenberg. She especially remembered the summer her family and the Garfinkels had adjoining beach houses there and her father and Mr. Garfinkel would come for the weekend.

It was strange to now see her mother with Mr. Garfinkel, walking together in the same way as he used to with his wife. Her mother looked so different. Her hair was styled in little curls and there was a sparkle in her face. She wore a yellow dress that Libka had never seen, with a lace ribbon tied at the waist. She almost looks young, thought Libka.

"And you know who this is," Sara said as Libka came up.

"Of course."

Mr. Garfinkel extended his hand, which Libka accepted.

"I shouldn't ask you how it is here," he said. "You miss Muizenberg? We had good times there, our families."

"Yes."

Libka was pleased she had worn her good peasant skirt with the lace blouse. Her mother seemed proud.

Libka's eyes fell upon her brothers and sisters. What a happy, complete family they appeared to be. Beryl's skin was golden from days under the sun, and he wore white shorts and a yellow shirt. He smiled easily as he acknowledged Libka. And Golda looked prim and dainty in pale green organdie.

"I have for you also such a dress," her mother said quickly. "Two from the same I make. One for each of my beautiful daughters."

Shneyer felt as though the grounds were his domain. "Come, everybody, follow me. I'll show it to you. Watch it, there's a worm hole somewhere, and I think I saw a snake."

Dina was the first to totter after Shneyer. She ran off balance, plopping onto the ground, desperately getting up only to plop down again. She cried and laughed as she tried to pursue her brother.

"Look," Libka called in glee, "she's walking so much better!" And she ran after the baby in the ruffled dress. "What a fatty!" Libka lifted the pudgy thing, who answered with a gush of broken words, spitting fervently.

"Let's see her bite." Libka offered the baby a finger. It was like tempting a puppy with a bone, and Dina sprang at this chance. She dug her teeth in with all her might. "Ouch!" Libka tore her finger away. The infant was insulted and began to howl as she saw everyone laugh.

When Libka caught Golda alone, she said, "You didn't have to lie to Mommy that I'm doing so well. How come you ran off that day you came to visit?"

Golda did not answer.

With her family present, Libka was permitted to go out of the school grounds. She had not been beyond these walls for many months.

"Take an extra sundress and a swimming costume," Sara said.

"Why?"

"A surprise. You will see."

They all settled into Mr. Garfinkel's spacious Packard. Beryl and Shneyer sat in front, and Sara sat in back with Libka and Golda, Dina on her lap. The baby was the life of the party. She gurgled and cackled and giggled, biting everything in sight. And from time to time Libka could not resist snatching her away from her mother.

Mr. Garfinkel had rented a house on the cliffs in Muizenberg. They drove for hours until they reached the seashore. Garfinkel opened the trunk of his car and Beryl helped him unload the food that Sara had packed for the weekend. Though Garfinkel had warned her not to fuss, she had awakened early that morning and made *kreplach* and *taiglach* and even chopped liver, brisket and *lokshen* pudding. She knew how Abe enjoyed these things, and his maid could no longer make them.

After they had settled into the beach house, Sara proceeded to prepare the evening meal while Mr. Garfinkel and Beryl went off with their fishing equipment and Shneyer tagged along. Libka watched Beryl walk beside the man. He strode with a confident gait, conversing easily, and Shneyer threaded in and out as they moved briskly along.

Sara busied herself in the kitchen, and Golda set the table with decorative dishes they found in the house. Dina had fallen asleep on the long drive and Sara tucked her into bed.

Libka changed into an orange sundress and stepped out onto the sands, silky beneath her feet. The air was pure and the breeze twirled her hair in circles. Far below she could see the waves bursting on the shore, sweeping upwards to the red and green and yellow bungalows that lined the beach. It was high tide. She remembered how in past summers she would rush down the cliffs, her feet sinking into the slippery sands, then race into the ocean, diving beneath the waves before they burst.

And on Friday nights she would wait for the sound of a car and run out to greet her father. He would come laden with confectionery and biscuits from the *landsleit's* factories on Sir Lowry Road. She would rush into his arms and dangle from him as he made his way into the house. Then as her mother would bustle in the kitchen, Libka could not resist tearing the tinsel wrapping from the chocolates and biting into them to test the fillings. "Enough already," Sara would reprimand her. "Your teeth will get rotten."

"Where are you, Libkala?" Sara now appeared from the doorway of the house, a ruffled pink apron over her dress.

"Where did you get that fancy apron?" Libka asked.

"Leave me alone."

Sara sat down on the marble bench beneath the yellow-and-orange sunshade, the fountains splashing. Palms and cactus plants enveloped them, with multicoloured flowers bursting from the soil.

"So tell me, Libkala, how is it at the place?"

"What place?" Libka pretended.

"Stop."

Sara drew close to Libka and reached for her hand. She asked about school, about her life, but Libka waited for something else. And at last she could not restrain the words, "So are you still thinking of America?"

Sara looked at her. "What you think, Libkala? What is your advice?"

"So it's up to me?"

"I will tell you, *mein kind*. I want to take you out of this school. It is not a good place for you."

"Why suddenly?"

"I know about the letter from the boy in England."

Libka searched her mother's face in astonishment. "What are you talking about?"

"The headmistress sent us a letter and I went to see her."

"You came to that place and I didn't know about it?"

"*Sha, sha, mein kind.* It was good I came. I saw what it is like, and if they condemn you because you write a letter to a boy in England, then it is not an improvement from Promenade High School. Tell me, this is maybe the boy from the Malay store?"

"It's his grandfather's store."

"I used to see the boy sometimes when I go into the store for fruit or vegetables. He look like a quiet boy, sitting in the corner with books."

"You didn't see him lately!"

"Not lately."

"He's studying to be a barrister in London. He goes to Oxford University."

"Like Mr. Garfinkel's son Andrew. Imagine."

Sara then recounted her visit to the headmistress.

"I will tell you, I even talk to Mr. Garfinkel about it. You understand I had to let it out. Beryl was a good boy. He telephoned the headmistress when we got the letter and made an appointment for me. These days he is much more considerate and helpful."

"Mevrou Vandermerve is a witch."

"A Afrikaner lady that don't like the Jewish people. She question me left and right. But I don't care. I made up my mind even when I was riding home in the train that this is not a place for you, Libkala."

After a moment, Libka asked, "And you told Mr. Garfinkel the whole story?"

"I can talk to him. You remember him, of course, from when you were small and the times in Muizenberg."

"He's a nice man."

"And he told me he didn't think it is a crime that you write to a Malay boy. You remember Mr. Garfinkel's son Andrew?"

"I always liked him."

"Well, like I say, he is now living in London, studying politics. And Mr. Garfinkel tell me he doesn't even want to come home to Cape Town. He doesn't like the system."

"I always thought they were a nice family. I remember how they used to treat their maid. She was part of the family, like Maputo was to us."

"And Mr. Garfinkel still got this maid. She's old already and can't do much, but he keep her."

"He's a nice man."

"Of course he's a nice man. Daddy always felt he could trust him with his life. And you know he made him manager of the bank in Rumshishok."

"Yes, I know. Too bad his wife died. She was nice too."

"Hena was a good woman. You know she was a distant cousin of mine."

"You told me a hundred times."

Around six o'clock Mr. Garfinkel returned with Beryl and Shneyer. By then the chopped liver and chicken soup with *kreplach* were ready, and Golda was putting a vase of primroses on the table.

"Come, everybody, sit and eat," Sara exclaimed, her eyes shining.

"I told your mother this was a well-deserved holiday," Mr. Garfinkel said to Libka, "but she's a very determined lady."

Sara laughed girlishly.

That night Libka shared a room with Golda, as in the old times. Beryl and Shneyer were roommates, and Sara slept with Dina in the third bedroom. Mr. Garfinkel had taken the small room adjacent to the kitchen, which appeared to be the servants' quarters.

The next morning Libka was up before sunrise. She pulled on her swimming costume and tiptoed out of the house. Racing down the sands at full speed, she plunged into the ocean, then swam until she could hardly see the shore. There was no lifeguard on the high post at this hour. The ocean was all hers and she felt she could reclaim the world.

· twenty-seven ·

Two weeks later Libka came home on a weekend permit. The family had decided that she would complete her term, but would not return thereafter. In a letter that Beryl had composed and scripted in his artistic handwriting, the message read:

> Dear Mevrou Vandermerve,
> I wish to advise that due to new developments, my daughter Libka will not be returning to Kirstenhof Girls' Academy after the close of this term. Though we hope she has benefited from this experience, she will be following a new path.
> We thank you for your courtesy and cooperation.
>
> Mrs. Sara Hoffman

Beryl and Sara had reviewed the wording of the letter several times and concluded it was best to part on amicable terms. They saw no advantage in expressing their displeasure and hoped the headmistress could read between the lines.

Sara would have preferred to withdraw Libka sooner but felt she should complete the term. Also, Sara required time to consider future options.

When Libka arrived on her weekend permit, she had barely climbed the steps when Beryl grabbed her satchel. "Let me help you," he said. She studied him speculatively. During the weekend in Muizenberg, he had been acting as if he had something important on his mind.

Dragging the satchel into Libka's bedroom, Beryl watched as she pulled off her sandals and removed a pair of white shorts and top from her drawer.

"Okay, what is it?" she finally asked.

"It wasn't convenient for Mom to tell you in Muizenberg but she agreed to let me break the news. We're rid of Motel Shmerl! He turned out to be a crook, as we suspected."

A feeling of relief swept through Libka.

"And it was Mr. Garfinkel who pinned him to the wall. He took me down to the factory the night the thief returned the equipment. Can you believe he actually stole bronze and brass and tools you can't get for money these days! He even took Dad's lathe! And now we know why he got rid of Fortune and all our loyal workers."

Beryl described how it had been prearranged that Shmerl appear at nine-thirty sharp. Mr. Garfinkel and Beryl had arrived a few minutes earlier, and just on the stroke of nine-thirty the lorry pulled up.

"I think he was terrified. He knew he could land in jail. You would never believe how strict Mr. Garfinkel could be. When the two helpers began dragging the equipment off the lorry, he yelled 'Stop' and ordered Shmerl to lug the stuff himself. 'You drag it, you filthy dog!' he shouted. Can you imagine Mr. Garfinkel talking that way?"

Libka had the feeling Beryl stopped strangers on the street to tell the story. He was so proud and excited. Now that Shmerl was out of the picture, Libka thought perhaps someday she would tell her mother what had happened.

"So what about the factory? Are we going to America?"

"You'll have to get the details from Mom," Beryl replied.

As Libka skipped into the kitchen, followed by her brother, everyone was waiting for her.

"Libka came home!" Shneyer announced as he ran to her. "Yoo hoo, everybody! Three cheers for Libka! Can we sing 'God Save the King'?"

"So he listens to news bulletins from London!" Libka laughed and ruffled Shneyer's hair.

She enveloped her brother in her arms; and when she released him, her face was streaked with tears.

It seemed strange to be in this house again after so long a time; and though she was drained from the journey, she felt jubilant.

———·———

When Libka appeared at Anya's house that weekend, she found the door ajar and the sunlight streaming into the passageway. It felt so inviting that she just walked in. She heard a spinning sound and caught sight of Mrs. Steinberg at the sewing machine. The woman's face seemed cheerful and relaxed, and when she saw Libka she did not jump up but only said, "Hello, Libka, don't stand on ceremony. You know where Anya is."

The door to Anya's room was also open and the gramophone played "There'll Be Bluebirds over the White Cliffs of Dover."

As Libka breezed into the doorway, Anya hopped up, grabbed her friend and twirled her around as she sang:

> There'll be bluebirds over
> The white cliffs of Dover,
> Tomorrow, just you wait and see.
> There'll be love and laughter
> And peace ever after,
> Tomorrow, when the world is free.

Libka had grown up hearing this song amid BBC broadcasts of bombs and burning towns and the voice of Sir Winston Churchill.

As the girls danced, they saw Mrs. Steinberg watching in delight from the passageway.

Anya pushed Libka into her room, where a suitcase was half packed with books and clothing.

"Are you going somewhere?" Libka asked.

"How come you're home?"

"They gave me a weekend pass."

"So you know what's going on, huh?" Anya said triumphantly.

"Beryl was so excited when he told me how Mr. Garfinkel made Shmerl lug the stolen stuff back."

"Your brother's improving," said Anya. "Mr. Garfinkel has been a good influence."

"Do you like Mr. Garfinkel?"

"He's fine. One of the few people who wasn't condescending towards my father. Notice something missing?"

"You told me your father went away. He didn't come back?"

"He won't come back. This was his present to my mom and me. Did you talk to her?"

"She looks different." Libka eyed the open suitcase. "So what's going on, Anya?"

"I'm off to London! My poor mother's been taking in sewing to help me save up for the ticket. I don't approve of her making fancy outfits for the conceited Jews, but she insists."

"You're already packing?"

"We have a far way to go, Libka, before we can put together the money, but the open suitcase keeps me going."

"What about your mother? Will she go too?"

"I go first, but she promised to follow!"

Anya shoved the suitcase aside and invited Libka to sit beside her on the floor. "What's going on with you?"

Libka took the chance to tell her about the letter from Sayyed and all that had transpired as a result of it.

"You can thank him for it," Anya said. "He helped get you out of that miserable place. And good for your mother that she wasn't intimidated by that Mevrou Vandermerve. She sounds even worse than Miss Bloemfontein. Anyway, did you answer Sayyed?"

"In my head I did."

"Write and tell him I'm coming!"

Anya jumped on Libka and they wrestled as they giggled and rolled on the floor.

· twenty-eight ·

Now that Libka's term at boarding school was drawing to a close, she wondered what her future would be. Her confinement had liberated her thoughts and enabled her to soar to new levels. She hoped that Maputo would also be roaming to far-off places in his mind. Though her heart ached when she remembered him lying in his cell, his eyes had glowed and perhaps his mind was journeying to the happy times in the Transvaal before his family was wiped out by the epidemic.

Sara had arranged for Libka to return home at the end of the term. Since that decision was made, even Mevrou Vandermerve had been less stern. "Hello, Libka," she said when she encountered her in a hallway. And her Afrikaans teacher, Mevrou du Plessis, avoided her eye. Libka was no longer attending Afrikaans classes and they did not force her to do so. She had responded to the letter from Sayyed, even though she had never been permitted to retrieve it. She assumed it was part of her records in the school office.

In replying, she thanked Sayyed for his letter, and did not mention the problems it had created, though she gave him her home address. She wrote that Anya was planning to move to London and expressed her own dream of some day going there too. "It would be nice to ride on a tram or train with you." Though she was not able to address him by his first name only, she signed her letter merely Libka.

The letters Libka received from her mother were cheerful and optimistic. She knew it was the presence of Mr. Garfinkel that had brought about this change. Though she hoped her mother still mourned Yosef, it was easier with her behaving normally. Beryl had told her she didn't talk to herself so much anymore and he had even caught her laughing one day. "Can you believe that?" he said. "What a surprise not to find her crying over those old Jewish songs. She's actually cheerful in the morning! And she makes decent meals, not only avocado salad with chopped egg. And she buys mangos and pawpaws from the Malay merchant on the wagon. He even lingers before our house and rings his bell. I'm sure, Libka, that Mom wouldn't send you to school anymore with mashed-banana sandwiches."

Libka sometimes wondered if her mother would marry Mr. Garfinkel. It was almost two years since her father had died; and though she could not imagine anyone taking his place, Mr. Garfinkel was similar to her father. He was reserved and didn't socialize with the Sea Point crowd. Being wealthy was no excuse to take advantage of the poor people. He seemed to have a special rapport with them, like her father had. Beryl even told her about the Sunday they spent at his home. "Mr. Garfinkel and Simon prepared all the meals! Of course Mom tried to help but they wouldn't let her. Their servant is so ancient and sick she can hardly move, but Simon told me his father will take care of her until the day she dies. That's pretty decent, don't you think?"

The more Libka heard about Mr. Garfinkel, the more she respected him. She felt sad that his wife had died, but grateful he was becoming part of her family.

· twenty-nine ·

One Monday morning the postman rang the doorbell. Usually he slid the mail through the slot, but this time he waited. When Sara came to the door he held out a blue envelope. "Registered from America," he announced. "I need your signature, madam."

The letter was from her brother Meyer. After signing, she moved swiftly to the kitchen and tore the envelope open.

> My dear sister,
> At last we know the fate of our beloved family. Though it is hard to write you the circumstances, it is still perhaps better that we know. We cannot put to rest the fact that our beloved ones met their end in such a brutal way, but we must comfort each other. From our whole family only our dear brother Eliahu survived, and it is from him that I have received the news. Eliahu survived because he and his wife Hinda worked as doctors in Russia. Before they left Kovna, they went to Butrimantz and begged Mother and Shleymi and his family to

run away into the forest with them. Mother said she was too old to run, and Shleymi refused to leave Mother behind. Thus, my dear sister, they met their fate in mass graves. Shleymi was first taken to Alytus with a wagon of other Jewish men. They were told they were going to work. Mother even received a letter in which he asked that she send money and other valuables. Of course she did. It turned out he was already shot and the letter was written by one of the murderers.

Eliahu writes that the Germans did not even occupy our shtetl. Our "loyal" neighbours, the Lithuanians, were happy to do the job, and then take over the Jewish homes.

Mother, Shleymi's wife and their two little girls lie in the mass graves in Butrimantz, and Shleymi met his fate in Alytus.

I enclose a copy of Eliahu's letter so you can read the whole story. You will see he and Hinda are working in Russia. They have a boy a year old. But it is no surprise that every day of their life they think of this catastrophe that befell our beloved ones and the Jewish people.

My dear sister, our family has become small and it is important that we join together to give each other strength. Now that you have lost your dear Yosef, please prepare to come to America. I will talk to the consul right away and I ask you to do the same in Cape Town. Though visas may not be easy to acquire, I will do my part to speed the process along. Your children will be better off here, and we will all be less lonely. The tragedy that has befallen our people should remind us that we must value each other and our family.

I look forward to your letter but will proceed to investigate without delay.

Hoping to meet you and your beloved children in person before long, I remain

Your dear brother Meyer

As Sara read the letter and the accompanying one from her youngest brother Eliahu, she was frozen. She wondered why she was bereft of feeling.

When Beryl returned from school, she showed him the letters. "If you can't make out all the Hebrew words, I will help." Beryl took the letters into his room; and when Sara went to his door after some time, she noticed it was closed and felt she should not intrude.

It was clear Beryl had been crying when he finally came into the kitchen. "It's barbaric," he said. "How can human beings behave in this way? So the rumours we've been hearing are true."

"You could read the Hebrew writing?"

"Unfortunately."

Beryl put the letters back on the table. "Mom," he said, "I'll go down with you to the American consulate."

———•———

A few nights later when Abe Garfinkel came to visit, Sara waited until the children had gone to sleep before showing him the letters. He sat down in the armchair and put on his glasses. He lingered over the letters for some time, after which he replaced them carefully on the tea wagon and sat in silence. As Sara looked over at him from the settee where she sat with hands clasped, her tears finally came. Not since the death of Yosef had she wept with such abandon.

Abe Garfinkel gently moved over to the settee. When he put his arm around her, she cried aloud, smothering her tears into his chest.

"Sara," he murmured in Yiddish, "I'm very fond of you, but I will understand whatever you decide."

When Sara had composed herself, she reached for his hand. "Without you, Abe, I don't know where I would be. What do you think I should do?"

Mr. Garfinkel shrugged. "How can I make such a decision for you, my dear? You know what I would want, but you have to decide what's best for you and your children."

Sara made a trip to Claremont to share the tragic news with Rochel and Reuven Shevah. After reading the letters from Sara's brothers, they sat with heads lowered.

"Perhaps it is still better to know the details," Rochel said, "but in our hearts we already knew what became of our people."

Sara spent the night with the Shevah family since she could now rely on her older children to tend to Shneyer and Dina. Late in the evening as she sat with Rochel in the kitchen, they discussed Sara's thoughts of

America. Though Sara opened her heart to Rochel, she was not able to confide her personal feelings for Abe Garfinkel. The Shevahs knew of his efforts to resolve the problems with Motel Shmerl, but did not presume there were intimate feelings between them.

"Are you prepared, Sara, to break up your home and move to a new country?" There was deep concern in Rochel's grey eyes. "Though our people don't feel very welcome with the Afrikaners, it could be worse, as we know. What will you do in America with five small children? Maybe take Dina and first go and see what it is like."

"We will find a way to survive," Sara assured her. "I want to join Meyer and it will be good for my children to be close to their cousins."

After talking with Beryl and Golda in the days that followed, Sara decided they should go to the American consulate to explore the possibilities of emigrating. When Sara told Garfinkel of her intentions, he offered to accompany them.

As an established manufacturer with a sound knowledge of the immigration policy of the country, Mr. Garfinkel made a fine impression at the consulate's office. He explained that Sara was a widow with five young children, Beryl at sixteen being the eldest, and she had no relatives in South Africa. She had just learned that her mother and other family members in Lithuania had perished, and she was eager to join her brother in America, who was urging the family to emigrate. Her brother himself was well established in the state of Massachusetts and was making efforts from his end to facilitate the process.

The consul explained that there was a limited quota for immigration to America, but he would look into the matter and see what he could do. Mr. Garfinkel offered to help in any way and gave the consul the name of his solicitors, the esteemed British firm of Edwards and Edwards.

In further discussions with Sara, it was decided that she would put the house up for sale. "The house is neglected and who knows how easy it will be to liquidate," she told Mr. Garfinkel. "Maybe I should put on the market, and if I find a buyer we can rent a place in the meantime."

"That won't be a problem," Garfinkel said. "You are all welcome to stay in my house if you decide."

Though the factory ran smoothly under Aaron Adelson's management, with the help of a highly qualified engineering consultant, Sara knew she had to sell it if they were to relocate to America. Again, it was Mr. Garfinkel who came forward with the solution.

"I'll buy it from you, Sara. As you know, Simon is graduating soon and he and Shoshana plan to marry next summer. They've chosen a December date. I can't think of a better wedding present to give them than Yosef's factory."

In subsequent sessions Garfinkel offered Sara a sum that exceeded her expectations. "It would make me very happy to see Simon take over Yosef's business," she told him, "but you don't have to pay me such a big amount."

"*Sha*, Sara! It's worth it to me."

Though Mr. Garfinkel acted with strength and optimism, he felt empty when he thought of losing Sara. All her struggles had brought him closer and he wondered how she and the children would fare in America. It had been over twenty years since she had seen her brother and he knew that the demanding life in America could change a person. Having discovered the tragedy of the family, the remaining ones yearned to be closer; but how would it be when Sara arrived with her five young children? Though the amount he had offered for the factory would be adequate to purchase a home and sustain them for several years, he knew that considerable funds would be needed to give them all a university education, as was Sara's intention. She would have to start some kind of business; and in the competitive environment of America it would not be easy for a widow with faltering English.

"It's not too late for you to change your mind, Sara," he told her one evening when they spoke of these concerns. "But whatever I may feel in my heart, I don't have a right to influence you."

She longed for him to express himself more directly, but said only, "It is a hard decision for me also, Abe."

"The thought of leaving Cape Town?" Here Garfinkel was seeking reassurance.

"It is not Cape Town," Sara said softly, "something else."

"Can you tell me?"

They looked at each other and their eyes provided the answer.

"Whatever the outcome," Garfinkel said, "for me your parting will not be goodbye."

"For me also, Abe," she answered shyly.

He squeezed her hand and held it for a long time. "You have brought me happiness, Sara."

· *thirty* ·

As the term at Kirstenhof Girls' Academy drew to an end, Libka prepared for her freedom. For a while Sara and Beryl had written about the developments at home, but in Sara's last letter she merely wrote, "Since you will soon be home with us again, *mein taier* Libkala, we will talk in person."

Instead of doing her school assignments, Libka would spend her evenings writing. She wrote poems about her childhood wanderings in the veld. She wrote a story about the Voortrekkers stoning her house in Newlands and how she and her mother and Golda hid in the chicken hok. She remembered how Wendy van Hutenbek and her brother Piet called her *Jood* and slammed their gate in her face.

As she wrote, other memories floated to the surface — Wendy's father driving his lorry over Scottie, and Mickey the Monkey found poisoned in their back yard. She recalled too how shattered Beryl was when he returned from school to find the cage open and all his parrots gone. For days he had searched the sky, hoping they would return.

She also began a story about a noble man who had left the Transvaal when he lost his family in a typhus epidemic and roamed through the townships and shanty towns, sleeping in squatter camps, until he came to Sir Lowry Road and stumbled upon the workshop of an immigrant from Lithuania. In writing about Maputo she relived her childhood, remembering how he would lift her high up in the air with his powerful arms. Though Maputo could not read or write, she hoped that from his prison cell he dreamt of those early days in the Cape Province when he worked side by side with her father.

As the time drew close for her departure from boarding school, Libka wondered what her mother had in mind for her. She was, after all, fourteen and had a longing to learn new things. When she returned to Green Point she would again be able to visit the library on Adderley Street and hoped Miss Higgins would still be there. She had not told the librarian that she was being sent away; but the lady had never questioned her, even when she asked directions to Maputo's prison, so perhaps she would not inquire where Libka had been for half a year.

It was Beryl who came to fetch Libka on the last day of the term. He helped her pack everything into the old brown suitcase. Her luggage consisted mostly of books, which she had bought with her allowance. She had gone to Jason's Rare Books, the store Anya had recommended. For a tickey she bought Tolstoy's *War and Peace*. She also found a tragic love story by him, *Anna Karenina*. In a collection of Chekhov's plays, she was excited to find *The Three Sisters,* remembering her mother had performed in that play when she was a girl. As she put the books back into her suitcase, Beryl noticed a pile of black volumes on the floor. "What about these?"

"The next inmate is welcome to these horrible textbooks."

"I don't blame you," Beryl said after reading the titles.

She opened the tiny closet and pulled out a few dresses, blouses, shorts and pedal pushers, leaving the tunic and blazer. "That stays too," she said. "That and the hideous oxfords that make me feel like a prison guard."

"Why take anything that'll remind you of this place?" her brother agreed, as Libka threw her personal stuff into the suitcase. Beryl clicked it shut and wound rope around it, securing it with a sailors' knot.

Libka hoisted her satchel on her back, and they set off across the grounds towards the gate.

"Do you need to say goodbye to anyone?" Beryl inquired.

"No, thank you."

Riding home in the train, Beryl said, "Libka, there have been a number of new developments in the family situation, but I'll leave it to Mom to tell you."

"Can't you give me a hint?"

"You'll have to wait until you get home."

During the ride he told her of the times he spent with Simon Garfinkel and their fishing and sailing expeditions. "I wish I could spend more time with him," he said, "but he's completing his education and will get married this coming summer."

Beryl also told her he had acquired a budgie. "When I walk into the room, he says 'Good day, Beryl.' He's quite a character."

Libka considered this a good sign. Since he had lost the animals in Newlands, he seemed afraid to get any new pets. Before his sixteenth birthday, Sara had offered to buy him a puppy, but he had refused.

Libka asked what Beryl's plans were now that he had matriculated from high school.

"I was tardy in applying to the University of Cape Town, but I was accepted, anyway. I guess I can thank Simon for that. He really inspired me to make an effort. Mom was thrilled. However, there are developments that may override this."

"Why all these secrets?"

"It's appropriate for Mom to tell you."

When Libka inquired about the factory and Mr. Adelson, Beryl reported that all was running smoothly and they had retrieved many of the contracts lost during Shmerl's management. "Everyone likes and trusts Mr. Adelson, and he's teaching me a lot too. And of course Dad's old workers know what they're doing. Now that I'm out of school I'll be spending more time there. I don't think I'll eventually become an engineer, but the experience may come in handy."

Libka was struck by the change in Beryl, but she thought it would embarrass him if she mentioned it.

It was comforting to ride the train with her brother and she couldn't wait to be home and see the rest of the family. She suddenly felt so lucky to have brothers and sisters, unlike Anya whose siblings were far away.

The moment they reached their gate, Sara rushed down the steps and enveloped Libka in her arms. "Libkala! Thank God you're home."

"Don't get so hysterical," said Libka, embarrassed by the display of emotion as they both laughed and cried. Golda, Shneyer and Dina had come out onto the stoep and Libka embraced them lovingly, even giving Golda a peck on the cheek. It was not that she didn't feel warmly towards her sister, but being so close in age they were shy about hugging and kissing.

"Out of my way!" Beryl pushed them aside as he lugged up the suitcase. "Do you always have to get so emotional?" Yet he was happy to see this family reunion.

Libka was eager to hear the new development, and as soon as she flung off her satchel, she skipped into the kitchen.

"Mommy, what's this new development Beryl mentioned?"

"Libkala," said Sara, stirring the chicken soup and *kreplach*, "I will tell you after supper."

"But give me a hint."

"All right, *mein kind*. We are going to America after all."

Libka tried to read her mother's expression. Did something happen between her and Mr. Garfinkel? she wondered.

She restrained herself during supper and helped her mother and Golda clear the dishes from the table. Golda had become so efficient that Libka couldn't keep up with her.

When the dishes were done, Sara said, "Libkala, we received a letter from my brother in America. Come, I will show you. You still remember your Hebrew?"

"I'll try."

Libka followed her mother into the dining room, where she removed a blue envelope from the sideboard. "Try to read for yourself."

Sara sat beside Libka as she read the letter, wishing she could spare her the tragic news, but Libka seemed strong and composed.

"So you've decided to take your brother's advice?"

"We think it is the right thing. What is your opinion, Libkala?"

"You're always asking me."

"Of course I'm asking you."

Libka was confused about many things, but she did not find it comfortable to ask her mother. How did Mr. Garfinkel feel about this and why had her mother made this decision? Did something happen between her mother and Mr. Garfinkel? she wondered again.

It was as though Sara had read her mind. "Without Mr. Garfinkel I could not have managed anything."

"So does he feel sad that you're leaving?" she asked.

"He wants me to do what is best for the family."

"Do *you* feel sad leaving him?"

"I feel sad, of course."

Why did life have to be so difficult? thought Libka as she went to her old bedroom and found Golda sleeping. Her blanket had slipped off onto the floor and Libka lifted it and tucked it around her sister.

· *thirty-one* ·

Five weeks later the auction of the house took place. Furniture was shuffled around as people prowled through the rooms, inspecting the contents. Libka watched in horror as a woman squeezed a feather pillow and another poked fun at the embroidered quilt Sara's mother had made. Amid the chaos an alley cat scampered about fearfully, disappearing into dark corners, and Libka wished she could do the same.

"Going! Going! Gone!" the ruddy-faced auctioneer shouted. "Five pounds ... five pounds, two shillings ... Going! Going! Gone!"

The stout figure presided from the stoep where the furniture was dragged out by three black men. He held himself like a great orator on the stage, keeping his audience captive as one by one he dispersed the Hoffman family's memories.

In front of the house stood dozens of spectators — neighbours with their children who had come to watch, merchants seeking bargains and the curious and idle. Most had come for the drama of the event. Weaving among the crowd were the deaf couple from next door. Their fingers were signing with such momentum that at times they stole attention from the auctioneer.

"Six pounds, four shillings ... Six pounds, six shillings ... Going! Going! Gone!"

Oh, how the neighbourhood children loved the crescendo. They had never witnessed such excitement on this dead-end street. Soon they began to join in. "Going! Going! Gone!" With each "Gone!" a man or woman charged up the steps to claim the bargain.

Sara occasionally appeared on the stoep, but mostly she remained inside the house, wandering amid the chaos. Golda had retreated beneath the primrose trellis, where she played with Dina. It was Beryl who stood beside the auctioneer, involved in every transaction. He kept a keen eye on the proceedings and questioned when in doubt.

Of all the children, the busiest one was Shneyer. For days he had sensed upheaval, and Libka would find strange assortments in obscure places. In her father's drawer that had been emptied by Elsie she came upon a crumpled bag patched together with chewing gum. Inside was a one-legged soldier, part of a vanilla toffee, a wing of a butterfly and mud-covered marbles. In a corner of the closet she found jars with dead insects and a chameleon crawling inside Beryl's old Boy Scout cap.

On the day before the auction when Libka was tidying Shneyer's room, she saw something move at the foot of the bed and uncovered a tortoise. Beneath the bed, among the confectionery wrappers and soldiers with broken heads, lay a puppet of Hitler and Mussolini. She went into the garden and buried it near the rabbit hok.

Libka watched the auction, but mostly her eyes were set on the peoples' faces and hands. Each time the auctioneer handled an item roughly or a spectator laughed or jeered, it was an insult to her family.

The children in the street were ecstatic. The auction of "The Haven" was a great event in their lives.

"Dey goin' to 'merica, Sayer and dem all ..." one little boy boasted.

"Where's dat?"

"Wid a ship ..."

"Going! Going! Gone!" they all chimed, swinging deliriously on the gate.

Halfway through the auction Libka became aware of a man in a maroon cardigan who seemed different from the others. He had gentle eyes and dark curls. He stood apart from the crowd. His expression was earnest and he did not erupt in excitement with every "Gone!" nor did he push and shove like the others. She had noticed him in the house earlier, studying her father's Russian and Hebrew books, and realized she had seen him at the store when she bought the books before going away. When he saw her watching, he remarked, "These are precious volumes. Did your parents bring them from Europe?"

Libka nodded as the man softly read the foreign names: "Bunin, Dostoyevsky, Gorky ... Ah, Pushkin ... one of my favourite poets."

He had replaced the books carefully, straightening up the pile, then nodded at Libka before stepping out on the stoep.

When the books were brought out, the auctioneer grunted at having to deal with such trivia. "Throw them down there," he ordered the workers. Then he thrust the books aside and motioned at the heap, laughing, for he could not read the foreign titles. There was a flutter in the crowd, mockery, then someone presented a bid to amuse the spectators. "How's a farthing?"

"Going ... Going ..." growled the auctioneer.

Libka was about to run up and withdraw the books when the man in the maroon sweater cut in with an offer that silenced the crowd.

After he claimed the books, she followed him.

"These have special value for you too," he said gently.

"Yes. My father used to read them."

"And where is your father?"

"He died." Involuntarily tears sprung into her eyes.

"I think I've seen you before. I have a bookstore on Adderley Street," the man said. "Jason's Rare Books."

"Yes, I know. You have very good books."

Libka felt a strange triumph that this man would care for her father's books.

—•—

It was not Shneyer alone who had rescued his personal treasures. When the chaos of the auction subsided, it appeared that every member of the family had salvaged private mementos. In Golda's heap Libka found a pile of letters from a dead friend. The girl's name had been Fanny Scott and she died of a mysterious illness when she was ten. The letters were written to Golda from the hospital.

Beryl too had his treasures, but he kept these hidden in his room and Libka knew she dare not touch them. She understood that his keepsakes would include tokens to remind him of Joyce and of Eleanor, who had adopted his budgie that was now blowing kisses.

Libka was passionately collecting petals from the garden and pressing them in her diary.

To her surprise she discovered that her mother had packed Yosef's old military jacket from Leningrad, which Elsie had not bothered to take.

Mr. Garfinkel stood behind Sara in all her dealings. She felt stronger with his support. He would often deliver orders in her defence, and then his voice would become tender when he spoke to her.

Libka began to wonder whether her mother should leave Mr. Garfinkel. Who could tell how things would be in the new country? And one day she found the courage to bring it up. "But you like him," she said. "Why are you giving him up?"

"You read my brother's letter. With our whole family wiped out, at least we will be together. And you will have cousins."

Libka could not imagine how it would feel to have cousins and an uncle and aunt. She knew she would never know how it felt to have grandparents, like the *oumas* and *oupas* of the Boer children.

"America never really appealed to me," she told her mother. "I would much rather go to London like Anya. She said the *Winchester Castle* sails from Cape Town to Southampton. Don't we have to change there to get to America?"

"Yes," said Sara.

"So can we all sail there together if Anya and her mother raise the money for the ticket?"

"That would be a good idea," said Sara, "so Anya would not go all alone. Maybe we can even spend a little time in London and then take the *Queen Mary* to New York."

Libka felt a shiver of excitement. Though America was not her chosen land, it would be an adventure. She had never been on an ocean voyage. Anya told her that it took three weeks to reach Southampton. She imagined standing on the deck writing poems about the sea. It now seemed that anything was possible.

· thirty-two ·

On a sunny morning in April Sara and the children climbed into Mr. Garfinkel's car. Beryl and Shneyer sat in front, and Sara, Libka and Golda in back, Dina propped on her mother's lap.

As the car began to move, all eyes were fixed in the same direction. They would imprint in their memories forever their house "The Haven." Empty and silent as it now stood, they knew it would soon be filled with the eight flaxen-haired Van Wyk children. They would swing on the primrose trellis, and their playmates from the street would join them. The doors and shutters of the house would bounce open, and the gate would pound joyously as it once had.

With slow dignity the car moved down the cobblestone street. Sara and the children sat silent in their stiff new clothes as memories fleeted before them. They wanted to retain every curve in the road, every house, every tree they may never again see.

As the vehicle turned onto York Road, Libka's eyes set on the coloured children playing in the gutters. Passing the alley where Maputo had laid his blanket before his arrest, she remembered how they had clung together when they found each other. With the magic in his soul, did he now see her going towards a new world with the same hope and mystery he held in her father's departure?

On this final journey through the place of her birth she yearned to see Sir Lowry Road. She remembered sitting on the high chair in the rooms above their workshop while Mrs. Shevah twirled her hair; and Miss Ingrid reading English fairytales. Libka had once read that as a person lay dying his entire life flashed before him, and she almost felt that sensation. She wondered if her father, in the moment of death, was carried back to his youthful days in Eastern Europe when he swam the Black Sea and dreamed of new horizons.

The car glided beneath the palm and silver leaf trees, and Libka wanted to jump out and pick one last leaf. Past the white mansions they cruised, the stately upper stories peering loftily over the hedges. Then they turned up an unpaved street of shacks and stopped before a grey dwelling with a tin roof, hidden by a gnarled old tree. No gate enclosed this house where Anya Steinberg lived, no gardens surrounded it.

As the car stopped before the house, the door opened. Anya stepped out in a dainty peach coloured frock with white shoes. Her hands seemed lost in the spotless white gloves, and she clutched a small matching handbag. The tag on her suitcase was inscribed with an address in London. Before lowering herself into the vehicle, she turned and looked for a moment at the woman who stood alone in the doorway. Then she crouched into the car beside Libka, and the vehicle proceeded on the downward path towards the sea.

· glossary of Yiddish words ·

boba grandmother
bulkas buns
challah egg loaf for the Sabbath
Channukah Festival of Lights
cheder Hebrew school
chutzpah nerve
dinst servant
farshteyst? understand?
fendele little pot
fraindlech friendly
ganef thief
ganovim thieves
gefilte fish patties made from ground fish
genug enough
goldene golden
goldene zach golden thing
Got in himel God in heaven
Habonim movement exploring Jewish life
hinten buttocks
hoiz house
imberlach carrot pastry
kazatska traditional Russian dance
kinderlach little children
klein kind small child
knaidlach dumplings
knip pinch
knishes dumplings filled with mashed potato
kop head
kreplach noodle dumpling filled with meat or potatoes
landsleit people from the same town
landsman (men) a person from the same town
lokshen pudding noodle pudding with dried fruit, raisins, apple, etc.
mein kind my child
maise story
mench an upright, honourable person
menchisdika honourable behaviour, proper
meshugaas madness
muzeltov good luck (a toast)
naches pleasure
nisht not
nu? what's new?

oy! oh no! (exasperated exclamation)
oy mein Got! oh my God!
oy vey! woe is me!
popke doll
popkele little doll
seichel sense
sha! shh!
Shabbes Sabbath
shein pretty
shiker drunkard
shivah week-long period of mourning
shlep drag
shlepers loafers
shmaltz herring herring in oil
shmate rag
shochet ritual slaughterer
shtetl small town in Eastern Europe
shtetlach villages
shul synagogue
shvartze blacks
skandal scandal
strudel crisp pastry filled with apple
taier dear
taiglach honey tarts
tsimis stew of carrots, prunes, raisins, etc.
ver vais who knows
zach thing

Note: The spellings used are the traditional ones felt to be more appropriate for the general reader, rather than those used in scholarly and formal Yiddish translations.

· glossary of Afrikaans words ·

aantrek   move on
baas   master
broers   brothers
dankie   thank you
domkop   dumbbell
doodskrik   scare to death
dorps   small towns
gaan   go
gewoon   lived
goed   good
hoeveel   how many
ja   yes
Jood   Jew
jou   your
jy   you
Kaffir   derogatory for blacks, like nigger
kinders   children
kopje   small, isolated hill or ridge
kry   get
lank gelede   long, long ago
meisie   girl
mevrou   madam
moeder   mother
naam   name
nee   no
ouma   grandma
oupa   grandpa
sjambok   a heavy leather whip
Suid-Afrika   South Africa
susters   sisters
tante   aunt
vader   father
veld   grassy plateau
voetsek   go away
Voortrekker   pioneer Afrikaners who left the Cape Colony to make the
    Great Trek into the interior between 1835 and 1854
vrou   woman, wife
waar   where
woon   live

· *Afrikaans expressions* ·

Dit gaan goed, dankie. It's going well, thank you.
Ek het hier gewoon lank gelede. I lived here long, long ago.
Ek sal jou kry, Jood! I'll get you, Jew!
Hier is my vrou. Here is my wife.
Hier woon my moeder en my Here live my mother and my
vader en my ouma en my oupa father and my grandma and my grandpa
en my broers en my susters. and my brothers and my sisters.
Hoe gaan dit met jou? How are you?
Hoeveel kinders het jou moeder? How many children does your
  mother have?
Jy is die vrou's man? Are you the woman's husband?
Jy woon hier? You live here?
Jou naam? Your name?
Kom uit, Jood! Come out, Jew!
Nee, nee, hier is my vrou. No, no, here is my wife.
Waar woon jy? Where do you live?
Wat jou naam, meisie? What's your name, girl?

Chorus of a traditional Afrikaans folk song "*Sarie Marais*," created during the Anglo-Boer War

O bring my t'rug na die ou Transvaal O take me back to the old Transvaal
Daar waar my Sarie woon. There where my Sarie lives.
Daar onder in die mielies Down among the maize fields
By die groen doringboom Near the green thorn tree
Daar woon my Sarie Marais. There lives my Sarie Marais.
O bring my t'rug ... O take me back ... *(refrain)*

From the South African national anthem "*Die Stem van Suid-Afrika*"

Uit die blou van onse hemel, From the blue of our heaven
Uit die diepte van ons see From the depths of our sea ...

· *notes* ·

A Word About the Epigram

"All the world is a narrow bridge...
and the main thing is not to be afraid."
RABBI NACHMAN OF BRESLOV (1772-1810)

Rabbi Nachman was the great-grandson of the *Baal Shev Tov* (Master
of the Divine Name) and was one of the most creative, influential and
profound of the Chassidic masters. To this day the mystery and depth
of his teachings attract thousands of followers. He believed stories to
be the pathway to the soul. He said, "There's nothing in heaven that
rejuvenates the soul, purifies the heart, stimulates depth of mind and
brings one closer to their father in heaven like a story."

"Die Stem van Suid-Afrika"

Uit die blou van onse hemel,	From the blue of our heaven
Uit die diepte van ons see,	From the depths of our sea,
Oor ons ewige gebergtes	Over our eternal mountain ranges
Waar die kranse antwoord gee.	Where the cliffs give answer.

The South African national anthem, *"Die Stem van Suid-Afrika"* (The
Voice of South Africa), was written by the Afrikaans writer and poet
C. J. Langenhoven as a poem in May 1918. In 1921 it was set to music
by the Rev. M. L. de Villiers. It was first sung publicly at the official
hoisting of the national flag in Cape Town on May 31, 1928.

"God Save the King"

God save our gracious King,
Long live our noble King,
God save the King:
Send him victorious,
Happy and glorious,
Long to reign over us:
God save the King.

The British national anthem is often credited to Henry Carey, 1740, although there is controversy with many votes, including the British monarchy's, for anonymous. It was first publicly performed in London in 1745.

"If You Were the Only Girl in the World"

If you were the only girl in the world
And I were the only boy
Nothing else would matter in the world today
We could go on loving in the same old way ...
A garden of Eden just made for two
With nothing to mar our joy.

This popular song, written by Nat D. Ayer, with music by Clifford Gray, was introduced on April 19, 1916, at the premiere of the musical *The Bing Boys Are Here* at The Alhambra, Leicester Square. It was republished in 1946. In the context of the deadly battles going on at the time, it seems representative of a need for escape from a nightmare of war.

"I Go Out on the Road Alone"

Marvellous and solemn are the heavens
And the earth is sleeping in a pale blue light.
Then why am I so troubled and so heartsick
    Do I still hope or do I feel regret?
    Do I still hope or do I feel regret?

This translation by Sarah Poritz, from which the title of the novel is derived, is an excerpt from a poem by Mikhail Lermontov (1814–41), a Russian Romantic writer and poet, sometimes called "the poet of the Caucasus." He was the most important Russian poet after Alexander Pushkin's death. The poem was translated into Yiddish by Avrom Reisen (1875-1953), and set to music by E. Shashina. The Yiddish text and melody can be found in Eleanor and Joseph Mlotek's *Songs of Generations*.

"Sarie Marais"

My Sarie Marais is so ver van my hart,
Maar'k hoop om haar weer te sien.
Sy het in die wyk van die Mooirivier gewoon,
Nog voor die oorlog het begin.

Chorus:
O bring my t'rug na die ou Transvaal
Daar waar my Sarie woon.
Daar onder in die mielies
By die groen doringboom
Daar woon my Sarie Marais.

Also known as *"My Sarie Marais,"* this is a traditional Afrikaans folk song, created during either the First Anglo-Boer War (ca. 1880) or the Second Anglo-Boer War (ca. 1900). The tune was taken from a song called *"Ellie Rhee"* dating from the American Civil War, and the words translated into Afrikaans.

In English, the song begins "My Sarie Marais is so far from my heart / But I hope to see her again. / She lived near the Mooi River / Before this war began." The chorus goes: "O take me back to the old Transvaal / There where my Sarie lives. / Down among the maize fields / Near the green thorn tree / There lives my Sarie Marais." It continues about the forced removal of Boer men, women and children to faraway concentration camps by the British.

"There'll Be Bluebirds over the White Cliffs of Dover"

There'll be bluebirds over
The white cliffs of Dover,
Tomorrow, just you wait and see.
There'll be love and laughter
And peace ever after
Tomorrow, when the world is free.

This is one of the most famous of all the World War II era pop classics. It became a sensational hit in 1942, as it reflected the feelings of all the Allies towards the British people in their brave fight against Hitler.

· *acknowledgements* ·

When I began writing this novel, my mother, Sarah Shapiro Poritz, was my first critic. She would feverishly read into the night, as she had always done as a girl growing up in a *shtetl* in Lithuania. I then had the involvement of Eleanor Nichols, a gentle woman who was editor-in-chief at McGraw-Hill in New York. Intrigued by the story of a young girl of Jewish immigrant parents from Lithuania adjusting to life in South Africa, she devoted many hours to helping me realize my vision. There was also the illustrious Bertha Klausner, founder of the International Literary Agency, Inc., in New York, who provided inspiration and guidance. Regretfully, these people are no longer alive, but I am indebted to them for their help and encouragement.

In my present world I was fortunate to encounter a woman who has made an impact on my life. When the esteemed Yiddish translator Miriam Beckerman visited Lithuania to attend the Summer Program in Yiddish Language and Literature at Vilnius University, she encountered a Holocaust survivor on whose testimony I had worked. As a result of this contact, Miriam became my literary colleague and devoted friend. When I shared the manuscript of my novel with her, she rushed it over to Sumach Press, a publisher that she admires, and thus it fell into skilled and compassionate hands. My special appreciation goes to my editor, Jennifer Day, for her insight, firm guidance and sensitivity.

Lily Poritz Miller was born in Cape Town, South Africa, and came to the United States with her family when she was fifteen. She began her editorial career in book publishing in New York at The Macmillan Company and later McGraw-Hill, then moved to Toronto, where she was senior editor at McClelland and Stewart for eighteen years.

She has written three plays, which were performed in New York and Toronto, and received a Samuel French national award for her play *The Proud One*. Her short stories were published in the anthology *American Scene: New Voices*. She has also written for film. She presently divides her time between Toronto and New York.